P9-EMC-312

"I SEE WE'VE COME AT AN INOPPORTUNE TIME."

That satyr's grin slipped, but only a little. The gleam in Roamer's green eyes was almost feral. Mattie thought of a predatory animal waiting, lurking just outside the glow of a campfire. "Scout, perhaps we should come back later."

For the first time Mattie became aware that Scout stood beside his uncle. He was staring at her with a crooked smile.

"Mrs. Smith, I brought some money to pay for your dress," he said, taking a step toward the open door. "A man has to pay his debts. Uncle Roamer told me that."

Mattie's eyes flicked down to Scout's hands. They were small and clean, the nails even. The hands of a child well cared for—well tended and well loved. And this . . . *man* before her was the one responsible for that.

Roamer took the money from Scout and placed it in Mattie's palm, slowly folding her fingers over it one by one. Where in the street his hands had been rough and punishing, now they were gentle, seductive.

Once again Mattie's perception of Roamer shifted, altered, and shattered into colors like those in the bottom of a kaleidoscope. Things were not so simple. *He* was not so simple. He was as far from her ideal of a gentleman as a man could be. He was big, muscled, certainly not the kind of man given to intellectual love.

Not with a body like that, Mattie thought, and she blushed.

Dear Romance Reader,

In July, we launched the Ballad line with four new series, and each month we'll present both new and continuing stories set everywhere from medieval England to the American West—the kind of passionate, romantic stories you love best, written by the most gifted authors. At the back of each book, we'll tell you when you can find subsequent books in the series that have captured your heart.

This month talented Cindy Harris introduces the charming new *Dublin Dreams* series. When an anonymous benefactor brings together four penniless women in one stately Dublin square, none of them expect to find love. Yet in the first book, the widow of a dissolute gambler meets her romantic match when she has **A Bright Idea.** Next, rising star Linda Lea Castle presents the second of a trio of spirited *Bogus Brides.* In **Mattie and the Blacksmith,** a schoolteacher who longs to be properly courted discovers that the most unlikely suitor may be the one who steals her heart.

Fabulous new author Lynne Hayworth is also back with the second installment of the *Clan Maclean* series, **Autumn Flame.** Will a spirited pickpocket make a proper wife for the overseer of a Virginia plantation? Finally, Cherie Claire concludes the atmospheric *Acadians* trilogy with the story of **Gabrielle,** a woman who will risk anything to save the bold privateer who had claimed her, body and soul. Enjoy!

Kate Duffy
Editorial Director

Bogus Brides

MATTIE AND THE BLACKSMITH

Linda Lea Castle

ZEBRA BOOKS
Kensington Publishing Corp.
http://www.zebrabooks.com

ZEBRA BOOKS are published by

Kensington Publishing Corp.
850 Third Avenue
New York, NY 10022

Copyright © 2001 by Linda L. Crockett

All rights reserved. No part of this book may be reproduced in any form or by any means without the prior written consent of the Publisher, excepting brief quotes used in reviews.

If you purchased this book without a cover you should be aware that this book is stolen property. It was reported as "unsold and destroyed" to the Publisher and neither the Author nor the Publisher has received any payment for this "stripped book."

All Kensington titles, imprints, and distributed lines are available at special quantity discounts for bulk purchases for sales promotion, premiums, fund-raising, educational, or institutional use.

Special book excerpts or customized printings can also be created to fit specific needs. For details, write or phone the office of the Kensington special sales manager: Kensington Publishing Corp., 850 Third Avenue, New York, NY 10022, Attn: Special Sales Department, Phone: 1-800-221-2647.

Zebra and the Z logo Reg. U.S. Pat. & TM Off.

First Printing: April, 2001
10 9 8 7 6 5 4 3 2 1

Printed in the United States of America

To my family and friends, and to lovers of romance and history.
As always, all glory to God.

One

"Tell us again about your husband, Mrs. Smith." Two small girls, the Hanson twins, giggled shyly from the school desk seat that they shared. Their smiling faces and shining braids made them look younger and fresher than the spring breezes washing across McTavish Plain.

"My husband, Captain Samuel Smith, is a handsome man. He is strong and kind, and of course he is a man of letters. Quite a romantic man." Mattie unconsciously turned the gold band on her finger. "But he can be a formidable leader. The master of a ship cannot show softness or fear on a long voyage." Mattie smoothed the front of her navy twill weskit and stood a little straighter. Thinking of her imaginary husband always had that effect on her. Her make-believe husband had taken on a life of his own. Mattie could almost picture him, standing at the helm of a ship with the wind in his hair, or sitting in his cabin composing poetry for her.

She took a few steps, the ruffles of her robin's-egg blue skirt whispering against the planks of the scrubbed pine floor.

Over the past few months, Mattie's mental image of Captain Samuel Smith had sharpened until she could almost believe he was real. But he was too perfect, in her heart of hearts she knew that. He was more dashing than any living man—more romantic, more capable of experiencing a pure intellectual love than any real man. For Captain Samuel Smith was only a story—an invention to allow three unmarried sisters to be a part of McTavish Plain, the wonderful charter town near the Black Hills.

Mattie couldn't remember now if the idea had been hers or her sister Lottie's, but whichever of them had come up with the notion, it was brilliant. It had of course taken a bit of time to persuade Adelaide.

Mattie thought of her eldest sister. Addie was now married to the town's founder, Ian McTavish, a gruff Scots mountain man with an iron jaw and a lilting burr. It was plain as a wart on the end of a hog's nose that Addie was in love—blissfully, completely, romantically head over heels in love. The odd part was that sensible Addie had fallen for a man as big as a bear and rough as bark, but who would slay dragons for his Adelaide. Ian was the only one who called her Adelaide now. Without ever having to say so, he had adopted the name as his own particular endearment. Mattie understood that the name held every tender thought and soft notion Ian felt for his wife but couldn't put into words. She always understood things like that because she was intellectual and had a grasp of things ethereal and pure—like love.

"Mrs. Smith?"

Mattie blinked and shook herself.

"Mrs. Smith?"

All the children were staring at her. She focused on the expectant face of the boy who had spoken. Scout Maravel looked up at her with a mischievous grin showing unevenly spaced teeth. A new crop of freckles sprouted across the bridge of his nose. He had a knack of catching her when she was woolgathering.

"Yes, Scout?" She said with a cock of her head. Did the little scamp think she was fooled by that angelic expression?

"May we be excused, ma'am?" he asked in his most respectful tone.

Mattie glanced outside at the lengthening shadows. The afternoon had passed quickly from arithmetic to geography. "Yes, class is excused—but don't forget tomorrow we will be discussing the impact of Kansas becoming a state last year and what changes that has brought to our country."

The ensuing thump and rumble of feet against the plain pine floor sounded like far-off thunder. In a flurry of skirts and trousers, children of all sizes headed for the door. Scout was jockeying with Clint Hollis for the lead position.

"All except for you, Scout Maravel," Mattie added in her starchiest voice. "You stay."

He stopped so quickly one would have thought an invisible hand had grasped him by the scruff of the neck. Slowly he turned, his face screwed up as if the action caused physical pain.

"Don't you have something to do?"

"Yes, ma'am." His tone was decidedly less respectful now.

"I think you were supposed to clean the schoolhouse for a month?"

"Yes, ma'am." His shoulders stooped and his head hung low as he shuffled to the corner to take up the broom.

"Your month is not yet up by my ciphering."

"No, ma'am." He kicked at something invisible as the last of the other children disappeared out the door. Their laughter floated on the breeze as they found happy pursuits.

Scout glowered out the door and then turned his attention to his task. The air was soon filled with dust motes, floating and swirling in the shaft of sunlight coming from the open door.

Mattie sat behind her desk. Soon she found herself watching Scout, wondering what kind of childhood the boy had before coming to McTavish Plain. His mother was dead, she knew, and Scout lived with his uncle, Roamer Tresh. Mattie had heard it whispered that Roamer had a past, but this was the frontier and almost every man—or woman—had some sort of a whispered past. Most folks came this far west to a wild territory to leave all of that behind and start anew. What they had been and done before was of little consequence in McTavish Plain . . . as long as the women were married according to the laws set down by Ian McTavish.

According to Mattie's brother-in-law, single women meant ruin in the form of gambling parlors, too much whiskey, and loose morals. How he thought one thing led to another, she did not know and was not about to ask.

"Don't neglect those corners, Scout." She said absently. She had a notion that Ian was just bone stubborn.

"Yes, ma'am." He squinted up at her before applying the broom to the corner.

She tried not to grin at Scout's barely concealed annoyance. The boy was a caution: polite to her, but the devil incarnate when it came to pulling pranks and stunts—and picking at the other students.

"Mrs. Smith?" He paused in his efforts and looked at her.

"Yes, Scout?"

He leaned on the broom while a halo of dust motes played about his flaxen thatch of hair. "What will you do if your husband never comes back from sea?"

Mattie blinked. "What on earth would make you ask such a thing, Scout Maravel? Are you trying to make conversation to get out of sweeping?"

"Why, no ma'am, I would never. I heard tell a lot of men die out at sea. I was just wondering what you would do if'n he died out at sea."

Mattie tried not to shudder. Scout's innocent question bore an uncomfortable similarity to the very words she employed last year while she was talking Addie into coming north to the wildest part of the territory. It had sounded so *refined* when Mattie said it. . . . Why did the same words coming from Scout's mouth have a bitter ring?

"If'n he doesn't come home, wouldn't you have to get married again, like your sister did? Wouldn't you have to pick a man from here in McTavish Plain?" Scout seemed to look right through her lies. He studied her for a long while with one brilliant blue eye squeezed shut, his head slightly tilted, like a hunter getting a bead on his quarry.

A cold finger of guilty unease trailed down Mattie's spine. She shrugged her shoulders, hoping the niggling worry could be removed with no more effort than shoving off her pale green wool shawl.

"Well, I suppose I would, Scout, but nothing is going to happen to my husband. Now, quit trying to shift my attention elsewhere. Did you apologize for putting rotten eggs in Marysue Martin's Easter display?" Mattie inquired sternly, keen to get Scout's thoughts on something besides her marital status.

"Yes'm." Scout started to sweep again; the air took on the familiar tang of dust.

"And what did your uncle Roamer have to say?"

Scout cleared his throat, pulled himself up as straight and tall as a six-year-old could manage, plastered a severe frown on his face, and in an exaggeratedly gruff voice said, "Boy, this is the last straw."

"Mmmmm." Mattie thought of Roamer Tresh. . . . He was as tall as Ian McTavish, and since the weather had warmed in the past few days, she had seen he was even *bigger.* Mattie was passing by his smithy on her way home. Roamer had been at the anvil with his shirt off. Rivulets of sweat trickled over rock-hard flesh and gleaming brawn like the thawing streams of icy mountain run-off over Redbird Mountain. She shuddered at the memory.

"He threatened to take me out behind the woodshed if'n I didn't stop deviling the girls."

"Surely he wouldn't do that?" Mattie said in half-feigned horror, trying to remove the image of half-dressed Roamer from her mind. Those muscles could do serious damage to a stripling child.

"No, ma'am." Scout rubbed the toe of his shoe in the dirt he had managed to pile up. "I think he just said that 'cause he has something else on his mind."

"Oh?"

"Uncle Roamer said, 'Boy, I think you better stop trying to marry me off.' "

Mattie choked. "He what?"

Scout nodded. "Yep, I have been trying to talk him

into it, but Uncle Roamer figures I don't need a mama and he sure as shootin' don't want a wife. He says they are too much trouble to court and too much trouble to keep."

"Oh, I see." Mattie was not in the least surprised. Roamer Tresh was big, brawny, and way too physical to have tender notions and sensibilities about love and marriage. It was her opinion that men of that bulk were little interested in refined thoughts and intellectual love. She had seen the like back in Nebraska—big healthy farmers groping girls, wanting kisses and *more.*

"But I figger what Uncle Roamer says he needs and what Uncle Roamer really does need are two different things. He sure as shootin' needs a little help with the cookin' and washin' and the like."

"No doubt," Mattie agreed, wrinkling her nose at the idea. She could barely boil water herself, but the thought of some poor woman marrying a man just to be his cook and housekeeper was appalling.

Scout leaned heavily on the broom handle, causing the bristles to fan out against the yellow pine floor. He rubbed his bottom lip thoughtfully. "Ma'am, do you cook?"

"No, I do not." Mattie said emphatically. "I never learned. My sister Addie is the cook in the family, and she keeps me well supplied with enough to get by on. And neither do I sew. My sister Charlotte makes all my frocks. So you see, there are some women who marry without turning into kitchen maids."

"Oh." Scout's voice rang with disappointment. "I thought all women were good cooks."

"No, Scout. It is not a skill we acquire at birth, and I prefer to read and improve my mind."

"Guess it's a good thing your husband stays at sea, ain't it?" Scout said without looking up.

Mattie didn't know whether to laugh or be offended by his sharp wit, but he was lost in his own thoughts, still thinking about his uncle.

"Uncle Roamer says he ain't—"

"Isn't," Mattie corrected automatically.

"—Says he *isn't* goin' to go courtin' no woman. 'Sides, he says he'd have to leave the smithy and go all the way to Belle Fourche to find a woman when he doesn't even want one. He says he don't have time to waste on such foolishness as courtin' or marryin'." Scout frowned and wrinkled his nose.

Now Mattie's suspicion was confirmed. Roamer couldn't have a romantic bone in his body. "Foolishness, is it?"

"Plumb foolish, Uncle Roamer calls it. Says most women are just trouble."

This was the very thing Mattie disliked about most men. They expected to treat romance and marriage like . . . well, like buying a horse. And that attitude was one of the reasons Mattie had wanted to come to McTavish Plain. She had no desire to get married and find herself tied to a cookstove and a house full of children. Being a teacher fulfilled whatever desire she had to be around children, without having to tend their cuts and mend their clothes. She and her sisters wanted freedoms that were only available in the far territory. So they had created pasts that enabled them to carve out a new life—one of their own making, not the one that society and men foisted upon them in the small Nebraska town where they were raised.

Everyone in McTavish Plain thought Mattie was

married, because every adult woman in McTavish Plain *had* to be married. That gave her the opportunity to shop around, find a sensitive man with a soul and intellect that suited her.

When and if she did marry for real, it would be to a man of her choosing, and he wouldn't be a muley-headed brute with a ready-made family, who considered courting and marriage to be a foolish waste of his time!

The sound of the broom rasping against the floor drew Mattie's attention back to Scout. He was making a halfhearted attempt to pile the dirt up.

"It sure would be a heap more simple if'n Uncle Roamer was willing to be married," he said softly.

"Even if he were willing, I think it would do him little good. Your uncle is right about having to go to Belle Fourche, since Mr. McTavish allows only married women to live here. It would be a long trip."

"Yep, that is 'zactly what Uncle Roamer said." Scout agreed solemnly. "He said there weren't none around anyhow and I just better stop being such a rascal to try and force him to get leg-shackled to some woman he doesn't want or need."

"For the life of me, Scout Maravel, I cannot believe your uncle says such things to you!" She laughed in spite of herself, a tiny part of her admiring Roamer Tresh for sharing some of her sentiments about marriage. She had managed to create a life here where she didn't need a man—a rarity for women in a male-dominated society. "You know, Scout, I think it is a good thing your uncle doesn't want a wife. I cannot imagine any woman, even a dried-up, desperate spinster, would want to marry a man who thinks marriage is nothing but a chore."

* * *

An hour later Scout was relating the details of his day to his uncle Roamer. He liked being near the forge and the smell of the burning wood. The heat of the smithy made his lungs burn, and his face felt like it was being roasted, but he enjoyed watching his uncle hit the red-hot iron and mold it with each mighty blow.

"And then Mrs. Smith said she couldn't imagine *any* woman would want to marry you, Uncle Roamer."

Roamer's hammer stopped in mid-swing, the steady rhythm disrupted by an over-starched schoolmarm's opinion of his desirability as a husband. Roamer took a deep breath, shut his eyes for a moment, and willed himself to be calm. It had taken him a long time to learn to tamp down his temper. He wasn't about to let Mrs. Know-it-all-Smith destroy all he had accomplished.

"Mrs. Smith is a citified woman, Scout—a citified woman who thinks too highly of her own opinion, it seems." Roamer smiled at Scout. "We are fine, just the two of us. We don't need a wife and mother and I think you'd best not talk about us with that schoolmarm."

"But she said you get a woman with sweet words."

Roamer winced. He could never forget the pain and misery his sister, Susan, had gone through because she had fallen for a sweet-talking man. Pretty words brought her a worthless man's name, followed by abuse and an early grave.

"For the last time, Scout, I ain't looking for a wife. And I don't care to hear about Mattie-the-marm's highfalutin notions about how to get one. Now stoke up this fire; I got a dozen shoes to make for Miley before sundown."

"Yes sir." Scout grabbed the huge bellows handle in both hands. He rose on his toes and then used his entire body weight to bring it down, air whooshing into the flames, fire rising higher. Roamer saw much of Susan in Scout's pensive expression while the boy worked. It bothered him that Scout had developed a soft spot for that marm with the honey-colored hair. Mrs. Smith was too flighty, too foolish, and entirely too free with her notions. It was bad enough Scout had decided he wanted Roamer to marry. The last thing Roamer needed was the schoolmarm encouraging those silly notions.

McTavish Plain needed an older woman to teach school. An older woman would be less foolish. But Ian had faith in her abilities, and Roamer trusted Ian's judgment . . . even if Mattie-the-marm was Ian's sister-in-law.

Hell-fire, Roamer did all right caring for Scout alone. He could fry a turnip and sear a steak. Gus had tins of peaches that they ate of a Sunday.

Did that snooty Mrs. Smith take notice of that? Did she realize that Roamer had learned how to thread a needle and darn a shirt so Scout would not go ragged? No. All she could do was belittle and encourage Scout that Roamer needed to marry. The last thing he needed was some nagging woman in his life.

"And Mrs. Smith said." Scout was speaking in a choppy rhythm, in between working the bellows. The coals in the forge were glowing a bright orange.

"Whoa." Roamer's hammer came down on the horseshoe he was shaping with a discordant clang. "I don't want to hear what Mrs. Smith says. Far as I'm concerned, she's already said too much." Roamer used the tongs to grasp the cooling arc of metal. He jabbed it back and forth into the bed of hot coals, taking his frustration out on the iron.

"Mark my words, Scout, there ain't nothing worse than a meddling woman . . . unless it's one that wants to give out advice to those who don't want it and surely don't need it."

"Yes sir," Scout said glumly. He would respect his uncle's wishes, but he was thinking hard about what Mrs. Smith said. It was going to be hard to convince Uncle Roamer that he really wanted a wife . . . but Scout was determined.

Two

"Lottie, the new sampler is beautiful!" Mattie said, fingering her sister's handiwork. She often dropped by Lottie's house in the evenings on her way home from the schoolhouse. The two of them would have sweet tea with bread and butter and discuss their day. It spared Mattie the chore of trying to cook herself a meal on the days that Addie didn't bring her something, and she enjoyed the gossip provided by Lottie's dress shop. All the women in town used the seamstress's house as a gathering place to trade receipts of favorite dishes and tell each other the woes of married life.

"Mmmm, it did turn out well." Lottie frowned absently, staring over the rim of her cup into space. Her pink-and-white striped frock with short, stiff lace along the high collar made her look neat and trim and very professional. Mattie refused to learn to sew, but since Lottie only charged her what the dress goods cost, Mattie was able to keep her own wardrobe right stylish on her teacher's salary.

"Tell me what gossip you heard today," Mattie said eagerly. "Is Velma Carter still making Harry sleep on the settee?"

Lottie remained silent, her lips pursed, her brow furrowed.

"What's wrong with you, Charlotte?" Mattie finally asked. "You are not paying a bit of attention to me. I may as well go home and talk to my hens."

"Ian came into the shop today."

"Ian comes by your shop most every day. It amazes me how romantic he is. How many dresses has he ordered for Addie this year? Good grief—did he commission another?"

Lottie's frown deepened and she drew in a taut breath. "It is nothing like that, Mattie."

"Is he ill? Is Addie well? Oh no! She didn't shoot him again, did she?" Mattie set her cup aside. " 'Cause if she did, well, it will just be the talk of the town for a month."

Lottie waved a delicate hand. "No, nothing like that, but he stopped by the dress shop today . . . just to be sociable, he said, but all he did was ask me questions about our *husbands.*"

Mattie sucked in her breath. "Our *husbands?*"

"Mmmm. I swear sometimes I think he *knows,* Matilda. There is something about the way he looks at me . . . such a sly glimmer of knowledge in those blue eyes of his, it gives me a turn. He is like a cat who knows where the birds go to roost."

Lottie drummed her fingers on the side table. The gauzy ecru curtain from the open window behind her fluttered over the arm of the yellow damask settee that she had shipped all the way from St. Louis. Somewhere in town a dog barked while the sisters sat in silence.

After a tense moment, Mattie collapsed back against the horsehair seat. "Lottie, you must be imagining things. I mean if Ian knew . . . I don't even think Addie could stop that man from doing his worst."

"I don't know—she could always shoot him again," Lottie said with a half smile, her head tilted in idle speculation.

"Lottie! What an unchristian thing to say. Ian is on the skinny side of civilized and I'll bet he's never even cracked a book of poetry, but you can't wish for Addie to *kill* him. After all, he is making her a good husband."

Lottie shook her head, her pretty blond ribbon-tied curls bouncing on the warm breeze. "Don't be so dramatic, Matilda. I don't wish for her to kill him. You are probably right. I am so bored that I do wish something, *anything* would happen to add a little excitement to this place."

Lottie sighed in a way that Mattie thought was a bit dramatic, but she held her tongue and refrained from saying so.

"I swan," Lottie continued. "I had hoped life here would be more exciting, but it is just as boring as Gothenburg ever was."

Mattie sipped her tea and listened to her sister's usual refrain with only half an ear. Her attention was on the platter of crusty fresh bread slathered with fresh-churned butter. She would have liked to have another piece of bread and butter, but her corset was pinching her ribs. Sometimes, not often but sometimes, she thought it must be nice to really be married. Then, if she wanted two slices of bread and butter, she could have them and not have to worry about getting fat. Mattie sighed and focused on her sister so that she wouldn't be tempted to indulge.

"Oh, you always want more excitement, Lottie. If

you had a shoot-out in your dress shop once a week, you would still moan that life wasn't exciting enough. You're feeling restless again. You always do in the springtime."

"I suppose," Lottie said, pursing her lips into a pout. "Tell me what you've been up to. Have you found your poet yet? I'll just bet the streets of McTavish Plain are teeming with poets this time of year." Lottie winked, but it didn't take the sarcastic sting from her words.

"Don't be a cat just because I pointed out your faults, Lottie. Besides, I am not about to apologize for knowing what I want. You won't be teasing when I am happy. When I find him, then I will write myself a letter like the one Addie got and reveal to the town that my poor, dear Samuel has gone to a watery grave."

"Just see you wait a respectable amount of time, my girl." Lottie waggled a finger in Mattie's direction. "Ian McTavish is no fool. If two sisters just happen to become widows too fast . . . I don't even want to think about getting tossed out of town when my business is doing so well."

Scout shifted his weight below the open window. He had been crouched there for a few minutes, listening to his teacher and her sister, Mrs. Rosswarne. Now the schoolmarm's words washed over him, tumbling his thoughts. For a moment, he couldn't get his breath.

Mrs. Smith's husband is dead!

It was difficult for Scout to think of any one thing. A hundred thoughts and ideas swirled through his mind. He forced himself to sit very still and concentrate, scrunching his eyes tight and trying to think.

Captain Smith was dead. And Mrs. Rosswarne was worried about what would happen to Mrs. Smith if Mr. McTavish learned the truth.

Mr. McTavish had made Addie, Mrs. Smith's sister, choose a new husband when she became a widow. The whole town talked about it. Even Uncle Roamer had said it was a shame she had to pick while she was still mourning her husband. But Mrs. Smith didn't sound like she was mourning. She said she was *looking* for a husband . . . the right man.

What kind of a man would be the *right* man? Scout wondered.

The couple sat in the sunshine and watched the dogs. Scout knew their names were Tay and Dee. The huge hounds had arrived a few weeks back in strong wooden crates with fancy labels and strange names painted all over the boards.

Uncle Roamer said the hounds were from Scotland, a faraway land where Mr. McTavish had been born.

Now the leggy female dogs frolicked with Darroch, Ian's big male, in the meadow grass, nipping at buttercups and startled birds that flushed from the bushes. The trio barked, hunkered down low in the front, and then bounded away like they had been shot from a gun.

Scout wished he had a pup . . . but most of all he wished for a mother. He wanted someone he could sit in the meadow grass with while Uncle Roamer was at the forge. He wanted someone to read to him and to hold his hand when he had a bad dream. Uncle Roamer tried, but he wasn't a mother.

Scout squeezed his eyes shut and tried to remember his mother. He couldn't recall her face or her eyes or anything like that. But a smell, a nice smell all soft and fuzzy around the edges, surrounded him and filled his nose. The scent tickled his nostrils and made his heart feel too big inside his chest. It happened each time he tried to remember his mother. And then he was filled with a terrible sense of loss—a deep ache that shut off the air to his lungs. He thought he might cry like a baby, and that embarrassed him even though he was alone and nobody knew he felt ashamed for not being more of a man.

Scout pressed the heels of his hands into his eyes to hold back the hated tears. He was six years old; he didn't cry anymore. But the remembered smell did strange things to him. It was his mother's scent, and it carried all the bittersweet memories of being loved and cared for. And how it felt to lose someone he loved.

Laughter carried over the greening meadow. Scout opened his eyes and listened to Mrs. McTavish. She had a nice voice, kind of husky but soft.

"The pups will be born in a month or so by my count, Ian."

Scout perked up a little, craning his neck to see the dogs.

"Aye, Tay will make a good mother," Mr. McTavish said.

"We will always have pups around so no dog will be alone again."

"No dog and no man." Mr. McTavish pulled Mrs. McTavish to her feet and kissed her. Scout closed his eyes real fast so he wouldn't have to watch. He counted to ten and then opened his eyes again.

Two fat otters darted in and out from beneath Mrs. McTavish's skirts. One of them had a crooked tail, and the other cocked his head and looked at things from an angle as he ran somewhat sideways. He sort of reminded Scout of the one-eyed tomcat that ate mice at the livery stable.

The dogs barked at the otters and chased them back under Mrs. McTavish's long skirts. Scout rose up a little more, trying to see what the otters were doing. Suddenly Darroch's head came around and he sniffed the air. Mr. McTavish's head turned. Scout could almost feel their gazes home in on him.

Mr. McTavish swept a ring of braided flowers from his head. Scout blinked and shook his head. Mr. McTavish would never do something as silly as wear a circlet of flowers. Would he?

"Ian, what is wrong?" Mrs. McTavish looked around, but Scout knew she hadn't spotted him—yet.

"I ken we have a visitor." Mr. McTavish narrowed his eyes. "Come on out, lad. Show yourself."

Swallowing his fear, Scout stood up. Immediately the three dogs bounded toward him. He braced himself as the two females slathered him with their tongues. It felt good to be crowded and jostled and hemmed in by their big, warm bodies. He tried not to giggle, but laughter bubbled up inside him.

"Tay—Dee, down." Mr. McTavish's voice rolled like thunder over the meadow. The dogs sat back on their haunches, panting in satisfaction.

"Hello," Mrs. McTavish said.

"Hello, ma'am." Scout dug his toe into a cluster of blooming clover. "I came to talk to Mr. McTavish."

The couple exchanged a look that made Scout want to squirm and run away, but he managed to stand fast and look Mr. McTavish squarely in the eyes the way Uncle Roamer had always told him he should.

"Say your piece, lad."

"I wanted to know—that is—I was just wondering . . ." Scout lost his nerve. He stared at the trampled grass beneath his feet, ashamed of his cowardice. Then he remembered Mrs. Smith and her dead husband. Scout drew himself up and cleared his throat.

"I was wondering if one of the married ladies in town found out her husband had died—"

"Aye?" Ian's voice was softer now.

"Well, if somethun' like that should happen, you wouldn't really make that lady leave town . . . would you?"

Mr. McTavish made a noise that Scout thought sounded a little bit like laughter. Mrs. McTavish elbowed him in the ribs hard, and he sort of coughed and cleared his throat.

"Ian. You promised. You swore you would never do anything to my sisters."

"And I have no intention of breaking my promise to you, lass, not ever in the world. But the lad has asked a fair question and he deserves a fair answer."

Scout didn't understand why Mr. McTavish's blue eyes were watering or what Mrs. McTavish meant about her sisters, but he was happy Mr. McTavish was going to give him an answer.

"If any woman in McTavish Plain is not married, then aye, lad, I would make her leave town."

"And you wouldn't care who that lady was a'tall?" Scout felt a hard lump growing in his belly.

"Not one bit. Even if it was my dear wife's very own

sister, for instance. Rules are rules. She would have to go."

Mrs. McTavish gasped. "Ian!"

"I'd have to put her out or make her marry. I can't bend the rules for anyone, lad."

"Yes sir. Thank you, sir." Scout turned away. Misery enveloped him.

"Lad, wait." The deep, burred voice halted Scout's feet.

"Yes sir?" Scout turned around and looked at Mr. McTavish.

"But before I sent her down the road, I would allow the lady to pick another husband from the men in McTavish Plain. Just like my own Adelaide did."

The thought ripped through Scout's brain. Mrs. Smith was too fine a lady to pick a husband like a horse or a rooster or a bull. He made up his mind right then and there. No matter what it took, he could not let Mr. McTavish learn about Mrs. Smith's secret.

"Yes sir," Scout said, feeling even more miserable than he had before. He walked away, kicking at little tussocks of greening grass. Then, in a blaze of insight, Scout knew his duty.

He had to save Mrs. Smith.

She needed to be married, and he needed a mama.

There was nothing else for it. He had no choice. It was as if God had planned it this way all along.

Scout had to find a way to get Uncle Roamer to want to marry, and he was going to have to want to marry Mrs. Smith before Mr. McTavish found out that her husband had died in a watery grave.

* * *

The next few weeks were a nightmare for Roamer. Scout seemed possessed by demons.

First he egged the church. Then, before the yolks were even dry, he put axle grease on the seesaw, which caused Archibald Marshal to slide all the way down, filling his trousers and his backside with splinters. Scout seemed bound and determined to turn Roamer white-headed overnight.

Roamer worked the bellows until the coals were glowing red. The truth of the matter was, Scout needed a good hiding. That was apparent, but Roamer would cut off his own arm before he raised a finger against Scout or anyone else ever again.

"And I think the little scamp knows it," he muttered to himself.

There were still times in the dead of night when the specters of his past and the consequences of his actions haunted him. Roamer could never raise his hand to any living creature again—not even if he knew deep down that it would do Scout some good.

"A coward, that's all I am," Roamer growled while he picked up the hammer and got to work on the lump of metal.

"Whoa, what did that piece of iron ever do to you?" Miley Thompson was leaning against the tall timber that supported the outside roof of the smithy, watching Roamer.

"Aw, Miley, how long have you been there?" Roamer was embarrassed that Miley had come up on him and he hadn't even been aware of the man's presence.

"Long enough. I heard that nephew of yours has been running you a merry chase. And from that hangdog look on your face, and your one-sided conversation, I can believe most of what I heard is true."

"He's been feeling his oats lately, that's a fact." Roamer used the tongs to slide the iron back into the bed of coals. "He's just bein' a boy. It'll pass soon."

Miley guffawed. "Well, I ain't one to tell you how to go about raising that nephew of yours, but I can tell you that you ought to consider getting that boy a mother, Roamer."

"What's that?" Roamer frowned and used his shirt sleeve to wipe the sweat from his brow. "What did you say?"

"You need to get married."

Roamer hit the metal—hard. "You too? Not likely, Miley. I don't want or need a wife. Besides I got to fix both leaf springs on your big wagon."

Miley yanked off his hat and scratched his thinning pate. "I guess I took Walker's Wash too fast." Miley's low voice rang with embarrassed guilt. "I was anxious to get home."

"You're lucky you made it to town." Roamer said with a grin.

Miley nodded in agreement. His big wagon was the town's lifeline. He hauled mail back and forth from Belle Fourche in addition to the supplies and things that could not be produced in McTavish Plain. The town could squeak by without the wagon for a while, but there would be folks who would feel the pinch.

"A good woman is awful nice to come home to, Roamer," Miley added when he clapped his hat back on his head.

"Miley, even if I wanted a wife—which I don't—how could I find a wife if I can't leave town? You and everybody else manage to keep me busy."

Miley smiled. "There are other ways. You could get one of those mail-order brides. Shoot, Roamer, if'n all you're wanting is a woman to help raise Scout and you don't care about the particulars, that might be just the ticket."

"Mail order." Roamer snorted. "I don't think much about marriage in general, but who would want a wife they could order like a pair of new overalls? That sounds like more trouble. If I decide to get one then I'll just propose to the first one that comes along."

Roamer was whistling a tune when he turned the corner and headed toward John Holcomb's post office. He was certain that Scout was only doing what boys did as they grew, and that he would soon settle down. It was at that moment, when Roamer was confident his life was about to become simple again, that the most god-awful stench hit him square in the face.

A dense cloud of low hanging smoke wrapped itself around his head and drove the air from his lungs. Roamer was well used to smoke, but this . . . this was a *stench.*

Through stinging eyes Roamer saw a string of cow patties smoldering in the middle of Main Street.

And there was Scout, grinning like a possum in a melon patch.

Roamer's neighbors came barreling out of shops and houses. Ladies with kerchiefs over their mouths trotted along the sidewalk, bumping into each other in the thick, choking smoke.

"Dang it boy, I warned you!" Otto Hudspeth, the barber-surgeon yelled. He had in his hand the leather strop that he used for putting an edge on razors. He ran stiff-legged toward Scout. "I told you, you little hellion, I was going to hide you good. Now I am going to blister the skin on your behind so you can't sit for a week!"

Roamer covered the distance between himself and the barber-surgeon in three long strides. He snatched the strop from the surprised man's hand and spun him around.

"I don't hardly think anybody is going to lay hands on this boy while there is breath in my body," Roamer advised him in a deadly calm voice.

The barber paled and shrank back. "No, don't hit me."

"I am not going to hit you, Hudspeth." Roamer released the hold he had on his shoulder. With a glower of disgust Roamer flicked the wide strap of leather, holding it by the metal end. The barber turned and ran for the safety of his storefront. For a moment everything was silent. Nobody coughed, nobody seemed to breathe, but most important, nobody threatened Scout.

Roamer heaved a calming sigh. He had tried to hold his temper but there had been a moment—just one fleeting moment.

He was glad the barber-surgeon did not have the backbone to challenge him. Roamer struck his open palm with the strop, feeling the sting of the leather in his callused hand, and he wondered whether he would have had the control to keep his vow if Otto Hudspeth had pushed the point—if he had managed to lay that strop on Scout just one time. . . .

"Don't you dare touch that child!"

Mattie-the-marm appeared in a flurry of yellow gingham ruffles and feminine outrage. Her eyes were flashing with fury when she reached Roamer. He had no notion what she was talking about until she grabbed the strop from his hand.

"Oh, you beast, how could you even think to do such an evil thing to this poor boy?"

"What the devil—?" Roamer blinked and tried to clear the smoke from his eyes. Slowly he realized the schoolmarm thought *he* was going to use that leather strop on Scout.

"I won't stand by and watch you abuse this child, you . . . you brute!"

Roamer backed up a step, the hissed insult ringing in his ears. The starchy schoolmarm's steps matched his. She was in his face—on her tiptoes to be sure—calling him a beast and worse.

The crowd stopped pouring buckets of water on the smoldering cow patties. Roamer saw everyone turning to gawk, but Mattie-the-marm was too busy to notice.

"How could you?" She poked him in the breastbone with a gloved finger. "A leather strop! How could you?"

"Now hold on a minute. You got entirely—"

"Oh you, *brute!*" She said again, and she rose up unexpectedly in his face. He accidentally snorted the slender blue feather on her bonnet against his left nostril. It tickled. He coughed and nearly sneezed, but the schoolmarm didn't even notice what her hat feather was doing as she continued to rail at him.

"Mrs. Smith, if you would hold on—"

"No, *you* hold on. I have a few things to say to you, *Mr.* Tresh."

Roamer was tired of backing up. He was tired of being yelled at and humiliated in front of the whole town. He glared down at her with a look that usually silenced most men.

"Never in all my born days—"

Evidently his fiercest stare had no effect whatsoever on the indignant woman. She poked him in the chest with her finger.

"How could you even consider taking a strop, a leather strop, to that poor little child?"

Roamer's gaze flicked to Scout. His nephew shrugged, his brows arching in helpless dismay, promising that he would be no help.

"Whoa, now, ma'am, you don't think that I—" Roamer held his hand out. She swatted it smartly with the leather strop.

"Ouch!" He jerked his hand back.

"Don't you dare raise you hand to me, you *brute.*"

"Now lady—"

"Mrs. Smith." she snapped.

"Mrs. Smith, I was not raising my hand—"

"Oh, I should've known you were the kind of man that would govern that poor, sad orphan boy with force. All the hours of hammering iron . . . A man like you wouldn't know how to use kindness instead of a switch or the back of your hand."

Something within Roamer snapped. He reached down and took hold of the leather strop and tossed it aside.

"I made a promise a good many years ago that I would never raise my hand in anger, Mrs. Smith, and so far I have kept my vow. But I swear you are the most contrary, outspoken, *nosiest* female the good Lord ever gave breath to. And if you don't shut up, I intend to turn you over my knee and give you a good spanking right here in front of God and everybody."

Mattie gasped, filling her lungs with the foul, pungent air. "You wouldn't dare."

"Just try me, schoolmarm." Roamer said with a wicked gleam in his eyes, leaning down until the tips of their noses nearly touched. "Just go right ahead and try me." He narrowed his eyes. "I am mighty tempted to show you some physical force right now, to demonstrate what kind of a brute I truly am."

Three

"Well go ahead, schoolmarm, dare me again," Roamer whispered close to her ear.

Mattie's face stung with heat. Sometime during the altercation with the brute, everyone who had been busy with other things suddenly turned all their attention to the ongoing argument. Feeling embarrassed outrage, she tried to slap him.

He clamped one hard, callused hand onto her wrist, his fingers circling the delicate bones and nearly overlapping. "Are you daring me, schoolmarm? Is that what you are doing?" His voice was low, deep, and menacing.

She struggled against his grip, making little mewling noises that were foreign to her. Hearing the strange sound coming from her own lips made her feel even more foolish. "Unhand me."

"With pleasure." He opened his hand so quickly, his abrupt release sent her staggering awkwardly back. Mattie did two or three rapid, awkward steps before falling on her bustle-padded behind. A little puff of dust flew up around her billowed skirts. Her once-fashionable hat canted across one eye as she glared up at her assailant. The broken blue feather dangled limply in front of her nose, a pitiful testament to her fury.

She blew out a puff of angry breath. The feather fluttered feebly upward for a moment, then drooped back down to rest on the very tip of her nose.

"You sir, are no gentleman," she said stiffly, snapping the feather off at the break and flinging it aside with a toss of her head.

"And you, ma'am, if I may be so bold as to point out right here in front of God and everybody"—Roamer went down on one knee and whispered in Mattie's ear—"are a tight-corseted busybody."

"Oh!" Mattie wished she was on her feet so she could . . . glare down at him, since he was still on one knee—a gallant position for such a rogue to be in. She balled her fists and hit the dirt beside her skirts.

A muffled chuckle reminded her that they were not alone.

Mattie had never brawled in the street with a common bully before. She had always managed to conduct herself like a lady. Even when she was a child and Lottie was trying to climb trees and skip stones, Mattie had kept her apron clean and her stockings up. She had never stooped to this kind of behavior before.

It was all his fault. All because of Roamer Tresh. Even his name was barely civilized.

Roamer. One who is homeless. One who wanders.

She glared up at him, still taller than her even though he was on his knees. His hard-muscled body was a wide, sturdy shadow against the brightness of the day.

Roamer Tresh had made her an object of curiosity

among her friends and neighbors. He was more of a crude degenerate than she had even imagined.

"Help me up this very instant," she commanded.

"My pleasure," he said, rising smoothly to both feet. He grabbed her hand and hauled her up.

"I demand a public apology," she said, drawing herself up, marshaling her dignity while she brushed dirt from her gingham dress. Drat it, she had spent a month's pay on this frock and now it was ruined. Not even Lottie's fine hand could save it.

His brows shot up toward his hairline. "You won't be getting an apology from me. You came butting in, jumping to conclusions, poking your nose where it isn't wanted or needed." Roamer folded his muscular arms across his chest, the seams of his homespun shirt straining as he did so, and glared stubbornly at Mattie. She continued to right her clothing, trying to think of some retort—some way of bending him to her way of thinking.

She glanced up at him again. He had not budged an inch. The line of his body, the very way he stood with his feet braced apart, told her that a good long time would pass before he would give in.

She frowned at him. Even through her anger she noted that under those tawny, scowling brows, his eyes were the purest emerald green she had ever beheld. When he set his jaw just so, a deep, masculine cleft sat in the middle of his square, resolute chin.

No, this was not a man to change his mind. But then neither was she the kind of person to back up.

"Mr. Tresh, I intend to stand here until you say you're sorry." She stamped her foot and made a face.

"Then I guess you'll be standing in the street until hell freezes over, Mrs. Smith."

"Oh!" She stamped her foot and sneezed when the puff of dust found her nostrils.

He chuckled and winked at her. He actually *winked,* as if he found her fit of temper amusing.

Her anger doubled.

"Oh, I should've known the next thing you would do is start spouting profanity!"

"Spouting profanity?" Roamer's arms dropped at his side. His expression sobered. He took a step toward her. "Now just a doggone minute, ma'am, I have never sworn at a woman in my life."

She backed up a step. "Don't you dare lay hands on me again . . . or I'll—"

"Uncle Roamer, Mrs. Smith . . ." Scout interrupted. He wriggled his small body between the pair of battling adults, looking up at them with an expression of worry.

"Scout, stand back before this hooligan strikes you," Mattie warned, taking his shoulders in her hands and trying to hide him behind her skirts.

Roamer rocked back on his heels and stared at her, wide-eyed as an owl caught in the sunshine. "Hooligan?"

"Hooligan I said and hooligan I meant." Mattie took satisfaction in her choice of words while she jutted her chin forward like she had seen Addie do when making a point.

"Women," Roamer said in a low voice; then he put his hand on Scout's shoulder, his fingers touching Mattie's for a moment. She jerked her hand quickly away.

"Come on, Scout, let's go home. If I stay here another minute I will be sorely tempted to do what this woman accuses me of and give her the spanking her papa obviously never did."

With that parting shot Roamer turned on his booted heel and stalked off toward the smithy. Scout gave Mattie an apologetic shrug and trotted after his long-striding uncle.

"Well, now, that was mighty interesting and pretty doggone entertaining," Gus Gruberman said, spitting into the street. "But it doesn't get this mess cleaned up."

Then and only then did the merchants and townspeople turn to stare at their street. Cow patties and puddles that looked like cannon balls had been tossed into the peaceful confines of McTavish Plain. A thin tendril of smoke still rose from one sodden cow chip.

Mattie didn't know if she wanted to laugh or cry. It was ridiculous—ludicrous and silly that she had been pulled into such a debacle. She vowed to make Roamer Tresh regret embarrassing her in this fashion.

"Mattie? Mattie, are you in there?" Addie's voice was full of concern. "Matilda either you answer me or open this door at once."

Mattie hobbled to the door, her backside still tender and sore. The bustle had left a few bruises on muscles that complained loudly each time she left the cushion of her rocking chair.

"I'm coming. Just hold your drawers a minute, will you?" Mattie said, wincing with each step. By the time she opened the door, Addie was practically kicking it down. "You don't need to shout; Lord knows I have given the town enough to talk about without having my sister screaming at my door."

Addie breezed by Mattie, with her usual woven basket slung over her arm. "I heard what happened."

The scent of fresh bread, spices, and roasted chicken wafted to Mattie's nose. She felt better already just knowing she would not have to tax herself in the kitchen. As usual, her older sister was taking good care of her.

"I am quite sure you did," Mattie said sulkily.

"Are you hurt?" Addie squinted and searched her sister's face as if the truth and extent of her injury could be found right there on her cheeks.

"It was awful, Addie, just awful," Mattie sniffed, fighting back tears.

"Tell me what happened. Gus said you were"—Addie rolled her eyes toward the ceiling—"and mind I do not believe this for a minute, Matilda, but Gus said you were sitting in the middle of Main Street, brawling with the blacksmith."

"I was not sitting. I fell. Well, actually, *he* allowed me to fall. Probably planned it that way, the brute." Mattie said sullenly. She rubbed her behind. "It hurt!"

"You were brawling? Well I never." Addie raised her brows in amazement. Then her expression softened. "Are you really hurt, or is it just your pride that is smarting?"

"Oh, Addie, it was just awful."

"Come along, Mattie, I think I might have something to make you feel better." With a knowing smile she turned and went into the kitchen, and Mattie limped after her. Addie started unloading small crocks and cloth-covered bundles of food. She shrugged off her poppy red shawl and draped it over the back of a kitchen chair. Her dress of printed calico bore traces of flour from her morning's baking.

"What you need is a cup of hot tea, Matilda, and some bread and butter. And perhaps a little reminder that you are woman grown and cannot go around fighting in the street."

"It wasn't my fault, Addie. That horrible Roamer Tresh was going to beat his nephew." Mattie blinked at the tears welling in her eyes.

Addie turned slowly. "Oh, Mattie, you have made a mistake. There is no way under God's blue sky that Roamer Tresh would lay hands on that boy. Now, what really happened?"

"It's the truth, Addie. That is what happened. Roamer Tresh had a strop and he was—"

"No, Mattie, it isn't possible."

"I was there. I saw. Why are you so sure?" Mattie sniffed.

Addie picked up the kettle and shook it, the water inside making a hollow glugging sound. "You better sit down. I'll make you a cup of tea and tell you how I know."

"Now you are frightening me," Mattie said as she gingerly lowered her bottom onto a chair. "How can you be so sure I made a mistake in assuming he was going to strop that boy?"

"Roamer Tresh would never, ever strike his nephew, or anybody else. Ian told me Roamer took a vow to never raise his hand against anyone—ever again."

Mattie shook her head from side to side. "Oh, but surely—"

"No, Mattie, you are wrong. Ian told me that

Roamer . . ." Addie opened the tea tin and pinched some up.

"Roamer *what?*" Mattie snapped impatiently. She couldn't have been wrong. She saw the strop in his hand. He was a brute, a big, brawny, hard-muscled cuss.

Addie glanced at her sister as if she had forgotten she was there. "Ian told me Roamer doesn't like to speak about it."

"About what?" Mattie's patience was all but gone.

Addie shook her head and sighed. "Roamer killed a man with his bare hands, Mattie. He killed a man, and he has never gotten over it. That is how I can be so very sure that he would never lay a finger on Scout."

The open grave yawned like a dark mouth in the greening verge. Jack Maravel looked down at the coffin crafted of the finest imported mahogany. It had been hand waxed and polished to a high sheen, outfitted with six shiny brass handles large enough to accommodate wide palms.

He wondered how much the foolish, vain old woman had squandered on the thing. How much of *his* money had been spent to see her leave the world and go to the great beyond? Her funeral had been a big event. Most of the town and a good part of the county around St. Louis had been lined up on the road in respectful silence as the fancy black hearse, complete with crepe fabric in the glass windows, rolled by, pulled by plumed matched grays.

Jack tipped his dusty bowler toward the hole and proffered a twisted smile. "Good-bye, Grandmother.

I hope you have a pleasant journey—and it is about damned time, I must say."

"I should've known you'd be here, Jackson."

The familiar gruff, condemning voice brought Jack spinning around.

"Nobody calls me Jackson anymore."

"I do."

"Yes, I 'spect you would have a long memory," Jack snorted.

Old Judge Mills looked the same: perhaps a little grayer, a little more disapproving, but still as straight and tall and formidable as his money, position, and Protestant morals could make him.

"I have a clear notion, but I may as well ask. Why are you here?"

"It is only right I come to pay my final respects to Grandmother," Jack said in a placating voice that rarely if ever failed to turn the trick. He sucked in his breath and waited, but the judge's expression never softened.

"Ah, yes, your final *respects.*" The Judge gave Jack a disgusted look. "Then you'll be available for the reading of the will after paying those final respects?" Judge Mills said caustically, evidently unaffected by Jack's charm.

"The reading of the will never even entered my mind." Jack flashed a smile out of habit, realizing too late that his charisma was lost on this canny, hard-eyed man. Even in his youth Jack had never been able to get around Judge Mills. "But now that you mention it, I will make every effort to clear my calendar and be available—"

"Save it, Jackson. I am not some doe-eyed female with a nice, fat inheritance to be plucked away, or some lonely old woman with deep pockets and no brains whom you are trying to fleece. You and I both know the will is the only reason you came back. After more than five years, why else would you be here—especially after the way you left?"

Jack shrugged. "Family devotion? A desire to see my last relative laid properly to rest?"

"Ha. When pigs fly," the judge snorted.

Jack bristled, but he quickly controlled himself. What did it matter that everyone in St. Louis knew him for what he was? As soon as he pocketed the old woman's millions he would be off to Paris. Never again would he be broke. He would buy himself the biggest, most vulgar diamond ring he could find. And he would order tailor-made suits and handmade boots crafted of the finest Spanish leather. Jack would finally be able to live the life he was born to live.

"I will be reading the will at two o'clock in my study." Jack looked up to see Judge Mills staring at the face of his gold pocket watch. When he snapped the case shut, Jack flinched. His own watch had been pawned for just enough money to buy a spavined horse and get back here to St. Louis.

"Be on time, Jackson," the judge added. "I don't intend to wait on you."

"Will Susan be there?" Jack asked absently, toeing a clod of dirt onto the casket. It hit the mahogany with a hollow thud, breaking apart in a burst of dust.

Judge Mills returned the watch to his broadcloth vest pocket. "I will give you the benefit of the doubt and assume you are sincere and do not know that Susan has been occupying that piece of earth yonder for four years."

Jack raised his head sharply and looked at the moss-flecked headstone next to his grandmother's open grave. He read the name cut into the stone for the first time.

SUSAN TRESH MARAVEL
TAKEN TOO SOON

"I didn't know," Jack mused.

"That in itself is a sorry recommendation, Jackson."

A long silence passed between them while Judge Mills clenched and unclenched his blue-veined fists. Finally he reached out and put a hand—a surprisingly strong hand—on Jack's shoulder, turning Jack toward him.

"Aren't you even going to ask how Susan died, or what happened to your child?" Judge Mill's rheumy eyes were sharp with anger.

Jack shrugged off the man's hand. "Frankly, I don't care how she died. And I didn't want the little brat in the first place. I made it plain to Susan when I left that I wanted nothing to do with her or the child. Not then, not ever." Jack sneered at the shock and disgust in the judge's face.

"My Grandmother has finally had the good grace to die, but that doesn't change a thing. As far as I am concerned, I don't have a child—maybe I never really did."

The longcase clock tucked in a corner against elegant wainscoting was tolling two o'clock when Jack entered the stately study, following a stripling youth in fine livery. Rows of books bound in fine Moroccan leather and embossed in gold-leaf lettering lined shelves of waxed oak from the parquet floor to the pressed-tin ceiling. The judge's private library smelled of old, respectable money and pious hypocrisy. Jack wondered how much the upkeep on the books cost the penny-pinching Judge.

"I hope it is a bundle," he whispered to himself as he stood on thick carpet and surveyed the sun-mottled space. His gaze lingered on the judge, who sat behind a massive, ornately carved desk.

A white-haired black man brought in a silver tea service and placed it on one corner of the Judge's desk.

"Thank you, Albert," Judge Mills said without looking up from the sheaf of papers in his hand.

Jack sat down in a tall, stuffed armchair. He stretched out his legs, staring openly at the servant. The dignified old black man cast a withering glance at Jack's boot heels and the marks they left on the pale Aubusson carpet.

Jack nearly snorted with laughter. He remembered Albert when the fool had still been a slave wearing a copper tag of identification around his neck like a cur dog. Judge Mills had bought Albert and set him free. It was plain to see the darky had gotten way too uppity with his betters.

"That will be all, Albert," Judge Mills said when he glanced up and found Albert and Jackson glaring at each other.

Jack gave the servant a mock salute before the pocket doors slid closed. Let the pompous judge's servants treat him like trash—their opinion counted for less than nothing. In a few minutes he would be rich as Croesus. Then Jack would thumb his nose at the whole town, from the lowest darky to the judge himself. In fact, Jack might rent one of the fine hotels on the river and throw a party to celebrate. Or he might drag out a few skeletons from some upper-crust closets—there were certainly more than enough to choose from. Not everyone in town was as pearly white as they liked to pretend. Jack had a long memory, and he knew where all the bodies and scandals were buried.

"I see no reason to delay any longer. I expect nobody else to come. The servants are aware of the portion they are receiving," Judge Mills said with a heavy sigh. "Your grandmother was a very rich woman . . ." He glared at Jack. "As you well know."

"I haven't been on the receiving end of her wealth or largesse for some time now," Jack quipped, steepling his fingers.

"And with good reason—"

Jack raised his hand to halt the Judge's words. "Spare me yet another lecture about my dissolute ways." Jack frowned and plucked at the fraying edge of his fancy lace cuff, noticing for the first time how tawdry his appearance was. Even the judge's servants were turned out better.

"Fine, I won't bother to read all the particulars to you, Jackson. Suffice it to say Rebekah Analise Maravel was of sound mind and body, her documents have been duly witnessed—"

"I am sure you saw that every detail was in order as always," Jack said mockingly.

Judge Mills did not react but continued to scan the documents, reading in a singsong voice. "She left her entire fortune, with the exception of a few odd pieces of jewelry and personal items that went to her maid . . ."

Jack's heart was pounding in his chest. He could practically taste the French champagne, feel the bubbles tickling his nose. No more would he have to cheat at cards or climb out a second-story window in the middle of the night to keep from being thrown in jail for unpaid hotel bills. He wouldn't ride spavined nags ever again. He would have the finest team and several carriages—

". . . the mining interests, the railroad stocks, the shipping interests . . ."

He was going to be rich, so rich he could buy and sell pompous little men like Judge Mills.

". . . the house and grounds in Amberson Square, the cash, and various deeds to the properties and farm interests in New Orleans—"

People wouldn't call him Laughing Jack Maravel with a snigger in their voice. When they spoke to him after today it would be with an air of respect. They would bow and scrape before him. Money was power, and if there was one thing Jack Maravel understood it was how to wield power. Finally he was going to be able to buy some dignity and respect and get what was due him from the narrow-minded little people of St. Louis.

He was barely able to suppress his grin.

". . . all property real and otherwise without encumbrance in the town of St. Louis . . ."

Now, any minute now . . .

". . . to Judson Walker Maravel."

Jack's heart stopped beating. He swallowed. His mouth had gone so dry, he nearly choked. He lurched forward in the chair, wanting to stand but not trusting his wobbly legs.

"What? For a moment I thought you said Judson

Walker Maravel, but you really meant to say Jackson. . . . Right?"

"No. I did not. I said and meant Judson Walker Maravel as it is written here and witnessed. Rebekah left her entire estate to Judson Walker Maravel." Judge Mills glared at Jack.

Jack lurched to his feet. His vision was blurring. He couldn't think, couldn't breathe. "Who the hell is Judson Walker Maravel?"

Judge Mills smiled, slowly, as if he were deriving great satisfaction from the act. It was a wicked expression that made the lines in his face deep. He laid the papers down and steepled his fingers together, leaning back in his comfortable padded chair. There was a gleam of malicious contentment in his eyes.

"Judson Walker Maravel is Susan's only child. Surely you remember, Jackson. I believe you referred to him today at the cemetery. You called him the little brat you never wanted—the child you denied only hours ago. That is Judson Walker Maravel," Judge Mills said dryly.

"But that isn't possible," Jack croaked.

"Why aren't you laughing now, Jack?" The judge said with a deep chuckle. "Don't you see the humor in all this? I certainly do. The child you deny is now rich—rich beyond imagining."

Four

"I'll give you two dollars for both of them. And Laughing Jack, *mon ami,* you should be very grateful for my generosity, eh? We both know these spoons, the finest silver and monogrammed, no less, they're stolen property, *n'est ce pas?*" Pierre winked. "But I am intrigued. How did you manage to get entree into a house fine enough and respectable enough to have such silver on the table? I had heard your name was not uttered in polite company."

Jack bit back the vulgar retort he so wanted to fling in the Frenchman's face. He had pocketed the pair of silver spoons from the judge's own tea service after the reading of the will.

The damned will.

Jack had been escorted to the door after he voiced his opinion of that document. Albert had called two burly stable hands to remove him, kicking and swearing, from the judge's house. The spoons that he managed to snag and put into his coat pocket were worth twice what Pierre offered, but Jack couldn't quibble. He needed a stake, and it gave him a bit of perverse pleasure to know that he had stolen them from the high and mighty Judge Mills.

"Fine, Pierre; since we're such old friends, I'll let you have them cheap. I will take what you offer."

Pierre chuckled around the cigar clamped between his yellowing teeth. His long moustache was heavily waxed and carried the attar of garlic. It repelled Jack that he had to deal with such a person now—now when he should be rich, now when he should have servants and lackeys at his beck and call.

He silently cursed his grandmother.

"*Oui,* Jack, you keep telling yourself that you are doing me a favor and we will both be happy with the bargain." With a beefy hand he slapped two coins down on the scarred slab of wood that served as desk and saloon bar. "I had imagined you to be up to your ass in fine whiskey and dancing girls since your *grand-mere* died. All your bragging about the fortune, it was just the wishful thinking, eh?"

Jack narrowed his eyes, but he was careful to keep the veneer of his smile in place. "I will have my rightful fortune soon enough. There are just one or two small legal details I need to tend to; then it will all be mine—as it should've been all along."

"*Mon dieu!* Still whining because your Papa did not leave his estate to you, I see. What did you expect after the life you have led? When your wife was murdered—"

"Murdered?" Jack realized too late his slip of the tongue as Pierre's dark eyes narrowed in crafty speculation.

"Ah, so you did not know?" Pierre spat into the dirty spittoon beside the bar. "She was beaten to death—they say because she had not the money to pay your debts."

"A story like that can be no more than idle gossip,"

Jack said lightly, but a shiver ran up his spine. Was it the truth? He had left before Harry Malone could get his thugs to break his knees. And though Harry had made threats, Jack had never suspected they would go after Susan.

Was Harry still looking for him?

"Gossip, you say? *Non.* After your wife was buried, her brother, the big one with the cat eyes, that one went a little crazy."

"The big ox always was crazy. Since you seem to be in the know on all of my family business, Pierre, what happened to Susan's brat?" Jack poured himself a drink; after all, Pierre was cheating him on the spoons.

Pierre laughed. "Poor Laughing Jack. You do not know much these days, do you? It is sad, is it not, to lose contact with one's family?"

"Oh, yeah, very sad. Now why don't you tell me, Pierre, since you are dying to give me every detail." Jack tossed back the drink and poured another.

"Your brother-in-law—the big one—he saw to the justice of his sister's death. He found Harry Malone and did to him what had been done to your wife."

Ah, so Harry won't be a threat. Jack let out a relieved sigh.

"And the child, Pierre?"

The Frenchman lifted his brows. "I hear your brother-in-law took the child and left. I have heard it said that he went west, but you know how these stories are. A man is killed, another disappears." He gave a shrug. "It is always said he goes to the West or to the North."

So Roamer killed Harry and took the kid—Susan's

brat. A brat named Judson Maravel. A smile tugged at Jack's lips.

At last his luck was changing. A man on the run wouldn't be too inclined to argue over giving up Susan's whelp. Roamer wouldn't have any choice but to hand him over. And then Jack would make sure all the papers were filed right and proper so he could control the money and then he could dump him.

No, Roamer wouldn't have any choice. But if Roamer didn't like it and wouldn't back off at the threat of being turned in for murder, then Jack would have to kill him, or have him killed. But assassins cost money, and good ones cost even more. Thanks to Jack's grandmother and his tightfisted, moralistic father, he had none.

"I hope they are both rotting in hell," he said and splashed back another drink. "Right beside sweet, simpering Susan."

Ian cast the fishing line out into the middle of the slow-moving current. Angus and Fergus ran back and forth along the damp loamy bank, chirping and grunting and making impatient otter noises. Three dark eyes winked in the lazy sun.

"Have some patience, lads." Ian said. "It takes a bit of time to tempt the fishies."

The sound of a stick breaking underfoot brought Ian turning around. The Salish had been quiet since Grass Singing's death, but Ian was ever watchful for trouble. His hand was on the hilt of his knife when a thatch of hair appeared beside a sapling. Ian was surprised to find Scout Maravel peeking at him from behind a newly leafing branch.

"Do you fish, lad?" Ian asked with a grin, unconsciously relaxing.

"Uh-huh."

"Then come and help me get dinner for these two walking glove liners."

"Glove liners?" Scout repeated.

"Yep, I have been promising to skin them and make a pair of gloves for years."

Scout wrinkled his nose and looked at the otters. They tumbled and chirped along the bank, their soft feet packing the earth smooth and shiny.

"Come on. They are always hungry, and today, impatient as well."

"Can't they catch their own fish?" Scout said, plopping down beside the water, unmindful of the mud that clung to his trousers and shoes.

"Heroes such as these fine lads should'na have to do their own fishin'. 'Tis only fittin' that I pay proper respect to them."

"Heroes? Those otters?" Scout wrinkled his nose in doubt. "But that one only has one good eye and the other one runs funny 'cause of his crooked tail."

"Aye, those are the marks of their honor." Ian cleared his throat and turned to Scout. "Do you know what a hero is, lad?"

"Sure, Mrs. Smith told us about the heroes that fought and got us free from England."

Ian scowled and spat. "Bloody damned English." Then he turned back to Scout and smiled. "Aye, that's one kind of hero, but there are others. Remember David and Goliath?"

"Yes sir, but he had a slingshot."

Ian chuckled. "Aye, he had that, lad. Do you have a slingshot?"

"No."

Ian laughed and pulled a rolled-up bit of rawhide from a pouch at the waist of his buckskins. "David had a slingshot and every good shepherd since has carried one." He unfurled the leather and put it in Scout's hand. "Now you have one as well."

The boy's smile was sheer sunshine as he closed his hand over the leather. Then he frowned at the otters as if just remembering them.

"What could a couple of crippled-up otters do that would make them heroes?" He smoothed out the thongs on the slingshot.

"Ah, lad, these two otters saved my wife's life. That is how Angus lost his eye and when Fergus's tail was ruined. She surely would have froze to death if not for them. They flung their bodies down a steep cliff for no other reason than their great love and heroic hearts."

Scout sat up straighter and stared at the otters with renewed respect. Uncle Roamer called Mr. McTavish a man of his word, so he couldn't be joshing about his wife nearly dying, or about what the otters had done.

"Really?"

"Aye. She owes her life to those glove liners." Ian chuckled and shook his head. "I will be truthful, lad, sometimes it surprises me too that a couple of furry nuisances could do what they did."

"I wish I was a hero," Scout said softly, experimentally giving the slingshot a twirl and smacking himself in the cheek.

"Ah, lad, anybody can be a hero. All you have to do is see a thing that needs to be done and do it; no matter the risk and the consequences, a hero canna be stopped. He keeps to his goal until the task is finished, even when it turns unpleasant, as life oft does."

Scout considered that for a minute. He thought of his uncle Roamer and Mrs. Smith—things had turned awfully unpleasant between them. The otters tumbled over to him and nudged his hand until he petted them. They looked different to him now. Whereas before Scout saw only their imperfections, now he saw their worth and he knew. If otters could be heroes, then so could a boy who wanted a mama. He could find a way to get a secret widow and a man who didn't want to be married together.

"You won't really make them into gloves, will ya?"

"No, lad, I willna. They have a home beside the fire and I will catch fish for them as long as they live, because they are heroes," Ian said softly, and he tossed the line back into the current.

"Oh, Mr. Jones, you are so knowledgeable about Lord Byron and his poetry," Mattie simpered and batted her lashes. It was not an entirely intelligent way to speak to a man, but she had seen young Mrs. Edwards do it to her husband. The man practically fell all over himself to do her bidding after that, so Mattie was trying it out. Of course she had to watch exactly what she said, for as far as Mr. Jones or anybody else knew, she was a married woman. Mattie was careful; she kept her flirting respectable but practiced the simpering voice and the little artful wiles that she was sure would eventually land her a sensitive, deep, thoughtful man.

"Do you mind? My hands are a little cold." She slipped her fingers into the crook of his arm just like she had seen Mrs. Edwards do. It was just innocent enough not to provoke gossip, but she saw a pink glow in Mr. Jones's pale, lean cheeks. He was not a big man, not much taller than she was, and lean built. And he was quite well-read—the kind of man who would understand a pure, intellectual love. Mattie rather fancied the shy young printer and thought he might be just the man she was looking for. She laughed at nothing in particular and drew a little nearer to him. Yes, he might just be the man for her. When enough time had elapsed and she wrote herself a letter saying she had become a widow, Mr. Jones would be there to comfort her.

Mattie had it all worked out in her head. She could have a nice, intelligent man who wasn't interested in all that sweaty groping and foolishness. They would share a love of the minds.

Her life would be perfect.

Scout hunkered down lower and pulled a face. He had never heard Mrs. Smith speak with that funny, kittenish mewling sound in her voice. He wondered if she had something in her eye because she kept fanning her lashes really fast, as if she couldn't keep them open—or maybe they were stinging.

She was acting all funny, laughing over nothing. Walking really close to Mr. Jones.

Moonstruck, Uncle Roamer would probably call it. But it wasn't even sundown yet, so he doubted that Mrs. Smith was moonstruck.

What if Mr. McTavish saw? What if he figured out that Mrs. Smith's husband was dead and she was looking for a new man on the sly? What if he made her leave town?

Scout stuck his hand in his pocket. The slingshot

Mr. McTavish gave him was all he had—but then it was all David had against Goliath, and look how well that turned out. In fact, David had become a genuine hero.

Scout took a deep breath and stood up, putting the stone in the sling of leather just like Mr. McTavish had shown him. Then he began to swing it over his head, the leather singing through the air with each arc.

The stone came from nowhere, hitting with a sharp plop that made Mattie gasp. Michael Jones's tall beaver hat flew down the street, and his eyes rolled back in his head as he collapsed and slid like warm molasses to the hard-packed street.

"Mr. Jones?" Mattie knelt beside him, fanning his face, touching his cheeks.

From the corner of her eye she saw Scout Maravel skinning out of the bushes toward his home as if Satan were nipping at his heels.

"Lord have mercy, that child is going to kill someone. It is high time I had another talk with that reprobate Roamer Tresh."

Michael Jones moaned and put his hand to the swelling bruise.

"And I am going to do it just as soon as you regain full consciousness, Mr. Jones, I promise you that."

Mattie raised her hand and knocked for the third time.

"Open this door at once, Roamer Tresh, I know you are in there. It is time you had a piece of my mind." Mattie knocked again, hard enough to make her knuckles smart from the effort. She was certain she heard someone moving around inside.

"Don't try to avoid me. It won't work." She banged on the door with her fist. "I am not leaving until we talk. You might as well open up and face me. Hiding behind a closed door will not prevent me from speaking to you."

Roamer was standing in the big half barrel he and Scout used for a tub, lathering up his hair. An accident with the worn bellows had left him covered with coal soot from head to toe. His clothes would have to be laundered, and he had to bathe in the middle of the week. He had just begun to work up a good suds upon his hair, noticing that he needed a haircut but loath to go see that weasel Hudspeth, when Roamer thought he heard something.

He tilted his head, his hands buried in suds, and listened.

Nothing.

He dismissed it as a trick of liquid in his ears and finished his lathering. He started to rinse with a pitcher full of cold water, and as the lather sluiced off his wet head in white sheets, he heard the sound again.

Roamer shook off the water and realized the noise was an insistent banging on his front door.

"Scout?" He muttered, pouring another pitcher of water over his hair. Suds slid down his back and over his buttocks, tickling his legs like a dozen spiders as the soap meandered through the hair on his wet thighs and calves.

"Maybe I put the bar across the door and forgot," he muttered when the loud knocking continued.

He stepped out of the tub and snagged a clean sheet off the pile of clothes that he had yet to fold. The scent of clean fabric dried in sunshine wafted to his nose, and he slung the sheet loosely around his hips. Cursing mildly under his breath, Roamer strode to the door, leaving wet prints on the pine floor.

"Damn, now I'll have to mop up a mess before I can get supper together." All in all, it had been a bad day, and the housework was piling up faster than Roamer could get to it.

Roamer opened the door. "Doggone it, Scout—"

"Mr. Tresh I am here—"

The breeze evaporated the water on his skin, chilling him. Roamer squinted and swiped at a bit of soap lather in his eyes.

"Mrs. Smith?"

"Oh my!" Mattie stared, too stunned and fascinated to look away. Roamer was mostly bare and he was huge. Well, she had known he was big, but she didn't know he was *big*.

A thick white scar ran from his collarbone to his right nipple.

Nipple?

Mattie blushed. She had never even formed that word in her mind until this moment. Nipples and breasts and wide expanses of bronzed flesh were physical—and astonishing—and things that a properly brought-up woman did not say or think. But lands! There was so much of him she could not help but think about it.

She stared in mute awe. Roamer was smooth, hard, and all male. His chest seemed to fill the doorway, his shoulders, corded and ridged from swinging a blacksmith's hammer, were solid as the peaks of Redbird Mountain.

She lowered her eyes.

That was a mistake.

A small squeak escaped her lips when her embarrassed gaze locked onto what she found below Roamer's naval. Big.

Big.

"Oh my. Oh, oh my." She said again and swallowed hard.

Roamer didn't know what to think of Mrs. Smith. She was wide-eyed, and two bright circles of color were flaming on each cheek. She just kept repeating those words: "Oh my."

Roamer glanced down to see what had tied her tongue in knots and was stunned to see the sheet had caught on one damp hip bone, not covering much of what God gave him. His altogether was right there, in the altogether. And the schoolmarm was looking at him like—well, like she had never seen a grown man before.

Embarrassed annoyance ripped through him as he gave the sheet a jerk and covered himself.

"What do you want?" he snarled.

Her eyes snapped up to his face. She was still open-mouthed and bug-eyed. For all the world, she acted as if she had never seen a grown man before in her life. A married woman had no call to look at him as if he were malformed or something. For pity's sake, he was just a man. And goll-dang! A married woman had no call to be blushing and staring like an awe-struck virgin. He wasn't that much different than any-body else—all right, so he was a tad on the large side, but it wasn't his fault; that was the way God made him. And the schoolmarm had no call to treat him like a freak of nature.

"Oh my," she said again.

"I asked you what you wanted, Mrs. Smith."

Never in her life had she imagined. When she read

poetry and looked at the classically carved statues from the ancient civilizations like Rome and Greece, well, she just never imagined. And those little fig leaves—well, how in the world could she have known?

Roamer was not prose or stone; he was flesh—large, hard-muscled flesh. Just looking at him had made her tingle all over—even in places where she didn't think a body was supposed to tingle.

"Mrs. Smith? Is there something I can do for you?" he repeated gruffly, tucking one edge of the sheet in over the top at his lean waist.

"Y-y-yes." Mattie blinked and tried to sort her jumbled thoughts. She shook off the amazement and pulled herself up straight. "Yes, yes, there is. I have come to speak to you about Scout."

Roamer's deep green eyes narrowed down to slits. Mattie could practically read his thoughts.

She interjected quickly, "I realize the last time I spoke to you about Scout—well, I accused you of being some sort of beast that beats children and women."

"Yes, I believe you called me a brute among other things."

"Well, I was wrong." She said.

"Now you think otherwise?" he said, raising one tawny brow. "All of a sudden you *don't* think I beat Scout?"

"Yes—I mean no."

"Why?" he demanded. "I am the same man. Why have you changed your opinion?"

"My sister—my sister Addie assures me I was wrong." Mattie could not bring herself to say she knew Roamer had committed murder. The very idea of it left a hard knot in her stomach.

"I am sorry I jumped to conclusions."

A shadow of some deep pain passed over Roamer's face. "What else did your sister say?"

"Oh, nothing really," Mattie lied. "Just that Ian knew you well and that I was entirely wrong."

He studied her face for a moment with the same keen intensity that Scout used. "Fine, I accept your apology. Is there anything else? As you can see I am in the middle of something."

Once again her eyes flicked from the top of his tawny head to his bare toes and back again. She had the good grace not to linger long at his groin—well, not *too* long.

"Scout needs guidance, Mr. Tresh," She blurted out. "May—may I come in and speak with you?"

Roamer's brows rose to his damp hairline. He was feeling just contrary enough to let her in, to let the foolish marm's reputation be ruined. "Be my guest," he said with a frosty smile.

Mattie squeezed by him, careful not to brush against him lest she touch what was nestled beneath that damp swath of linen.

"Thank you." Mattie marched to one of the chairs positioned in front of the fireplace. She perched stiffly on the edge and swept a quick, assessing gaze over the room.

"Jumping to conclusions again, Mrs. Smith?" Roamer strode across the room and took the chair opposite her. "Did you expect to see chicken heads laying in heaps? Perhaps a hog or two running tame about the house?"

Mattie held her tongue, but she couldn't stop her cheeks from burning. She had expected something far from this tidy, all-male domain, and she certainly hadn't expected the fresh scent of line-dried laundry to fill the room. But she sure wasn't about to admit that to Roamer Tresh.

"Uh-huh, I thought so," Roamer said with a satisfied grin. "Well, Mrs. Smith, I can't say I am sorry to disappoint you."

Mattie wanted to look away from those twinkling green eyes but was afraid her gaze would fasten on the sheet, and she couldn't, just *couldn't* do that again even though her curiosity was begging her to take one last, long look.

The image of his form was still there, behind her eyes, lurking, waiting to be examined closely. His private parts had astounded her. He was so different from her—beautiful and a little frightening—and she knew a proper lady shouldn't be thinking about it, but she was.

Oh, she was. Her natural curiosity was nudging at the edges of her mind, taunting her, wanting her to explore this new mystery.

"You wanted to talk about Scout?"

"Oh . . . yes. He is just too full of the devil and he needs a woman in his life."

"A woman?" Roamer said, stretching out his legs, making himself comfortable in his chair. "Why? As you can see, we do just fine alone. I don't need a cook or a housekeeper, if that's what you are thinking."

Mattie sat up straighter, forcing herself to maintain the proper attitude. "Yes, well . . ."

Don't look at his bare legs. And don't think about what is between them.

"Scout needs a mother."

Roamer's tawny brows furrowed. He took a deep breath. Mattie-the-marm was the most contrary, nosiest woman he had ever met.

"A mother? What filled your head with that nonsense?"

"I have been watching Scout, and you and I—"

Don't look at his feet or his thighs beneath that sheet.

"Ma'am, I don't make a habit of discussing my personal business with just anyone," Roamer said coldly, pulling the sheet tightly together just below his thighs.

Mattie felt her cheeks heating again when she realized she had been staring at those rock-hard legs. They were long and big as tree trunks, but there was a strange, raw beauty about them. His feet were big—everything about him was big and male and fascinating.

"Ma'am?"

She looked up. "I am sorry. This was a bad idea. I should've known that . . ." Her words trailed off.

If only he had some clothes on.

"This situation with Scout is getting worse each day. Mr. Tresh, you don't like me very much, do you?" she suddenly blurted out.

Roamer blinked. Her directness had taken him by surprise. "Well, now—"

"No, it's all right. I don't like you very much either. But I care for Scout very much. He is a lonely little boy. I believe he is acting up in an attempt to get attention. He needs a mother."

"I have to disagree with you. He is a healthy, ornery boy. Soon enough he'll settle. There is an old saw, Mrs. Smith. The wilder the colt, the better the horse. I have an idea Scout will be a fine young man."

"But—"

"No." Roamer shook his head, damp strands of hair snaking around his square jaw. "Mrs. Smith, since you have laid your cards out on the table, I will be honest as well. I don't much care for you but I can see you are genuine in your feelings for Scout, and I appreciate that. But I won't tolerate you—or anyone—interfering with me and Scout. We are the only family we've got, and we do just fine alone. I have no intention of getting married—now or ever. Marriage, as far as I can see, is a bad bargain at best and a living hell at worst. No, I will never marry."

Silence hung in the room. Mattie could hear the ticking of a clock from the bedroom. She should go. She lifted her hand from her lap, looking at the gold band on her own finger.

"Is there anything else?" Roamer asked.

"No."

"Then, Mrs. Smith, it is time for you to go." He grabbed up the edges of the sheet to keep it in place around his waist. "I have to get supper ready for Scout."

"I hope you understand, I was only trying to help—" She halted and turned so abruptly they almost collided.

Roamer glared down at her, his deep green eyes lit by indignation. "Thank you, but I think I can manage my nephew's upbringing without any help from you."

"Perhaps, but in spite of the fact that you can keep a clean house and can evidently cook, I still think Scout needs a mother." And with that, Mattie opened the door and stepped out, slamming it soundly behind her. Only when she was halfway home did she realize that she had forgotten to tell Roamer Tresh that Scout had knocked Michael Jones unconscious. In fact, she barely could remember what Michael Jones looked like, since the picture of Roamer Tresh naked and glorious was occupying every bit of her mind.

Five

"Scout, you can come out now." Roamer flipped off the sheet and pulled on his union suit.

The towhead appeared from behind the kindling box. "How did you know I was there?" Scout asked, scratching his knee.

"I smelled you." Roamer said with a grin. "Where have you been boy, wrestling with a coon? Or is it polecat I smell?"

"I found a hollowed-out place near the creek. I thought something was living in it. Maybe a fox with little kits and I could get one for a pet." Scout scratched his mud-caked cheek with a dirty finger. "It would be awful nice to have a pet, Uncle Roamer."

"You stay out of those hollowed-out dens 'afore you find yourself facing a mama bear." Roamer slid into a clean shirt and trousers. Then he turned to Scout. "Now tell me what you've been up to that has got Mattie-the-marm up in arms again."

Scout stared at the toe of his shoe.

"Come on, boy, look at me." Roamer said softly.

Slowly, reluctantly, as if the movement were difficult to manage, Scout finally raised his head. He wrinkled up his nose and scratched his cheek again.

"Now what have you been up to?" Roamer crossed his arms at his chest and looked stern.

"I was practicing with my slingshot. I'm gettin' real good, too."

"Where did you get a slingshot?"

"Mr. McTavish gave it to me. He said heroes used them."

Roamer tried not to grin at the serious expression on Scout's face. The boy was a caution, but it was difficult to be angry with him when Roamer's heart was overflowing with love.

"And just what were you using as a target while you were practicin'?" Roamer sat down in the chair and patted his thigh, and Scout sidled over and scooted up on his leg.

"Well, I was sorta aiming at Mr. Jones's beaver hat. But I swung a little harder than I intended and it kinda' knocked the hat off his head."

"And?"

"And it kinda' knocked him out cold. I didn't know a body's eyes rolled back until all you could see was whites," Scout said with all the true curiosity of a small boy.

Roamer nearly guffawed. Now he knew what had brought the marm to his house. And now it explained why Mattie-the-marm was fit to be tied. He had seen her making strange calf eyes at Mr. Jones, though why a married woman would look twice at that pale, shy man was a mystery. She was a strange woman. She seemed to pay an odd amount of attention to single men and other people's business in general. Her husband needed to get his butt home and keep her in line.

The image of her face flashed through Roamer's

mind. An odd satisfaction thrummed through his chest as he imagined Mattie Smith's eyes when she had her temper up.

"Uncle Roamer?" Scout's quavering voice drew Roamer's thoughts from Mattie-the-marm to his nephew. Scout's face was puckered up in deep concentration as he stared up at Roamer.

"You ain't awful mad at me, are you?"

"Well, I am disappointed in you, Scout, but no, I ain't awful mad. But promise me you won't use anything living for practice again. You coulda' killed him, you know."

"I kinda' thought he might be dead until I heard him moaning, then Mrs. Smith saw me and I knew I was in for it," Scout said softly.

"Promise me, Scout. No more slingshots, no more nonsense to get the marm all het up and poking her nose where it don't belong."

"I promise, Uncle Roamer."

"Good. Now go and skin off those clothes. The tub is probably cooling, so hurry and hop in. Use plenty of soap and wash up to get that stink off you. I don't want to contemplate my dinner with your perfume up my nose."

"A bath? But it ain't even Saturday, Uncle Roamer."

"Do as I say, boy," Roamer said gruffly. "And don't do anything else to upset Mrs. Smith."

Mattie stepped inside her tidy little house and tossed her bonnet and shawl on the back of the rocker. She found the matches and lit a lamp. Then she went into the kitchen and unwrapped the bundle that Addie had dropped by earlier.

Inside were two crusty loaves of bread and a small crock of fresh butter.

Mattie sliced off the heel and slathered on the butter. But halfway to taking her first bite, she paused while memories of Roamer Tresh danced through her mind.

"Oh, bother," she said, sagging into a kitchen chair.

All the way home, with every step, in fact, she had told herself that she was being silly. But the picture of his tall, hard, damp body would not be banished.

"I never imagined," she mused, still holding the bread and butter near her mouth. "How could I?"

Mattie had spent her life reading poetry and romantic sonnets. She had savored every word written about passion, but never in any book had she encountered anything that heated her blood and captured her fancy like Roamer Tresh's body.

"I wanted to touch him," she admitted softly. "I wanted to touch him and find if his skin is smooth, like touching polished stone."

For that was what he had looked like: a statue hewn from living rock, fashioned from man's highest ideal of what mortal man should be.

"For surely, no man of flesh and blood should look like *that,*" she said with a wistful sigh, and finally she took a bite of bread and butter.

Scout hunkered down in the lilac bush and waited. The outhouse was empty, but it wouldn't stay that way long. At recess there was always a steady procession of giggling girls who traveled in small troops, followed by teasing boys who would heed nature's call before they had to go back inside the schoolhouse.

He looked down at the flour sack at his feet. He had a time getting the critter, but it was going to be worth it. In fact, he was hoping that this would bring Mrs. Smith back to the house, and that this time when she suggested that Uncle Roamer needed to get married, she would tell him that her husband had died and he needed to marry *her.*

Scout nudged the sack with his foot. It moved. Gingerly he reached down and picked up the sack, disturbing it as little as possible. Then, with one last look to be sure nobody was about, he hurried to the outhouse with his sack.

Quick as he could manage, Scout untied the knotted string at the top. Then he carefully put the bag inside. It would only be a matter of minutes before the inquisitive animal nudged the neck open and escaped into the cool, dim confines of the privy.

If he was lucky, he would have Mrs. Smith for a mama by the weekend.

Dashing back under the cover of the lilac bush, Scout squatted down and waited. If this stunt didn't convince his uncle Roamer that he needed a mama, then surely nothing short of a lightning bolt would.

Mattie finished her buttered bread and the buttermilk that Addie had sent to the schoolhouse while she read the sonnets Mr. Jones had sent her. She stood up, carefully brushed the crumbs from her pale blue silk frock, careful not to damage the delicate lace that Lottie had pin-tucked into rows down the front.

It was by far the most expensive and most stylish frock Mattie had ever owned. The material had to be shipped all the way from St. Louis, and Lottie had fingered it as if it were spun gold. They had spent hours poring over the pattern book, deciding whether or not it was too fancy for a schoolteacher in a small town. Mattie had finally decided that she needed the dress for the time when she announced to McTavish Plain that she had become a widow. She had been counting the weeks, waiting until a respectable time had elapsed since Addie was "widowed."

Mattie put her hands on the small of her back and stretched. She could see the children playing tag and blindman's bluff outside the open window, dodging around a cottonwood tree, giggling and squealing with delight.

"I better go to the privy and then ring them back in before they wear themselves out and can't do their sums for fatigue," Mattie muttered to herself, cleaning a handful of crumbs from her desk.

The book of sonnets had been a nice gesture and a lovely present. And for the first time in many long days, she found herself thinking of the erudite Mr. Jones instead of the physical Roamer Tresh.

Mattie was humming a merry tune when she opened the outhouse door. Momentarily blinded by the darkness, she stepped inside and turned the wooden block that served as a latch. She bumped something with her foot.

And then, even before she had her skirts and heavy petticoats hitched up—

Mattie screamed, but screaming only filled her lungs with the stink. Her nose stung, she tasted vile, slightly oily musk on the back of her tongue. Her lunch threatened to come up.

She groped for the wooden block to free herself from the dark, smelly prison, but couldn't seem to find it. Gagging, choking, weeping, she banged on the door with her balled-up fists and wondered if the critter was going to run up her leg any moment.

"Help! Oh, please, help!"

She heard the children squealing her name, but they sounded far, far away. Other voices—deeper, louder—soon followed. She was ill; she was choking. Her eyes burned so much she had shut them against the pain. She might have been inside the privy for moments or for hours.

"Hurry, help me!" she croaked. "Oh, somebody, please open the door."

Then suddenly the door was wrenched open. Mattie staggered out into the sunshine. Gratitude at her faceless rescuer flowed over her. Her throat and nostrils were raw. She couldn't see through the tears, and her nose was burning like fire. She rubbed at her eyes, but they only stung and burned worse so she gave up, flailing her hands in front of her as she walked.

She stumbled against something solid. "Oh, thank goodness." Her arms went around whatever it was, grateful to have found someone to cling to while virtually blind and helpless.

"Whoooeeee! Mrs. Smith," Roamer Tresh said with barely suppressed horror as he reached out and steadied her. His hands fit nicely around her corsetted waist. "You have been skunked. And judging from the guilty look on his face, I think I have a good idea of who did it."

* * *

Roamer looked up from the forge and saw them coming. He saw Horace and Harriet Miller, Gus Gruberman, Nate Pearson and his brood, and even the lanky, pale Michael Jones, the small bluish bruise on his forehead still visible. The whole town—in buggies, wagons, and on foot—was trooping up Main Street. Each member of McTavish Plain cast one withering glance his way and headed straight for the church.

"Scout." Roamer put the iron he was working back into the coals and looked at his nephew.

"Yes sir?"

"I want you to go into the leanto in back. I want you to think real hard on what you done today."

"Yes sir." Scout said, avoiding Roamer's stern gaze.

"And I want you to know I am mighty disappointed in you."

"Yes sir." Scout's bottom lip quivered and his eyes welled with tears. It was hard for Roamer to keep from hugging him up and telling him that it would all be fine in the end.

"Why'd you do it, boy?" Roamer finally asked, giving in to his yearning, bending down on one knee to be eye-level with Scout. He put his hand gently on the small shoulder. "What possessed you to put a polecat in the privy? You have always been feisty, but I have never known you to be bone mean."

"I—I want a mama," Scout said thickly, blinking back tears. "I didn't do it to be mean; I did it 'cause I want you to get me a mama."

"You want one that much? So much that you would risk losing friends and seeing Mattie-the-marm in a fine, high temper?" Roamer frowned and raked his hand through his hair. "Do you really think you would be happier with a mother?"

Scout looked up and nodded. His forlorn expression cut a wide swath all the way to Roamer's heart. He remembered the marm telling him Scout needed a mother, and now Scout was saying he *wanted* one. There was a significance that Roamer was hard-pressed to ignore.

"All right, we'll speak more about this later. Now go to the leanto and stay there until I tell you to come out."

"Yes, sir." Scout turned and ran to the leanto in back. It hurt Roamer to exile the child, but seeing the throng of people filing into the church had set his nerves on edge. They were probably meeting to decide who was going to hide the boy.

"But it will be over my dead body," Roamer said as he picked up his hammer and retrieved the glowing iron. "Scout has been through too much. Nobody is going to cause that child more pain while there is breath in my body."

The church was abuzz with conversation. Nobody had ever called a town meeting before, not since they all came to McTavish Plain. It was quite a sight to see.

Ian had almost chuckled aloud when a half dozen angry citizens appeared at his stone castle on the hill. They had barreled out of buggies and wagons, and leading the mob was his own sister-in-law, Matilda, in a fine, high dudgeon and a mighty high stink.

Red-faced and demanding, she had marched up to him. "Ian, I insist you do something about that miserable, no-account Roamer Tresh."

Her eyes were red-rimmed, her nostrils swollen. Ian

tried not to recoil at her scent. His eyes watered and his own nostrils burned just being near her. He wondered how she could stand herself, but then he supposed she had no choice. He stepped outside and shut the front door behind him so the entire house would not be filled with the musk of polecat. Thank God, Addie was out in the pasture with her milk cow. She would likely want Mattie to wash the stench off here, and Ian didn't fancy his home smelling like a ripe polecat for six months.

"Now Roamer is a blacksmith and a fine one, so I dinna think you should be calling him no-account."

"That is not why I am here. It is not his skills in question but the way he lives," Mattie snapped.

"What has Roamer done?" Ian said, edging his way around Mattie and getting upwind before he inhaled a deep breath.

"Ian, don't be thick. He hasn't *done* anything. That is the problem," Mattie hissed. She swiped at her running eyes and a strand of hair that had fallen free of the bun she usually wore. "If he would *do* something then things would be just fine."

"I dinna know what you are saying, Matilda," Ian said with a grimace. His eyes were beginning to tear.

"It's that nephew of his," Otto Hudspeth said. "That urchin is a menace—an out-and-out menace."

"Have a care," Ian warned.

"I am afraid it is true, Ian. Something must be done before the child maims someone," Gert said, wrinkling her nose against the stink as she stepped nearer Mattie.

"Well, I canna force the man to beat the lad."

"I don't want him beaten," Mattie said in horror. The memory of Addie telling her that Roamer had killed a man with his bare hands made her shudder. He did have hands that were lean, strong, and *lethal.* They were big enough to do a lot of damage.

"You dinna want the lad whipped?"

"Of course not! Don't be thick," Mattie snorted, swiping at that unruly strand of hair.

"Then tell me exactly what you *do* want, lass," Ian said with an innocent smile.

"I want you to make Roamer Tresh find a wife!"

Like noisy, annoyed geese patrolling a barnyard, they arrived at the front of the smithy. Roamer had been expecting them for more than an hour. When he saw them leave and head up to Ian's stone castle, he knew the writing was on the wall. Now he crossed his arms and waited at the wide-open arches of his forge as they came nearer, chattering, discussing Scout and what should be done.

Nobody was going to lay hands on Scout. Not even Ian. Roamer would leave town first.

"Ian," he said stiffly when his friend stopped at the threshold of the smithy.

"Roamer." Ian's eyes were twinkling. A mischievous wink took away a small measure of Roamer's anger. Perhaps he had misjudged their intention—at least Ian's.

"Is there something I can do for you, all of you?" Roamer asked, raking a gaze over every man jack and old biddy among them. Otto Hudspeth couldn't meet his gaze, but he noticed that Mattie-the-marm had no problem glaring at him as if he had sprouted horns and a tail.

"Something has got to be done before it is too

late." Mattie stepped forward, which meant everyone else stepped back. Like birds kiting away from a predator, the entire group shrank from her. The stench was enough to knock down a full grown pine.

Roamer blinked and tried to hold his breath. It didn't work. He stepped back toward the forge, much preferring the aroma of smoke and tempered iron to skunk perfume.

"You have got to get married," Mattie said, shaking her finger toward Roamer. "And you have got to do it quick."

"Married? Why?"

"Just look at me." She picked up a handful of blue fabric in her hand and shook her stained and stinky skirt. "My best dress is ruined and I . . ." Mattie teared up. "And I *stink.*"

Roamer tried not to laugh at her. With her nose red and her eyes watering, she didn't look quite so prim and proper. And though she reeked to the high heavens, there was something appealing in seeing her like this. The severe bun that usually lay at the nape of her neck had come undone. Most of her honey-colored hair was tumbling over one shoulder. There was something . . . earthy about her.

"What you say about your dress and your scent is true, ma'am, but I don't know why that means I have to get married."

"Oh!" Mattie fumed and stamped her foot. "Scout is responsible for my condition, and well you know it."

Roamer nearly laughed. He was put in mind of a young girl in a fit of anger. Mattie's cheeks pinked and her eyes blazed and the funniest thing happened: In spite of being skunked she seemed *attrac-*

tive. It was ridiculous, he knew, but for one fleeting moment he had the urge to hug her up like he would Scout, to cradle her head on his shoulder and let her cry out her frustrations.

"I'll see he apologizes to you, ma'am," Roamer said softly. "And he will pay for the frock."

"We all signed this petition." Otto Hudspeth darted forward. Roamer's notions of comforting Mattie vanished. The barber's small, dark eyes were wide and rimmed in white as he held out the paper toward Roamer. "The whole town signed. You've got to do what it says." He glanced back at Ian, Miley, and Gert. Roamer could practically see the man drawing courage from having them nearby.

"You have three months to find a wife, or you have to leave McTavish Plain," Hudspeth said with undisguised satisfaction.

Six

"Three months?" Roamer bellowed. "Now how in blazes could any man find a wife in three months, especially when there isn't a single woman within a hundred miles of here?"

"You could get you a Salish squaw," Joe Christian said with a wicked grin.

"Guess you better get cracking," Otto chimed in until Roamer turned to him. He glared until Otto's snigger vanished. The barber-surgeon melted back into the crowd.

"Sorry, Roamer, but the town voted," Ian said with a grin. Since Ian had shaved his beard off, Roamer found that he grinned often, but this was one time he didn't appreciate the Scot's sense of humor.

"Now wait a doggone minute. This just ain't fair. You can't do this," Roamer began.

"Actually, I see no difference in this or making my poor sister pick a new husband when she became a widow," Mattie said with a sniff. "Why should a single man with a child be any different?"

Roamer blinked and looked at Miley. Then at Gert. One by one he glanced at his friends, his neighbors. And one by one he saw they agreed with the school-marm's sentiment.

He was to be leg-shackled, like it or no.

"Well I'll be—" He glared at them all and slapped his thigh with an open palm. "How in tarnation am I supposed to find a wife? There ain't no single women in town, and I sure can't go to Belle Fourche for such foolishness and leave both Scout and the smithy untended."

"Foolishness, indeed," Mattie harrumphed.

"Yes, Mrs. Smith, foolishness." Roamer took half a step toward her before recoiling from her perfume.

"Roamer, I don't think any woman in town would want the job anyway," Miley said, scratching his head in deep thought. "Scout has put the fear of God into folks hereabouts."

"Yes, a stranger might be a better choice," Michael Jones said, rubbing his bruise lightly.

Roamer turned on Miley.

"Now don't go getting all het up," Miley said, holding up his hands. "But Mike has got a point, Roamer; a stranger might be a mite more willing."

"And how in tarnation am I going to marry a stranger?" Roamer asked in disgust.

"I—I told you once before about the mail-order brides."

Roamer glared at the teamster; then he thought of Scout: the way his bottom lip had quivered, the sadness in his voice. The child wanted a woman in his life. He wanted and deserved a mother's love and care.

Roamer narrowed his eyes at the crowd. It galled him that they would think they had bullied him into finding a wife, and that was exactly what they were going to think, because he would endure anything, *anything* for Scout.

"You could use my Heart and Hand book." John Holcomb's voice filled the silence.

As of one mind, the group turned to look at the postmaster. He blushed a ruddy hue under their combined scrutiny.

"I been thinking about finding a wife myself," he explained apologetically. "A man can get lonely out here."

"So it is to be a mail-order bride?" Roamer spat the words out as if they were choking him. "You want me to write a letter to some woman I ain't never met and ask her to marry me?"

"I think you will have a lot better chance of getting a stranger to marry you than a woman who knows you." Mattie said caustically. She almost forgot her own indignation as a few people chuckled and Roamer's face took on a dusky flush.

"By the way, Mattie, all this talk of letters makes me wonder," Ian said with a coy smile. "Have you had a letter from that seafaring husband of yours lately?"

"N—no," Mattie stammered. "Why?"

"Hmm, just thinking that it has been a while since you heard from him. I hope matters with him are as they should be."

Mattie swallowed hard. Could Lottie's suspicion that Ian might know be true? But he didn't—he couldn't.

"I was just thinking that you have a lot of time on your hands without your man in town to look after. Addie does most of your cooking and Lottie does all your sewing. I bet you often wish for something to occupy you so you dinna miss your husband so much."

"Well . . . of course I do miss him."

"And you are a very romantic woman, or so Addie

tells me. I canna think of anyone who would be better at helping Roamer write a proper proposal than a schoolteacher with a romantic nature."

"Now that's the first sensible thing I heard all day," Gus said heartily.

"Oh, yes, if Mrs. Smith helps Roamer, he is bound to get it right first time. And the quicker the better—for all of us," Gert said with a smile. "We all know that Mattie is right handy with poetry and fancy words."

The mention of fancy words made Roamer's blood run cold. To woo any woman with promises like the ones that captured his poor sister Susan was repugnant to him.

"I am a plain-speaking man," Roamer said. "I wouldn't want anybody to get the wrong idea about me because I had help spouting a lot of nonsense."

"No, no, of course not, Roamer, but we want—that is, you need a wife and fast," Miley said, nodding. "Three months is not a lot of time when you figger the slow mail in and out of Belle Fourche."

Roamer scratched his jaw. "I guess you are right about that."

"So, Mattie, will you help Roamer write a letter to the mail-order bride service?" Ian asked with a lift of his brows. "You can help him be as tender and winnin' as that seafaring husband of yours must have been to capture your sensitive heart."

Mattie glared at Roamer and he returned the favor. It was plain that the last thing either of them wanted was to spend evenings in close proximity. But the sooner Roamer got a woman to help keep that rascal Scout out of trouble, the better off everyone in McTavish Plain would be—especially Scout himself.

"Fine. I'll do it. . . . For Scout," Mattie said sullenly, plucking at the ruined blue silk frock. It would take two months to save enough to replace it, another month for the fabric to come, and six weeks for Lottie to finish sewing up a new one.

"Agreed. For Scout," Roamer said sullenly. "The sooner this business is done with, the better."

Scout watched his uncle pound the hard square of iron. It was nearing dark, and as the light outside faded, the fire appeared to glow more brightly. Now each blow of the hammer caused a shower of sparks to fly.

Roamer never missed a beat. He worked from sunrise to sunset, and after he closed the smithy, he would fry up a turnip and a slab of beef, or maybe a bit of mutton that they would have with bread purchased from Gus at the mercantile.

But tonight would be different. Tonight they would be going to Mrs. Smith's house. A little trill of excitement went through Scout at the thought.

"What say we knock off a little early tonight?" Roamer said suddenly.

Scout shook himself mentally. He must have been wishing so hard that he heard what he wanted to hear. "Aw, it ain't even full dark yet."

Roamer shrugged. "Near enough." He took off his heavy leather apron and went about cleaning up his tools. "Sides, I think we need to get to Mrs. Smith's a bit early tonight."

Hope blossomed in Scout's chest at his uncle's eagerness. Maybe his plan was already working.

"I think it is high time you paid her for that dress.

I think you need to get into that money your grandmother gave you when you were a baby."

Scout wrinkled his nose. Uncle Roamer had told him about his grandmother, an old lady in a town back east someplace. When he was just a baby she had given him some money, but Uncle Roamer refused to touch it. It was Scout's money, he said, to do with as he pleased—when he was grown up, he said. Never before had Uncle Roamer told him to use it for anything.

"Scout?"

"Yes sir?"

"A man pays his debts." Roamer raised his brows and waited for his nephew to think about it. "A man works hard, does what is right, and he pays his debts."

"Yes sir," Scout said. He knew the money was packed away in a leather bag deep within a chest of things that had belonged to Scout's mother. He didn't care a hoot about the old money, but the thought of touching something that his mother had touched made him happy inside. Suddenly he was eager to get into the trunk. "Yes sir. I should give Mrs. Smith some money to pay for her ruined dress."

"Good boy. I am proud of you," Roamer said, resting his hand on Scout's shoulder. "Maybe the town is right. . . . Maybe spending a little time in a woman's company will be good for you."

Scout held the fabric under his nose and breathed deeply. There was a sweet, warm smell on all the clothes in the trunk. When he closed his eyes, he got a strange feeling inside.

It was like Christmas morning and sunshine and all the good things he could imagine.

But when he opened his eyes, he felt a wave of sadness so deep, so raw that he sat down—hard.

His hands held the lacy material so tight, he could see his knuckles. Scout didn't know what was wrong with him, but something surely was, because he felt like crying all of a sudden.

"Scout?" Uncle Roamer's voice drifted over him and he sniffed, not wanting him to know that he was near tears.

"It's all right, Scout. I get the same way when I look at your mama's stuff. I feel like I swallowed a lump, and my eyes sting and burn and are wont to water."

Scout looked up at him, relief and gratitude shining in his face. "You understand?"

"Uh-huh."

"You know what it means, Uncle Roamer?" Scout asked, rubbing the soft, pale cotton lawn against his face.

"Uh-huh, I know what it means, Scout."

"What is it, Uncle Roamer? Why do I feel so heavy that I can't move and so sad that I want to blubber like a baby? What is it?"

"It is missin' someone you love, Scout. It is grieving and loneliness and wanting to turn back the clock to a happier time."

Wearing only her chemise, Mattie was washing her hair for the second time. Most of the skunk smell was gone after the bath of vinegar and a few other things she preferred to forget mixed in. But when she brushed out her hair she still got a faint whiff of skunk odor.

It was more than she could stand, so she mixed up eggs and vinegar and suds again. It seemed the clock hands were moving faster than she was. Lottie was also supposed to come by for tea and bring some of Addie's fresh-baked gingerbread before Roamer and Scout arrived.

Mattie was looking forward to seeing Lottie and having a good chat. She had come close to telling her sister about Roamer—about his body and the way she felt.

But she hadn't—not yet.

Roamer's body was Mattie's own secret, and she held it close to her heart and guarded it greedily. She should have made an effort to blot it from her mind, but she did just the opposite. There were times when she closed her eyes and willed herself to remember.

Every detail.

A man's body had never before been anything more to her than a work of art, something detached and poetic and unreal. Or something to be avoided like she had avoided those healthy young farmers back in Nebraska when they had wanted to hold her hand or steal a kiss.

"Or marry me, so they could do even more," she said sullenly.

Men's bodies had held no interest for her. They were hard and hairy and brought a panic that went so deep, she couldn't breathe.

But Roamer was different. Even the thick, white scar had been fascinating to her. What should have been ugly and repulsive had made her itch to touch it, lightly, just once . . . well, maybe a few times.

There had been a frightening, out-of-control moment there when she *had* almost reached out to trace her fingertip along that scar and then over his flat, hard nipple—and maybe down his belly to where *it* jutted from his body.

"Oh my," Mattie said with a shudder as she realized exactly what she had wanted to do that day.

She snatched up the crockery pitcher full of white vinegar and doused her hair. The pungent odor stung her nose and made her eyes water, but the scent of skunk became less noticeable.

In her mind the vision of Roamer remained pure and unchanged, though it still had the most unsettling effect on her mind.

She was just wrapping a clean length of linen towel around her hair when she heard the knock on her front door. She glanced at the squat little clock in her parlor. Lottie was overdue, and that almost never happened when it was Mattie's turn to brew tea.

Mattie started for the door, slipping on her sturdy wrapper as she went. She had one arm in a sleeve. With the other she opened the door.

"Lottie, you're late, but I don't have the bread sliced yet, though the kettle is on—"

"Uh, we met Mrs. Rosswarne coming up the street. She decided to go on home since we had something to speak with you about, but now I think coming early may have been a mistake," Roamer Tresh said with a tight grin after first allowing his eyes to skim not once, but twice over Mattie's half-clothed body.

Mattie stilled, the wrapper dangling from one arm. She found herself frozen in time. She wanted to move, but try as she might, all she could do was imagine Roamer's naked form.

Then, as if he could read her improper thoughts, his grin altered and seemed to shift from being a tad embarrassed to a tad *wicked*—no, more than a tad wicked—as his gaze lingered on the breasts showing too clearly through the thin chemise.

No man had ever looked at Mattie like that before. And just as her image of the male form had been transformed by one glimpse of Roamer's nearly naked body, now she experienced a compelling reaction to Roamer's perusal of her form.

Did he have the same thoughts that she did?

Her bosom felt heavy. The rasp of cloth against her nipples as they contracted was almost painful. It was as if his eyes had made her more sensitive, more attuned to her own body. She could almost hear her own heart. She could certainly hear the rush of her own blood in her ears. She felt the floor beneath her bare feet in a way that was new and different. Mattie had never stood before a man with her feet bare.

She swallowed hard. Roamer looked into her eyes. In those mysterious green depths, she saw her own reflection, and *possibilities.* And every one of those possibilities was the opposite of what she had planned for herself. Mattie had no intention of becoming a feisty boy's mama—particularly when the man involved didn't want a wife and had said so in the most emphatic terms.

Roamer had no use for a wife—perhaps for women in general.

And Mattie wanted more than just cooking and cleaning and darning socks. She had aspirations that stretched beyond a mop, broom, and cookstove.

But wasn't that what she saw in Roamer's eyes . . . more? More than an average life with an average man? More than she had ever wanted, ever allowed herself to think about?

With a mental jerk she forced herself back a step. "Roam—I mean, Mr. Tresh."

"I see Scout and I have come at an inopportune time." His satyr's grin slipped, but only a little. The glow from his green eyes was almost feral. She thought of a predatory animal, waiting, lurking just outside the glow of a campfire. She thought of all the primal, earthy things that glow promised. "Scout, perhaps we should return later."

For the first time, Mattie became aware of Scout, standing beside his uncle. He was staring at her with a crooked smile.

"Mrs. Smith." Scout took a step toward the open door. "I have brought some money to pay for your dress."

Her eyes flicked to his hands. They were small and clean. His nails were even. The hands of a child well cared for—well tended and well loved.

And this man before her was the one responsible for Scout's tidy appearance.

Once again Mattie's perception of Roamer shifted, altered and shattered into colors like those in the bottom of a kaleidoscope.

Things were not so simple. *He* was not so simple.

"Uncle Roamer and I didn't know what a lady's dress cost for sure. I don't know if this is enough. . . ."

"Oh, I can't." She stepped backward another step and, gathering her thoughts, finally had the presence of mind to put her other arm in the sleeve and pull the wrapper together. Roamer's gaze flicked greedily over her breasts before they disappeared beneath another layer of cloth.

But she realized with dismay that for each step she took backward, Roamer and Scout had come forward the same amount. They weren't getting nearer, but neither was she able to put any extra distance between them. A hot, charged feeling had entered her serene kitchen. And with every inch that Roamer invaded, it doubled, until Mattie could feel the small hairs on the back of her neck rising as if a violent storm was brewing over the mountains.

"A man has to pay his debts," Scout said. "Uncle Roamer told me that. I caused your dress to be ruined, so you have to take the money." He leveled a sober look at her. "You have to."

Roamer took the money from Scout's hand. He gently grasped Mattie's hand and put the money in her palm. Slowly he folded her fingers over it one by one. Where in the street his hands had been rough and punishing, now they were gentle, seductive.

Mattie felt an odd tingling in her body, as if a lightning bolt had hit nearby. She didn't want to feel that wild, restless pull when he looked at her—didn't want to have her stomach flip-flop when he touched her. But truth to tell, she did feel all those things and more.

More.

"Thank you, Scout. Mr. Tresh. Have you two eaten?" she asked, feeling awkward and excited and nervous. Mattie didn't know what to make at the physical reaction she experienced when Roamer was near. He was as far from her ideal of a gentleman as a man could get. He was big, muscled, and certainly not the kind of man who would practice intellectual love.

Not with a body like his.

She glanced at his eyes again. They seemed to glow

with an inner heat. Her temperature hiked up a notch or two.

No, Roamer Tresh would be the kind of man to pull a woman's hairpins out and run his fingers through her hair. He would strip her bare, body and soul. He would take her with that hard, large body of his. And when it was over, there would never be room for the thought of another man.

Mattie moaned softly.

"Mrs. Smith, are you all right?" he asked in a voice gone husky and deep. He reached out as if to steady her, but in Mattie's mind she saw his big, callused hand going to her breast.

She wanted him to touch her.

"Yes. Yes, I am fine. Just faint from hunger," she stammered. "I—I haven't eaten yet."

Roamer glanced down at Scout. "Gert offered us a pullet for the frying pan. Would you like to share it with us?"

Mattie thought of her minimal cooking abilities, and her belly drew into a hard, tight knot. "Well, I—"

"We'd pitch in and help, of course," Roamer said, and for a moment she almost thought he could read her mind, could sense her apprehension and her conflicting eagerness to be near him.

"That would be just fine," she heard herself say.

"Scout, run over to Gert's and get that pullet."

The boy's happy smile nearly blinded Mattie. "Yes sir!" And he was off like shot. Leaving them alone.

Alone. Alone with her carnal thoughts and her consuming hunger.

"I think he is a mite excited about eating somebody's cooking besides mine," Roamer said with a shy smile.

She allowed herself to really look at him then. Her eyes lingered on him in a way she had never before allowed herself. His sandy hair curled around his earlobes, hanging too far over his collar to be considered stylish—or even neat. His face was symmetrical and pleasing, with high, strong cheekbones and a strong, manly jaw.

Those green, catlike eyes bored into her again.

"I put on a fresh shirt and trousers—did I forget something? Do I need a shave?"

"What? Oh, no, you look fine . . . just fine." She swallowed hard. That was not an appropriate thing for her to say.

"You look fine, too," he said, and he stepped a bit nearer. "And you smell nice, all clean and fresh-scrubbed."

Suddenly her breath was coming in short drafts. Her breasts felt heavy again, and her flesh had sort of warmed all over. It was almost the way she felt when she had come upon him fresh from his bath.

It was a singular experience. Her heart seemed to soar, the way it did when she read a particularly romantic part of a poem, or a story about lovers. Could he see that she was trembling beneath the soft material of her wrapper?

She should go and put some clothes on, but a part of her did not wish to leave that compelling gaze—and the reaction that it stirred in her soul.

"I better go get dressed and brush out my hair," she finally managed to say.

Roamer cleared his throat. "Y—y-yes, and while you're doing that I'll learn my way around your kitchen and see what you've got that we can put with that pullet for dinner."

* * *

"Are you sure you won't have another helping of chicken and dumplings?" Mattie asked Scout.

"Oh, no ma'am." He spoke around a mouthful. "I am about to pop."

Though the chicken was tough and stringy and the dumplings a far cry from Addie's fluffy, light-as-a-cloud morsels, Roamer and Scout had eaten as if Mattie were the finest cook in all of McTavish Plain.

And that gave her a burst of pride that reached to the core of her soul. Although a week ago Mattie would have denied the possibility, there was something gratifying about seeing her food disappear into two hungry mouths. Roamer and Scout acted as if the meal were delicious, when Mattie herself knew it was only on the passable side—if one were being charitable.

"You know, Mr. Tresh, since we will be doing your lessons every evening, perhaps we should eat supper together every night," she heard herself say boldly.

"Oh, that is kind, but the trouble—"

"Nonsense. It is no more difficult to cook for three than for one." Well, at least that was the truth. Mattie struggled with even a single portion. But Roamer and Scout need not know that her sister Addie kept her fed and her sister Lottie kept her clothed.

They need not know that Mattie's only skill was with books and teaching. Or that she could barely fry an egg without burning up two pans—or that she couldn't sew a stitch to save her life.

They need not know she was so inept at being a woman—not when their faces glowed with satisfaction and she felt this warm, wonderful sensation each time she looked at her kitchen, crowded and full of company.

"Please, Uncle Roamer," Scout said.

"Well—"

"Please," Mattie said.

"If you are sure." Roamer gave her a crooked smile that made her heart stumble a bit.

"Good, then it is settled. Tonight we will begin by reading William Morris's work, *The Defense of Guinevere.*"

"Poetry?" Scout wrinkled his nose.

"Both poetry and literature, Scout. I believe, Mr. Tresh, if you hear romance in word and prose, the more likely you will be able to repeat it in your letters," Mattie explained.

"Well, before we begin, let us repay you for a fine meal. In fact, the best I have eaten in a mighty long time," Roamer said, snatching Mattie's empty plate along with his own.

"Oh, no—" Again Mattie basked in the glow of his praise and his willingness to do for her. It was a new experience for her. To have Roamer—or any man—compliment her on an earthy, capable skill like cooking was unique, because, all her life she had always been described as the flighty-dreamy sister.

"I invited you to eat, not wash up."

"Scout and I don't want to wear out our welcome. Besides, we're old hands at this. Won't take but a minute," he said with a smile. "C'mon, Scout, you dry."

Mattie stood back in silence as the huge man and the tow-headed boy went about tidying up her kitchen. Quick as a cat's wink, they had the place scrubbed, dried, and in order. With the ease of long practice, Roamer took a cloth to the scrubbed pine table. When he was done, he gave her a dazzling smile that made her knees go liquid.

"All right, Mrs. Smith, I think I am ready for my first lesson in being romantic."

But as Mattie watched him flick the dish cloth over a wooden peg, she began to doubt that she could teach him anything, for strange as it was, she found his cleaning up in her kitchen very romantic.

Very romantic and very, very dangerous.

Jack Maravel chewed the stogie from one side of his mouth to the other as he studied the cards in his hand. They were good, but were they good enough?

It was the story of his life. A little luck would come his way. Just enough to tease a man and make him think he had the world by the tail, then Jack would bet it all only to find the other guy holding a handful of aces.

It was as if he had been born under an unlucky star.

"Ante up or fold, Laughing Jack," the sharp across the table said, his gold tooth winking like a summer firefly when he grinned.

"Don't rush me." The hated name of *Laughing Jack* galled almost as much as lady luck's fickle nature. Jack had been in a bad mood since he sold the spoons to Pierre for a fraction of what they were worth. He certainly didn't need any tinhorn sharpie breathing down his neck tonight.

"Look, we all know you're busted, so get out of the game," another player grumbled. He had an evil-looking scar that ran across one brow and turned his eye a milky white. Jack's own gaze flitted to the wicked-looking blade strapped to his ribs.

"Not so fast," Jack said. "I still have this." He dug into his vest pocket and pulled out a diamond stick-pin. It was the last thing left that his father had given him—and in Jack's opinion the only thing of any value. The lectures and reprimands were not worth the breath and time it took to say them. Maybe if the old man had given him more things of value, like the diamond, Jack would have a kinder spot in his heart for his father's memory.

But he hadn't, and Jack didn't.

"Is it glass?" The sharp asked, squinting at the stickpin.

"Hell, no. It's a flawless diamond, but I suppose not having ever seen any before, you wouldn't know that," Jack said caustically. "It's worth at least five hundred dollars."

"And that's about what is in that pot right now," the sharp said lazily. "So what are you offering?"

"This against the pot. Winner take all." Jack flicked a glance around the table.

"I'm out—too rich for me."

"Me, too."

Now everyone else was out. It was between Jack and the cardsharp.

"Fine, Laughing Jack, I'll agree to it," the sharp said with a wink. "But you better know I shot the last man that tried to cheat me at cards. If you are pulling anything, or if that gee-gaw is glass, I'll put a bullet between your eyes."

"Just give me a card." Jack tried to ignore the dry-ness of his mouth. Some sixth sense told him he was risking more than a hand of cards if he slid the hidden ace from under the lacy French cuff of his sleeve. But he had always cheated, and so his instinct was to cheat now.

The sharp flicked a card at Jack. He turned it over and looked at it, unable to believe his eyes.

It was an ace. He didn't need to use the one up his sleeve after all. Perhaps at last his luck was turning.

"Show me what you've got," the sharp said.

"More'n enough," Jack said, grinning. He laid his cards down on the table, taking deep pleasure in the stunned look on his opponent's face.

Funny, it was the first time he could remember ever winning without cheating. But now that he had the experience, he didn't know why men put such store in it. It felt no different than any other win; there was nothing magical about it, no extra sense of accomplishment. In fact it was a bit of a hollow letdown. At least when he cheated there was the exhilaration of knowing he had taken his fate in his own hands.

Jack looked at the pot and decided that only fools put store in winning on their own. He reached out for the pot. The ace up his sleeve fluttered to the felt-topped table.

"You sorry son of—" The sharp bolted from his chair. Too late Jack realized there was a derringer in his hand. A pop, the smell of cordite, a plume of smoke. Searing pain blazed through Jack's body.

"And just when I found out what direction Roamer Tresh had gone," he said weakly as the hot trickle of blood rushed over his hand.

Seven

"So you think this Elizabeth Barrett Browning is a romantic woman?" Roamer asked from where he sat on the other side of the thick plaid blanket.

Mattie rolled her eyes heavenward. "Of course. The world lost a wonderful poetess when she died," Mattie sighed. "If only I could write like that."

"And if you could, Mattie, what would you say? Would you moon over a man, or would you have something else to tell the world?" Roamer leaned on his wide, callused hand and smiled at her with that crooked grin that always made her belly tighten.

Mattie couldn't help but return his smile. "I would write great odes to heroes and love everlasting." She was stretched out on her belly with the book between them.

"Is that what women want—love everlasting?"

"Yes," Mattie frowned.

"And what is everlasting love?" He reached out and put a wayward strand of her hair back behind her ear.

"Well . . . it is a love that weathers the rigors of life. It is a love that lasts."

"But I thought women wanted that reckless passion that your poetry talks so much about."

"Yes, they do. Don't men?"

Roamer furrowed his brows and gave her a shy grimace. "It's hard for me to know."

"But you're a man, Roamer." *More man than a body has a right to be.*

"Yes, but I have never been in love. I can't talk about something when I know so little about it."

"But why?" Mattie propped her chin in her hands and looked at Roamer's face. It was a nice face, all angles and grooves. It was a man's face. There was nothing soft or poetic about it, but when she looked at him she thought of strength and honesty and things that she shouldn't even allow herself to consider. "Why haven't you been in love?"

"I had a sister," Roamer said softly.

"Mmmm, Scout's mother," Mattie supplied.

"Yes. Susan. She was a sweet woman, but she listened to the words of a sweet-talking man. I swore I would never be like that . . . say words I didn't mean. And I have kept myself busy with Scout. I don't have time for some grand romance." Roamer drew in a painful breath and tried to hold back the memory.

"Roamer?" Mattie slipped her hand over his. Roamer's hand was warm and rough and huge, sun-darkened in contrast to her small, white one.

"It was a long time ago that Scout's mother died. I should be over it by now."

"But the memory still gives you pain?"

"She died too young. Her life would've been so different if she hadn't listened to the smooth lies of a man who knew how to sweet-talk a woman."

"But this is different. You are doing your best to find Scout a mother."

"But is it so different? Or are these women expecting a man to love them, to give up a piece of his heart to them? To provide, as you say, a love everlasting?"

Mattie thought about that for a moment. Of course that was what the women who advertised in the Heart and Hand books wanted. It was what all women wanted—to be cherished, to be special to a man. They wanted romance and poetry and moonlit nights, but they wanted a warm, strong body in bed with them each night. And a smiling face across the breakfast table in the morning.

It was what she wanted.

She allowed herself to consider it—Roamer and Scout as part of her life. Breakfast and dinner with their voices, their laughter. And the nights . . .

He slid his big hand from under hers and looked at it. "I know how to bend and forge iron to last. I can fry a turnip and burn a slab of meat, but not much else, Mattie. I am not a man that can look into a woman's heart or let her see into mine. It's just the way things are."

"Haven't you ever known anyone who was happily in love, Roamer?" Her heart cried out to him. She wanted him to consider a future that included her; she wanted Roamer to have the same dream.

"No." He made a fist of his hand and rolled over. "My chance of finding that kind of life is dead and gone."

She stared at his hand. The memory of what Addie had said came unbidden to her thoughts. How could a man so gentle and thoughtful kill someone with that hand?

He glanced over at Scout, sprawled out on the greening grass, practicing his letters on a slate.

Roamer leaned nearer to Mattie and spoke in a low, intimate voice.

"The only woman I ever saw fall in love was Susan, and it killed her—it truly did. And her death paved the way to more death and more unhappiness."

"You loved your sister very much." Mattie was stating a fact, not asking a question.

Roamer smiled in a melancholy way that made Mattie's heart flutter.

"I thought she hung the moon."

"Would you like to talk about it?"

"I never have—to any living soul. Ian knows a bit of what happened, but not all—not all. I have never met anybody that I wanted to share that with."

"I understand." Mattie picked up the slender volume of poetry and started to rise from the blanket. "Some things are too private to share."

"I never wanted to share . . . until now." He gently covered her hand with his. Once again she was struck by the hard, rough warmth of it.

"I'd like to tell you, Mattie."

Her heart nearly leaped from her chest. He had used her given name before, but today that one word held a feeling of kinship and endearment and trust. Her body trilled with excitement.

"I'd be more than happy to listen."

His expression was bland, but there was a tautness to his body that told Mattie how painful the recollection truly was. He spoke softly, flatly in a monotone of remembered agony.

"Susan was five years older than me. She was beautiful. Where your hair is the color of warm honey . . ." He reached out and took hold of a strand of Mattie's hair.

She nearly fainted when he rubbed the strand gently between his thumb and forefinger.

". . . her hair was the color of moonbeams. Soft as yours is, though, but hers was like a silvery cloud. Scout gets that pale hair from her. Her eyes were blue—pale and kind."

"What happened?"

Roamer suddenly came back into himself with a lurch. He looked at his fingers and self-consciously dropped the lock of hair.

"She met a man. He had charm, came from an old and moneyed family. He had a way of putting words together that would melt a woman's heart—Susan's heart. I never trusted him; I thought he acted like he was too good for the rest of the world, but she wouldn't listen."

Roamer sat up and stared out across the prairie as if he were looking back in time. Mattie sensed he was remembering painful events.

"Our parents were long dead. There was only me and her. But the more I tried to tell her about *him*, the more stubborn she became. They eloped one night. When she returned, his family cut him off in a fit of temper for marrying beneath him. Can you credit it? She was so far above him that he wasn't fit to touch the hem of her skirts."

Roamer glanced at Scout, who had fallen asleep, his pale hair fanning out on his forearm.

"The bastard wasn't good enough to lick her shoes, but they thought she was beneath him because they were a prominent family and we were just farm people. Rich folk are like that, I learned. Susan was soon carrying Scout. I saw the bruises, but she always denied he was mistreating her. I should've done something."

"Did he—"

"Kill her?" Roamer's eyes were ablaze with old fury. His fists clenched and unclenched at his side. "No, the sorry excuse for a human being didn't strike the blows, but he may as well have. He owed money—a lot of money from gambling, but the cowardly bastard left town before his creditors came calling. They came to Susan. She was so badly beaten I didn't know who she was except for her hair."

Mattie saw one solitary tear spill from Roamer's eyes. It cut a path through the lean, craggy features of his face.

"She died in my arms. Her last words were to care for Scout. To take him far away and keep him safe."

Roamer grabbed hold of the blanket, crushing a hank of it in his hand as if he were trying to keep himself from flying apart. His knuckles were white, his eyes full of anguish.

"I went looking for her husband. But he had vanished. I did find the man who had beaten Susan."

"Oh, Roamer," Mattie said with a chill.

He spoke softly, as if he were talking in sleep. "It only took a minute. There are times in the dead of night I find myself wishing I had made him suffer the way Susan suffered. But I didn't. I hit him once—only once."

"Roamer." She would have said more, but suddenly her throat closed off. She could only make a sound—nothing intelligible, nothing coherent—just a sound of rage, pain, and sorrow so deep it went beyond words.

The blanket ripped in Roamer's hands. He blinked

and looked down at the shredded threads as if his hands didn't belong to him—as if he had no control over them.

"Oh, God." He dropped the ruined plaid. "I didn't mean to do that."

His voice was so full of pain and regret that Mattie could not stop herself. She was across the blanket and in his arms. She touched his face, dried the single tear with a kiss. And then, with a moan that nearly broke her heart in two, Roamer held her to him.

"Oh, Matilda." He said softly. "I never want to feel like that again."

"You won't." She smiled at him.

And then he kissed her.

She felt as if she were falling down a long, deep hole and would never touch the bottom. Her hands skimmed over his shoulders and the hard bulk of his muscular neck.

For the first time in her life, Mattie understood what the poetry was really about. She understood that romance was words and thoughts and imaginings. But touching a man and being touched back was raw, primal, and animal.

This was not sedate or genteel or in the least intellectual. The feel of Roamer's lips upon her own had nothing to do with a higher plane—it had to do with heat, hunger, and physical longing.

Mattie's heart was beating so hard that she could hear her own blood rushing in her ears. Holding Roamer and kissing him was reckless, dangerous, and the most wonderful sensation she had ever experienced.

She felt her lips part in a contented sigh. And then Roamer's tongue darted between her teeth. His hands caressed the nape of her neck, the back of her head. Hairpins fell, plunking softly to the blanket.

Suddenly Roamer stiffened. Slowly he raised his head. His breath was coming fast and harsh. He stared at Matilda Smith and felt something inside his chest explode.

Dear Lord, she was a married woman! What had he been thinking? It didn't matter that she understood in a way nobody ever had. It didn't matter that she managed to soothe his soul.

She was another man's wife.

"Mattie—Mrs. Smith . . . I—I—" Roamer shuddered and stood up quickly, putting distance between them. "I apologize."

Mattie blinked and forced herself to focus. She could see he was gathering himself, putting the wildness of the moment under his steely control.

"Forgive me. I—I—lost my head." Roamer stood for a moment, breathing roughly, his shoulders stiff, his eyes still brilliant with unspoken emotion.

Mattie heard her own breath, harsh and revealing. She reached up to her hair, only to find it resting on her shoulders and trailing down her back in heavy, tousled curls.

"I—" She lifted her hand in a gesture of pure helplessness.

What could she say?

That she didn't want it?

She did. She wanted that and so much more.

That she hadn't enjoyed it?

She had. The promise of bliss beyond her reckoning was still glowing hot in Roamer's green eyes.

But she needed to master her own emotions just as Roamer was controlling his.

She had plans.

She had a prospect. Michael Jones was lettered, soft-spoken, finely mannered. He didn't make her feel like she was standing on shifting sand when he looked at her. His eyes didn't hold unspoken mysteries and forbidden promises in each glance.

Michael Jones was *safe.* He was predictable and steady.

Roamer was danger, passion, and every hazard a woman could risk. She *couldn't* let herself think of him any other way.

"Do you think it was the poetry?" Mattie said suddenly with a spat of nervous laughter.

Roamer smiled weakly, grateful for her saying something—anything—that would release the tension of the moment. He was disgusted with himself. All these years he had prided himself by thinking he was so much better than Laughing Jack Maravel, and now he realized he was not. For only the lowest son-of-a-buck would kiss another man's wife.

"Probably the poetry. That stuff is potent as whiskey. I better get Scout home; he'll be so tuckered out tomorrow, he won't be able to keep his eyes open."

"Yes."

"Sorry about your blanket, I'll have Gus see if he has one in stock at the store."

"Don't give it another thought."

"No, I insist."

"That will be fine. Thank you." She went about folding the blanket and gathering the books and the slate. She watched in silence as he gathered Scout into his brawny arms. The child barely stirred.

"I will see you both tomorrow at my house for supper?" Mattie said, a bit of doubt creeping into her voice.

Roamer hesitated for a moment. "Sure. We can't stop now—I only have two more months to find me a wife."

Of my own, echoed in the back of his guilty mind.

Roamer opened the door to the mercantile and stepped inside. The odor of scorched coffee and soot filled his nostrils. Funny how there was a completely different smell from the wood burning in the pot-bellied stove in Gus's mercantile than from the same wood crackling in Roamer's forge at the smithy.

When he built the fires and stoked it with the huge bellows, the fire smelled crisp, cleansing. Here it smelled musty and too close.

Or was it just his mood?

"Mornin', Roamer," Gus said, lifting his battered speckleware cup in salute. "Coffee?"

Roamer eyed the pot. He and Scout had gotten a late start this morning. By the time the chores were done and Scout was scrubbed and combed and shoved out the door for school, Roamer had decided not even to bother with coffee before he went to the smithy. He was still cotton-headed and scratchy-eyed.

And guilt-ridden.

"Sure."

Gus poured the thick, dark liquid into a cup and Roamer took it, savoring the feel of the warm metal against his palms.

"Hear you been spending a heap of time with Mrs. Smith," Gus said between lip-smacking sips. "The town has been breathin' a sigh of relief."

"What do you mean?" Roamer's guilt folded over him.

"The boy, Scout, ain't nearly kilt anybody in days," Gus said with a wink. "How is the wife trappin' goin'?" Gus asked boldly.

"Wife trapping?" A frisson of guilt flickered up Roamer's spine. Was that what he had been doing with Mattie—trapping another man's wife?

"You know, Roamer, all those lessons that Mattie is teaching you so you can learn to be a romantical man."

"Oh, I have been doing some studying," Roamer said, trying not to think about how it felt to hold Mattie.

"Studying?" Gus eyed him over the rim of his cup in the same way a hawk looks at a mouse. "I been wondering 'bout this from the first. How 'zactly do you go about this studying?"

Roamer squirmed inside. He didn't want to be having this talk with Gus. And he didn't want to be reminded of how he had kissed Mattie—*Mrs. Smith.* "We do a little reading is all," Roamer lied quickly. He certainly had no intentions of revealing to Gus, the biggest bag of wind in town, what he had done.

"Only reading is it? And is a bunch of words on paper goin' to be enough to turn an ornery galoot like you into one of them there, ladies's men?" Gus squinted one eye and chuckled. Roamer could practically hear the gears turning in that grizzled head. Gus was a meddler at heart, and since Mattie and her sisters had arrived in McTavish Plain he seemed to have appointed himself their guardians—or at least their head busybody.

"I suppose it will have to, won't it?"

"Not much like her sister, is she?" Gus said suddenly.

"What?" Roamer's head snapped up.

"Mrs. Smith—she ain't much like her sister Addie, is she?"

"I don't know Mrs. McTavish all that well." Roamer took a big gulp of coffee, nearly choking on the hot, bitter liquid.

"Addie is feisty. Kind of a sassy woman, but Mrs. Smith, she seems . . ."

"Thoughtful and kind of soft. Like she needs someone to look after her."

"Now you mention it, I think her sisters have looked after her most of her life. It'd be nice if that husband of hers would hurry and show up. I think Addie worries herself sick, and Mrs. Rosswarne too."

"What kind of a man leaves his wife for such a long time?" Roamer asked before he could stop himself.

Gus frowned. "Don't know."

"Funny, Mattie is the middle girl, but she kind of seems like the youngest in some way. You must be getting to know her pretty well—I mean with doing all that *studying.*"

"Well, we don't have time to visit. Scout is there and she talks a lot about her husband—he is a sea captain, you know," Roamer lied. Mattie had said nothing at all about her man, and that had pricked Roamer's curiosity about him.

"Yep, I heard that. Seems a powerful strange kind of man for her to have chose, but you can't predict love, I guess."

Roamer sipped his coffee and avoided Gus's discerning gaze. But with his own words had come a question. Why didn't Mattie-the-marm talk about her seafaring husband? In fact, why hadn't she mentioned him at all?

Roamer blotted the page, then picked it up and blew on the paper to dry any remaining wet spots of ink.

"Do you mind if I read it?" Mattie asked.

He laughed self-consciously and handed her the piece of paper, holding it gingerly by the edge as if it were something that might come to life and bite him.

"I was going to ask you to read it and tell me if you thought this one might convince a woman to come to McTavish Plain and marry me." A stain of color rose in his cheeks.

Mattie took the letter and began to read aloud. "I am a single man just over thirty, looking for a woman with a heart big enough for a man and a small boy."

She glanced up to see the slightly embarrassed but hopeful look on Roamer's face. He was right; it wasn't poetry.

It was better than poetry. It was honest and earthy. The revelations from a man's heart about what he hoped for the future.

Mattie ducked her head, wishing her heart would quit bucking in her chest. She continued to read. "I am a simple man with simple tastes. I am not a drinker, a wanderer or a gambler. I can promise to be there through sickness and health. I can promise to see you have hearth and home."

Mattie paused and swallowed around the hot, dry lump that was forming in her throat.

"I will share what I have and try to give you all that

you may want. All I ask is that you open your heart and be a mother to a boy and wife to a man. Keep our house clean, our clothes mended and a hot meal for us in the evening. And for your trouble I will be at your side through thick and thin, whatever life may bring."

Mattie looked up, swallowed hard, and laid the paper carefully on the table in front of her.

"What do you think?" he asked.

"I think that you will get yourself a wife, and I think it will be very, very soon."

Jack stretched and opened his eyes. The cracked ceiling above his hard, narrow cot hadn't changed a bit during the night. The same spidery network of flaking mortar and plaster met his bored gaze. The same long-legged spider spun her web in the corner, waiting to trap something—just like Jack was trapped in the small, dank jail cell.

"Hey, when is breakfast?" he said, swinging his legs off the bunk to the rock floor. He was bored stiff. Even eating the grub that was barely passable would be a way to pass the time.

"Pipe down in there. You'll get fed when you get fed," the gruff voice of his jailer advised. "The hotel ain't even open yet. How in tarnation am I going to order your breakfast if the cook ain't even up?"

Jack heard a chorus of songbirds as they took wing and flitted by the cell. He went to the barred window and tried to see out, but even on his toes the small, mean portal was too high. He could, however, see a slice of sky, pinking gray streaks, bringing another day. One more day of confinement, and one less before he would be free.

Spring was here in all its glory, or at least it seemed so from the birds and the afternoon heat that baked him in the small room. He wouldn't know, not having personally seen it himself. But here he sat, unable to do anything but think.

Think about Roamer.

Think about Judson Walker—and the money that was now his.

Jack cursed under his breath. The shot had made a clean in-and-out wound. The hole was healing nicely. He rotated his arm as if to convince himself of it, feeling only a little pinch of pain now and again. Jack had been damned lucky the sharper had poor aim, but unlucky as hell that the double-dealing four-flusher's brother-in-law was the sheriff of this one-horse town. The sheriff had decided that it was Jack who would cool his heels for thirty days and forfeit the entire pot that had been on the table at the time of his arrest.

"And who says blood is thicker than water?" Jack muttered. In this case it was in-laws that were thicker than thieves.

"Damn them all," Jack swore. "When I get out I will find Susan's brat and I will get my due." And he mentally added the cardsharp and the sheriff to the list of people he would settle up with once he was rich.

Eight

"Would you like another piece of fried chicken?" Mattie asked Scout as he plopped down on the blanket.

"Well, maybe just one more." He grinned at her, revealing the gap left from a newly pulled tooth. She felt her heart swell with affection for the boy.

Since the madness of the kiss, she and Roamer had kept their urges under control. They had made sure not to allow themselves to fall into that pit of passion again. At any rate, they were now stiff and politely cordial with each other. There was safety in their rigid manners—an invisible wall of civility as if, by addressing each other formally and never making full eye contact, each one could somehow make the memory of that moment vanish. But just beneath the surface there was a bubbling, hot awareness that Mattie was hard pressed to ignore.

When Roamer was near, her nerve endings came to life in a way that was both annoying and fascinating. She did not even need to look up and see him to know that he was near. Her body was tuned to him. An invisible connection had been formed on the day of the kiss. And although Roamer kept his distance, doing everything in his power to limit the time they spent alone, and making sure he never touched her, she saw the way he looked at her when he thought she didn't see.

It should have been reassuring for Mattie to know that Roamer would not tempt her, but it wasn't. She found herself growing impatient and cross. She wanted to be tempted; deep in her heart of hearts she craved his touch; she wanted him to kiss her again—and more. Though what that elusive *more* was, she couldn't say—only that she ached to know his touch, his soul and his heart.

She glanced at him now. Though he was sprawled out like a kitchen tabby on the blanket, she was not fooled by his posture. To the casual observer he would appear relaxed, on the verge of sleep. But Mattie knew him too well now to be deceived. His long, hard body was held tightly in check. His jaw was harsher than the craggy stones of Redbird Mountain, and his gaze focused with too much intensity on those snow-capped peaks. Mattie realized he might spring up and bolt at any minute.

Was he thinking of her? Mattie's heart cried out: *Please, let him be thinking of me.*

Roamer could feel Mattie's eyes upon him. His body tingled with awareness of her. Every movement she made, every breath she took, touched him. Since the kiss they shared he had been walking on a knife-edge of pent-up desire. He thought of her constantly, berated himself for his lustful thoughts, but continued to think of her all the same.

It was something he fought with every fiber of his being throughout the day, but at night, when he was asleep and unable to control himself, she came to him in dreams.

Last night she had been shrouded in mist, calling his name. He had never seen any evidence of danger, but gaining insight without substance in the way that dreams do, Roamer knew Mattie needed his help.

He had awakened shaking and had to fight the impulse to dress and go to her house in the middle of the night. And now, while she fed Scout and cast fleeting, curious glances his way, he felt a searing, taut desire enter his loins.

He hated himself for it. He was powerless against it. She was married.

She was another man's wife. And the fact that the man who claimed her wasn't even in the same town—was not here to comfort her and protect her—made Roamer angry in a way he would not have thought possible.

"Reverend Miller came by the schoolhouse today," she said suddenly.

"Oh?" Roamer turned to look at her, regretting it instantly. She was aglow with sunshine, the rays glinting on her warm, honey brown hair, kissing her cheeks to a soft pink.

He wanted to touch her. He wanted to pull out those hairpins and knead his fingers through that hair. He wanted to pull her down beside him and taste sweet sin on her lips.

"He said the whole town was happy to see Scout a little less rambunctious."

"Oh." He wanted to rub his palm against the creamy smoothness of her cheek.

"He also wondered if—" She looked down at the linen napkin she was folding and unfolding.

"What did he wonder?" Roamer's belly pulled taut.

Had anyone seen him kissing Mattie? He would not, for anything in the world, tarnish her good name.

"He wondered if you have had any answers to the letters you have been writing to the matrimonial agency."

Roamer frowned. He had not thought much about the nameless, faceless women he was courting. Mattie had been too much in his mind for him even to give a fleeting thought to them. He simply poured out his heart in the letters, folded them up, and sent them off.

But now he wondered.

How many had he sent? Six? Seven? More?

Why hadn't there been a single reply?

Each time he and Mattie finished a new letter, Scout delivered it to John Holcomb to be sent out with Miley on his next journey to Belle Fourche. And though the mail was slow, it was not so slow that a single reply could not have reached McTavish Plain.

"Look, wagons coming!" Scout suddenly shouted.

Roamer rose to his feet with a quickness that belied his size.

Mattie's traitorous eyes drank in the sight of him. The mountain breeze had plastered his shirt against the hard bulk of his chest, sculpting him in as much detail as any classic statue she had ever seen rendered in quill and ink.

Long legs and lean, powerful thighs braced apart, he squinted against the sun. His skin was burnished to a ruddy glow. The man was solid, strong, and so male she nearly licked her lips in hungry delight.

Her heartbeat quickened, and though she tried to think in terms of genteel, romantic poetry in the hope of recovering the foolish detachment she once felt about Roamer, she could not.

All her life Mattie had believed romance was words and shy smiles. But as she stared at Roamer, she knew what it truly was. It was raw emotion and gnawing need. It was the desire to touch flesh against flesh and the yearning need to be held. She wanted to hear her name on his lips. She wanted to explore the mysteries of the body she had glimpsed at his home.

"Please, don't let this be love," she prayed under her breath. "Not for Roamer Tresh."

Scout dashed toward the lead wagon. It had been many long months since any visitors had come through McTavish Plain. He was anxious to meet whoever was in those three covered wagons.

"Scout, you hold up there," Roamer's voice cracked across the prairie. It had the desired effect.

Scout halted.

"But I wanna see who it is." The boy jumped up and down as if staying in one spot were impossible.

"And you will, just as soon as I say you can."

"Yes sir," Scout sighed, and he waited while Roamer strode toward a man on horseback who Scout guessed was the guide. He was old, much older than Uncle Roamer, with a big red nose and funny-looking eyes. He spat tobacco juice from between his broken, stained teeth when he spoke, the juice dribbling down into his scraggly brown-and-gray beard. Even at a distance he smelled worse than the polecat Scout had put into the privy.

"Howdy," the guide said in a funny, slurred way. He swayed on his horse and kept grabbing up the

reins in a manner that made Scout wonder if he fell off sometimes.

Roamer nodded. "Where are you headed?"

The man spit brown juice on the ground. "Taking these pilgrims to Oregon."

Roamer's brows rose up. "A bit far north, ain't you. Easier trails to the south of here." Roamer scanned the small train. "Why are there only three wagons in your party? Have you had to leave some behind?"

Before the man could answer, another man, wearing a flat-brimmed hat, walked up. He was grinning with his hand extended.

"Praise the Lord, I thought we'd never see another white man." He grasped Roamer's hand and pumped it up and down so hard, Scout wondered if Uncle Roamer might not spout water right there.

Behind the man plodded a pair of speckled oxen pulling one of the wagons. Scout had never seen an ox with such a deep brisket. The thick hide nearly dragged the grass when the animal leaned forward, putting his weight against the heavy yoke.

"Roamer Tresh. Pleased to meet you." Finally the man stopped shaking his hand, releasing Uncle Roamer in a way that made Scout think he didn't really want to.

"A white man. I can't take it all in. I am Clarence Wilson. Pay no mind to our guide. Mr. Calston is a bit rough round the edges, but we had it on good authority that if anybody could get us to Oregon, he was the man. We had been led to believe there were only Indians this far north. Where you from Mr. Tresh?" The man looked over the empty grassland as if it were something to fear, his wide-eyed gaze lingering on the buggy and Mrs. Smith.

"McTavish Plain, about two miles south. My nephew and his schoolteacher were enjoying a picnic lunch. There is not a lot left, but you are welcome to join us."

"Mr. Tresh, we never expected to find any towns out this far—and certainly not people so comfortable that they can enjoy a picnic. I do declare, a picnic—just like this part of the country was all civilized and safe."

"McTavish Plain is a charter town; the land was settled by Ian McTavish after he made a pact with one of the Salish tribes. We have few problems with them. Ian is always looking for able-bodied folks to settle. If you decide Oregon is too far, you might consider signing up and joining the town."

"I heard the Indians hereabouts were fierce." Mr. Wilson said, his gaze flicking to the peaks of Redbird Mountain. "In fact Mr. Calston said—"

"Indians are unpredictable. They can howdy-do you one minute and lift your scalp the next," Calston interrupted.

"We treat them fair and they leave us alone," Roamer said, with a hard edge to his voice.

"Only good injun is a dead 'un." Calston spat tobacco juice near Roamer's left boot. "I wouldn't put much store in what this greener tells you, Mr. Wilson. Like as not the savages will have his purty yeller hair on their belt 'afore fall."

Roamer's nostrils flared and Scout knew that his uncle disliked the man. In fact, when he saw his uncle ball his hands into big, meaty fists, he wondered if he wouldn't hit him.

But he didn't, and Scout felt a wave at disappointment. His uncle was big and strong and shouldn't let a filthy man like that guide talk to him that way.

"Makes me no difference what you decide, but you

and your people are welcome to come to town, talk with folks. Make your own mind up about how safe the town is. McTavish Plain folks are always ready for news and gossip from the East."

"I'd advise against it," Calston said. "Pure waste of time. And I have more years experience than this young greener."

"We'd be mighty happy to follow you in," Mr. Wilson said, ignoring the guide. "We are in need of fresh water, and my woman would purely love to have someone new to talk with besides me and our young 'uns. It's been powerful hard on her all cooped up like we are, and one of them was feeling poorly today. It would be a pure pleasure to see her smile."

"I told you drinkin' water would kill you," The drunken guide said. He tipped up his canteen and swallowed, his whisker-dotted Adam's apple working. "Whiskey has what it takes to kill the impurities in barreled water. I am telling you, a cup a day will keep you fit."

Roamer turned away. "I have to help Mrs. Smith get the picnic basket packed up. You can fall in behind the buggy when we're loaded."

"Why don't your boy there ride in the back and maybe talk to my young 'uns?" Mr. Wilson offered.

"Would you like that, Scout?" Roamer asked.

"Yes sir." Scout was already in motion, scampering to the back of the wagon. Several children peeking over the tailgate of the wagon were watching him with shy grins on their faces.

"Howdy. I'm Scout Tresh." He scrambled over the back. "Got any water? I'm feeling a mite thirsty."

Mattie watched Scout disappear into the lumbering wagon. While Roamer had been talking, she forced herself to turn away and keep busy. She packed the remains of their picnic and climbed into the buggy. Though she wanted Roamer's hands upon her, she was too much a coward to risk the momentary joy by waiting and letting him hand her up. She saw him say a few more words to the two men, and then he was striding toward her.

"Who are they?" She asked when he climbed into the buggy. His brow was furrowed into a deep frown.

She wanted to smooth it away.

"Settlers headed to Oregon." Roamer picked up the lines. His body gave off a comforting warmth and aura of strength.

Would she ever meet another man who could make her feel safe just by being with her?

"I invited them to follow us to town. Their guide is a drunken fool. I suggested they think about signing Ian's charter and joining the town."

"And of course, Scout took every opportunity to make some new friends," Mattie quipped.

Roamer turned to her, his green eyes alight with humor. "You know that boy; he never met a stranger."

"I know, he is a trusting child. It's good you and he live out here in McTavish Plain. In the city it could be hazardous for a child to be so friendly."

Roamer nodded in agreement. "You're right. It worries me sometimes, that he isn't more cautious with strangers. Maybe I better have a talk with him."

"Good idea," Mattie said absently. She had scooted as far over on the seat as she could get, as if she were reluctant to let so much as the lace on her skirt come in contact with Roamer's leg.

But it wasn't enough. She sighed and realized a hundred miles between them would not be enough to sever the connection.

Roamer glanced at Mattie. An expression of sadness flitted across her face. It plucked at his heartstrings.

Did she fear him? Is that why she watched him so closely but pretended not to? Her actions made him think he should do more to make amends for his lapse of control.

"I wanted to apologize again."

"Oh, no, I was as much at fault as you," she said, her cheeks staining a bright pink when he turned to really look at her.

Lord, she was a beauty! Each day she seemed to become more alluring. Her hair was a peculiar brown that seemed to capture the sunlight and split into a thousand shades. Her skin was smoother than cream, dewier-looking than a flower after the rain.

Each day he spent a deal more time reminding himself that she was married—to someone else—and that she could never be his.

He ripped his gaze from her face and flicked the reins, wishing he did not draw in the sweet essence of her each time he inhaled. The scent of flowers that she wore, mixed with the smell of fresh air and starched clothes in sunshine, was making him hard as a post.

He wanted her, in a way that he had never wanted another woman. It was wrong; it was sinful; but it was also the sweetest, rawest hunger he could imagine.

His reaction to Mrs. Smith stunned him. It also disgusted and frightened him.

Roamer had always prided himself on doing the right thing but when he was around Mattie, he wasn't so sure what that was anymore. How could anyone so fine be so forbidden?

"Could I ask you a question?" he heard himself say.

"Of course." She glanced at him, and the momentary flash of her embarrassed smile made his chest contract around his heart. Or did his heart actually skip a beat?

"Is there—that is—" Roamer frowned. "What I mean to say . . ."

"Please, just say it."

He nodded. "Are things between you and your husband as they should be?" His voice was dry and low with lust.

Mattie swallowed hard. What should she say? What *could* she say? In her dreams at night she had imagined such a moment, when she would tell Roamer the truth. She wanted with all her heart to unburden herself—to tell him that Mr. Samuel Smith, sea captain, perfect product of her silly imagination, did not exist, and that she had never been married and never known a man. That she was free to be kissed, to be loved—and that she wanted Roamer to be the man doing the kissing and loving.

Then she remembered her sisters.

Ian McTavish was a stubborn Scot through and through. If he found out that his wife and her sisters had lied, out and out *lied* . . . the result could be disastrous. Mattie couldn't do it. No matter how much she wanted to see where this wild, reckless attraction to Roamer might take her, she could not take that opportunity at the expense of her sisters' security and happiness.

"Of course, there is the distance between us." She took a long, deep breath. "It isn't easy being the wife of a sea captain," she lied. "But soon he will give up that life and join me here in McTavish Plain. It won't be much longer."

Roamer heard the taut note of Mattie's voice and felt himself being ripped back in time. Susan had sounded exactly the same way each time he questioned her about the bruises, the torn clothing, the broken furniture in her shabby, small house.

"When?"

"What?" Mattie blinked, stunned by his harsh question.

"When will he join you?"

"I—I can't say."

"Ah, it's only the distance and nothing else, but you can't even say when he is coming to join you," Roamer said.

"I see." But what he saw was making him ill inside. He didn't want to think it, did not want to imagine Mattie's sweet, frail body with bruises like those he had seen on his sister, but the image came tearing through his mind anyway. "So what you are saying is that your husband has not told you when he intends to join you here."

"Yes—no. It sounds so hard when you put it into those words," Mattie said softly.

He shifted his position to make room for the uncomfortable notion taking root in his mind. And he felt a hot push-pull in his heart. Until this instant he had not wanted to admit to himself how badly he wanted Mattie to say her marriage was unhappy. He had wanted her to tell him that her husband had left her, that being at sea was more than his profession. God forgive him, he wanted her to be an unhappy victim of a loveless union, so that his feelings for a married woman would be acceptable. But never, not in the darkest corners of his lust did he want her to be abused and mistreated—and that was the conclusion he had come to.

He glanced at Mattie again. She was ripping tiny bits of lace from the bottom of her fancy reticule as she stared, unseeing, out across the prairie toward Redbird Mountain.

She was on the verge of tears. The only possible reason for such a reaction was that her husband was a cruel bastard no better than Laughing Jack Maravel, and she did not want Roamer to know.

It made perfect sense. She never spoke of him; she never smiled and told some little story of their life together.

He abused her.

That knowledge sickened Roamer. Anger, disgust, and a feeling of being helpless sluiced over him. He had watched his sister flounder and die in such a situation. He would not let that happen to Mattie.

Roamer flicked the reins and hurried the horse toward town. He made a silent vow. The moment her husband showed up in McTavish Plain, he would find a way to help her—no matter what that meant or whom it hurt.

Three wagons of strangers gave McTavish Plain a reason for a holiday. A fat weanling pig was spitted and set to roasting, and Addie McTavish and Mrs. Miller set to baking pies, cakes, and tarts. Every able-bodied man in town went about helping the settlers repair and replenish their stores while Nate Pearson resined his bow and tuned his fiddle.

By late afternoon, couples were dancing on the grass and in the street. The warm spring breeze kept the night-flying biters away. Folks laughed and exchanged questions about events at home. There was still talk of secession in the South—the reason Clarence Wilson and his kin from St. Louis, having no desire to be forced to choose, were heading west.

Everyone, it seemed, was festive but Roamer. Feeling the way he did for Mattie Smith did not make him fit company. He didn't deserve to be around God-fearing folk—not when with a word he would embrace sin and ruin just to hold her in his arms. So when Clarence brought a cracked wagon wheel to the forge to be mended, Roamer was glad of it.

As soon as Roamer had his coat off and his sleeves rolled up, Scout came tearing in with three children in tow. He was out of breath, and it took a moment before he could speak.

"Uncle Roamer, while you're fixing that, can I take Joey and his brothers and show 'em the beaver's dam and the new spring lambs?" Scout's cheeks were bright circles of rose.

Roamer frowned at him. It was not like Scout to be in such a dither that he colored up, even when he had been running all day. "You feelin' all right?"

"Sure," Scout said brightly.

Roamer glanced at the other boys. Their cheeks were rosy too. Maybe it was just the excitement of having someone new to play with. He was glad the boy was happy; it was the one wish Susan had for her son, and the one thing Roamer intended to do no matter the cost.

"Go ahead, but no farther than the dam. And I expect you to be here when you hear Gert ring the bell for victuals."

"I will," Scout said over his shoulder. "And I'll be hungry, too."

When Roamer finished the wheel, he headed toward the glow of light and laughter. He was tired, but his mind was still whirling, thinking of Susan and Mattie. At some point while beating on the hot iron, his anger had fled to be replaced by cold, unyielding hatred.

It wouldn't do for him to come face-to-face with Mattie's husband. If he did, Roamer was afraid he wouldn't be able to keep his vow.

I've already killed one man, he thought to himself. *I don't know that I could live with another on my conscience.* But he knew in his heart he would suffer any torment to free Mattie from a marriage of abuse. When he thought of Susan and now Mattie, his heart screamed for revenge.

He clenched his hands into fists and forced them to his sides. He would not lift his hand against any man. He had taken a vow before God, and he would not—*could not*—break it.

"Well, ain't you the purty little darky." The slurred words brought Roamer to a sudden halt. He peered into the alley behind Gus's mercantile. Slowly he made out two shapes.

"Let me go." Nate Pearson's wife was struggling to free herself from the drunken guide, Calston.

"A little poke first," Calston said.

Roamer was moving before his mind even registered the thought. He grabbed the stinking guide and spun him around.

"Whoa, now, there's 'nuff to go around. I won't take more'n a minute or two."

"Are you all right, Mrs. Pearson?"

"Ye—yes." She was shaking like an Aspen leaf as she drew her shawl tight around her shoulders.

"Go find Nate and Ian. Tell them what happened."

Roamer turned to Calston while he heard her run from the alley.

"You ought'n done that. She was just a darky." The man's fetid breath made Roamer's stomach roil. "Lemme go." He struggled to be free.

"You aren't going anywhere."

The man pulled out a knife quicker than Roamer would have thought possible. Even in the dim alley there was enough of a moon to glitter coldly along the blade.

"Lemme go."

Roamer held onto the man while he fought the rage building inside him. He wanted to hit Calston. He wanted to take that pigsticker and snap the blade from the haft. He wanted to pummel this disgusting excuse for a man until he was pulp. He wanted to do all that and more, but he was held by his vow.

"I'll cut out yer liver with this," Calston threatened.

Without conscious thought Roamer's hand tightened in the rough buckskin, pulling it taut across Calston's throat. The guide coughed and his eyes bulged a little. The man swiped at Roamer with the blade, but Roamer's reach was much longer, making his pitiful attempts to cut him useless.

"Roamer?" Ian's voice was like cool water over hot metal. "You can let him go, Roamer."

"He's a piece of filth."

"Aye, lad he is, but he is dying, Roamer."

Roamer's fingers unclenched and he shoved the guide away from him. The drunk fetched up against the solid bulk of Gus's store, out cold.

"I wanted to kill him, Ian," Roamer said softly.

"I know, lad, but you dinna and that is what matters. Go now and have something to eat. I will see this fool causes no more trouble until they leave at first light."

A few minutes later, still feeling cold with fury, Roamer joined the noisy town. It took a moment for him to find Scout, sitting near the table where Mattie was dishing up portions of duck stew. Looking at both of them made Roamer's heart ache. He wanted to keep them both safe and happy, but how could a man with such a dark past manage such a task?

He made his way through the crowd and smiled down at his nephew. "Scout? Have you eaten, boy?" Roamer squatted beside the child.

"No sir."

"Why not? I see they got all your favorites here, even berry pie."

"I just ain't hungry," Scout shrugged.

Roamer frowned. It wasn't like Scout at all. He tried to coax Scout to have some food.

"How about some of Mrs. McTavish's pie?"

"Naw, I don't want any."

"Scout, when you turn down berry pie, I worry. Are you ailing?" Roamer looked at the boy's eyes; they were not as bright as usual. His skin had a yellowish tint to it, and he seemed all done in.

"What's wrong?" Mattie had left the table and was squatting beside them. She pulled her calico skirt out of the way and touched Scout's cheek. When her arm innocently brushed against Roamer's thigh, he felt his heart flip-flop painfully inside his chest.

"He isn't hungry," Roamer said in a voice gone husky with need. "And when he isn't hungry I worry."

"Now, Scout, I just put out two roasted prairie chickens. And there are dumplings with them. Sure you won't try some? I am sure they're better than mine."

Scout smiled weakly. "Ain't nobody can cook better than you, Mrs. Smith."

Mattie's breath caught in her chest. She wanted to laugh, to cry, to hug this child to her. She wanted—

"I think I best take him home," Roamer said softly.

"Yes. That probably is best," Mattie agreed, but her heart was crying out for another possibility.

"Aw, I'm just a little hot. Can't we watch the dancing for a while?" Scout mumbled as Roamer hefted him up.

Mattie stood up and took Scout's chin in her fingers. She turned his face and looked into his eyes in the firelight. They were shot through with blood. She felt his forehead.

"He's fevered, Roamer."

"Too much sun and play, like as not. I shouldn't have let him run off all day with those new children," Roamer said as he shifted Scout in his arms. He wanted to believe his own words, but he felt an icy finger of dread. "Where are those children, Scout?"

"Their mama put them to bed a while ago. Joey's got a powerful ache in his belly."

"Did you eat any berries when you went to look at Ian's new lambs?" Roamer asked.

"No sir."

"Then it's probably nothing to worry about."

"If you need anything, please let me know." Mattie ran her palm over Scout's back, wishing to give him some comfort. She looked at Roamer's green eyes and saw fear in them. "Anything, Roamer. I mean it."

"He'll be fine—" Roamer began.

"Perhaps so, but promise me that you will fetch me if you need anything," Mattie insisted.

"I promise—and thank you."

The pounding was loud. Too loud to be part of the dream Mattie was having. She dreamed that Roamer asked her to dance. His arms around her were hard and strong. She felt safe and . . . *loved.* Then, in her dream they were at his forge and there was the steady clang of the hammer.

Roamer was calling her name. But in her dream he was with her. Then she heard the pounding again. It was more than just feet pounding in time to the music, or clapping hands, or his hammer on the anvil.

It was real. Someone was calling her name and pounding on her kitchen door.

Mattie shook off the heavy cloak of sleep. She opened her eyes and sat, fumbling for her wrapper.

"Mattie. Mattie, wake up, it's Roamer."

Groggy and disoriented, she swung her feet to the floor and ran to the door. The pounding was so insistent that she didn't even take the time to cover herself before she unlatched and flung open the door.

"Mattie. I knocked for a long time."

It was Roamer, with his shirt untucked, his hair wild.

"What is it?"

"Scout is very sick. Mattie—I'm afraid he may die."

Nine

"How long has he been like this?" Mattie dipped the cloth in the basin of cool water and sponged Scout's burning cheeks.

Scout moaned and writhed upward. The child gave one helpless look to Roamer. He nodded and picked up the chamber pot, positioning it in front of Scout. He lovingly stroked the child's head as he vomited. When he was finished, Scout collapsed back on the bed, curling into a tight ball of moaning pain.

"At first he was running to the privy every five minutes. Then the vomiting started. I have never seen him this sick."

"Could you get me some fresh water from the well?" Mattie asked Roamer, tossing off her shawl. She wanted him to get out of the room for a few moments so she could really look at Scout.

"I should stay—"

"I will be here, and I think you could use a moment." She laid her fingers on his forearm. "Please, Roamer."

"I'll hurry."

She had dressed hastily, without a corset, her plain calico buttoned only half way up. Now she finished the buttons with one hand while she pulled the chair nearer the bed with the other.

"Scout, can you hear me?"

His eyes fluttered open. They were glazed over, his cheeks pale with two bright circles of feverish color.

"Yes ma'am. I can hear you." He whispered. "Please stay. I think Uncle Roamer needs you."

"I'm here for you both, Scout, and I am not leaving."

"Promise?"

"I promise. We'll get you through this."

But how?

"Yes ma'am." He said weakly but with all the confidence of a child.

Mattie held his small, frail hand while she gathered her wits. Her heart was beating as fast as the wings of a bird in flight. She knew less about doctoring than she did about cooking. How could she help?

How can you not?

Surely, she could think of something that would help Scout. Didn't every woman have natural instincts that would help her in this kind of situation?

Mattie thought back to her childhood. No matter what the illness, the woman that raised her and her sisters swore that the girls must keep drinking throughout the feverish time. To stop taking fluids was the first step toward death.

Roamer returned with the bucket of water. "What do you think it is?" His voice was low and raw with worry.

"I don't know, Roamer. I know so little about children and the things most women know. But no matter what it takes, we have to get liquid in him to replace what he is losing."

His face fell and she saw fear in his green eyes. "Dear Lord, Mattie, tell me he won't die," Roamer said in a husky, painful whisper. He felt the cold hand of loss, so well remembered, settling around his heart. "Please don't let him die, Mattie."

"Not while there is breath in my body," Mattie said with a weak smile. She reached out and put her hands on his shoulders. "We'll care for him together, Roamer."

"Bless you, Mattie. For the first time in many long years I don't feel all alone."

The sun was a bright crimson disk rising in the east when Roamer went to Reverend Miller's house. The door opened before he even knocked.

"Roamer, you look awful." The churchman had a heavy lather of soap on his face and his shirt was half buttoned. "I saw you coming." A straight razor gleamed in his hand.

Roamer raked his fingers through his hair and rubbed his hand down the side of his face. It was bristly. He had not slept, had not taken the time to wash or comb his hair. Every muscle and sinew in his body was taut with worry.

"Scout is very ill. Mrs. Smith, the schoolmarm, is helping me tend to him. She wanted you to get word around that she won't be holding school today—maybe for a few days."

"My wife can take the classes. Tell Mattie not to worry."

"Thanks." Roamer turned away but felt a hand on his arm.

"We will pray," Reverend Miller said softly.

"Yes, do that."

"Roamer, would you like some breakfast? Some coffee? Maybe you'd like to take something back to Mrs. Smith. Or should I have my wife go to her house and get her some extra clothing. I know how women can be."

Roamer blinked. "I hadn't thought—that is, I am sure Mrs. Smith would appreciate the kindness."

Within an hour most of the town had gathered outside the white picket fence that surrounded Roamer's front yard. They had begun to gather just after the minister and his wife brought a basket of food and a bundle of things for Mattie. Fear pinched the faces of Roamer's neighbors. He opened the door and came out onto the stoop, chilled to the bone in spite of the spring sunshine.

"What is it, Roamer?" Tightly leashed fear made Nate Pearson's voice taut. "What's brought your boy down?"

"I wish I knew, Nate."

"He's always been such a frisky little scamp, it don't seem natural that he's down sick."

"Would you care for me to have a look?" Gert offered. Before Roamer could answer, he heard a sound and turned. Mattie appeared at the door. Dark smudges of fatigue ringed her eyes. Roamer felt a sharp stab of both affection and guilt that she was doing so much for him and Scout.

"No, Gert, you shouldn't," Mattie said. "We don't know what it is, and if it is catching . . ." Her words trailed off as Lottie stepped forward, a determined glint in her eyes.

"That means you too, Charlotte. I don't want you here." Mattie blocked the way and met her sister's glare with her own.

"Now, Mattie—"

"No. Roamer and I are doing just fine and if it is—well, if it is catching, there's no need for you or Addie to have it."

Lottie's eyes widened. There was a moment when Mattie thought she might argue, but then she gave one stiff nod of her head. A tense silence fell over the crowd. There was no need to say aloud what they were all thinking: Everyone in town could become infected. McTavish Plain had no doctor yet. They could all be dead and nobody outside their small circle would even know before it was over.

"I think we should send Ian to the Salish for a cure," Nate Pearson said. "The Indians might have herbs."

John Carpenter pointed to the horizon. "Look, there's Ian now."

Mattie turned and looked at the road that led from the stone castle where her eldest sister now lived. Ian was astride Dow, and he was alone except for the pair of big Scottish deerhounds.

"I wonder why Addie isn't with him?" Mattie said softly, looking up at Roamer. Fear for her sister made her shiver involuntarily. "You don't suppose she has come down with something, do you?"

"Don't borrow trouble, Mattie," Roamer said quietly, giving her hand a little squeeze within the folds of her skirt where none could see. "Like as not she's busy with some task. There is no reason to suppose Ian even knows Scout is sick."

"You're right, of course." She drew strength from

his touch, from his nearness. "Ian is just coming to town like any other day. He wouldn't know." During the night, when Mattie's faith was teetering and she allowed herself to consider that Scout might really die, she had drawn a measure of comfort just from being with Roamer in the tidy little house.

It was good to have him with her at a time like this.

"Ian, we're glad you're here." Gert met his horse before Dow had come to a full stop. "Scout is mighty sick. Can you ride to the Salish and bring back their healer?"

"Nonsense, we don't need those savages here," Otto Hudspeth snapped. "I have skills as an apothecary. Tell me his symptoms and I'll fix something to cure him."

Roamer glared at Otto. He wasn't sure he wanted anything going into Scout that that pinch-faced weasel brewed.

"How dire is the lad?" Ian dismounted.

"He is very ill, Ian. The worst I have seen. He has vomiting, his bowels are watery—I think I saw a stain of blood," Mattie said, trying not to break into tears.

"Good Lord. The child has cholera," Hudspeth said with a pale face. "I ain't going near him." He spoke while walking backward at such a pace he was awkwardly trotting, his eyes round with fear.

"All of you better start boiling your water and stay away from this house of pestilence or you'll be next. You hear? Cholera will spread like wildfire and we'll all be dead." Then he turned and dashed toward his storefront. As soon as he was inside the building the door slammed shut. The "closed" sign was in the window and the shades were drawn down in the blink of an eye.

"Well, I guess that apothecary ain't going to be helping," Gus said with disgust.

"Cholera? Isn't that from bad water? Ian, is our water gone bad?" Gert asked, wringing her hands.

"Is anyone else sickening?" Ian asked loudly.

A murmur of sound as people inventoried their own families and those of their neighbors. Finally someone said no.

"There's naught wrong with the water here, then, or else others would be sick as well."

"Ian, where is Addie?" Mattie asked.

"I dinna want her to come to town. She is not up to snuff this morn."

"Scout and Mrs. McTavish are both ill," someone gasped. "Then it is the water."

There was a rush of fear that passed through the crowd, tangible and strong. Mattie's stomach clenched. If anything happened to Addie . . .

"Nay. Scout is the only one sick. My wife is not ailing." Ian frowned at the crowd. "Dinna be daft and full of terror as that little apothecary. If the water in town was tainted then more than just little Scout would be poorly—in fact, most would be in the same shape if he has been sickening since the dance. Use your heads."

"Then where is Addie? Why didn't she come to town if she ain't sick?" somebody yelled from the back of the crowd.

"Are you keeping the truth from us, Ian?"

Ian frowned and whirled on the assemblage. "I am keeping naught from you."

"Then where is your wife?"

"My wife is goin' to be none too happy when she finds out I let the cat from the bag."

"What cat? Ian, what is the matter with her?" Lottie demanded. "Is my sister ill or isn't she?"

"Nae, lass. She is weak in the mornin' because she is carrying a bairn. I dinna want her riding and bein' jostled around."

"A baby," Mattie and Lottie repeated simultaneously. "Addie is having a baby?"

"Aye, lass, your sister is with child and she is sufferin' with the mornin' sickness. But if you need her, I know she will want to come."

"No. Keep her at home, Ian." Mattie shook her head, her disheveled hair falling down in her eyes as she did so.

"Lie to her if you must; tie her down if you need to, but don't let her put her child at risk."

"Are you sure it is not the water, Roamer?" Lottie asked again softly. "What did Scout eat or drink that the rest of us did not?"

Roamer thought for a minute. He remembered Scout's cheeks and those of the other children from the wagon train.

"Scout was with Clarence Wilson's children all day. He must've gotten something to eat or drink from the visitors. Mr. Wilson said they needed fresh water."

Ian's face turned stony. "I best ride out and find their trail. If they are sickenin' and alone they may need help." He turned to the crowd. "Go on home. The water in McTavish Plain is sweet and fine. Tend to your families and leave Roamer and Mattie to nurse Scout."

One by one, the townspeople began to leave. Some headed toward their own homes, their own families; others went to open their businesses.

"I'm going with you to find that train," Miley said. "Gert can see to things here."

"There is no need," Ian said.

Gert stepped up and jutted out her chin at Ian. "I ain't no shrinking violet. If my man says he is going with you and I can handle things, then he is going with you, Ian."

"I will go, too." Roamer stepped off his stoop.

"Nae. You stay with Mattie and Scout. The lass looks all done in. Her sister wouldn'a take kindly to her being left alone when she is so poorly." Ian nodded toward the house. "And you may be needed if the lad turns for the worse."

Ian's words fell hard on Roamer. He had not said what Roamer might be needed to do, but the image of digging a grave and building a small casket flashed through his brain, causing him so much pain he nearly sagged to his knees from the thought.

"Take care of Mattie and the lad. Miley and I will be back soon as we know something," Ian said as he mounted Dow and rode off.

Roamer watched them until they were no more than dark specks on the green horizon. He heard a tiny whimper and turned to see Mattie leaning heavily on the doorjamb. He moved toward her.

"Mattie, are you all right?"

"I am fine." She smiled weakly, then went white as snow. Her eyes rolled back in her head. She seemed to fold in half, her legs going liquid before Roamer had her up in his arms.

"Yes, darlin' I can see how fine you are."

And his heart kicked a little in his chest at how fragile and precious she felt in his arms as he carried her to his bed.

* * *

They settled into a routine. Mattie would keep Scout's fevered brow cool with a cloth. Roamer kept a kettle of water boiling, which was then cooled and given to Scout on a cloth. He had to suck the fabric because he was too weak to drink from a cup.

Roamer took the precaution of burning Scout's soiled bedding. He didn't know if that would be enough to halt the illness, but he remembered his mother and his grandmother saying nothing should be saved from a house where fever had been.

Mattie and Roamer clung to each other in silent vigil, as parents have done at their children's bedsides since the dawn of time. The hours since Ian left no longer had meaning as they watched little Scout fight for his life. They ate little and slept even less while they worked in tandem to keep Scout as comfortable as possible. And never once did they mention the wagon train and what they feared Ian and Miley would find.

The heavy wagons of the small train left a trail that a shortsighted man could have followed in the dark. Miley and Ian pushed their horses hard, covering ground at a pace that would far exceed that of the lumbering wagons loaded with all that the travelers needed to begin a new life.

Before noon they saw the buzzards in the sky—winged harbingers of death, hovering in a wide circle over the endless landscape. Ian and Miley looked at each other in grim silence. Then they spurred their mounts and hurried on.

The three wagons were in line in the bottom of a valley. Without shelter or protection, they appeared to have simply stopped moving.

"That looks quiet—" Miley said.

"—As death," Ian finished.

As they neared the wagons, they found the oxen still hitched to the heavy wooden yokes. The grass beneath their feet was trampled to dust, and they lowed pitifully from thirst and discomfort.

"No campfire was ever built," Miley commented grimly.

"Likely they were all too weak."

"I'll take the last wagon."

Ian nodded and rode to the next one. Dow snorted, blew, and shied sharply from the wagon, his eyes round with instinctual terror. Ian dismounted and held the reins firmly.

"I know, lad, 'tis the scent of death."

Ian yanked the tartan sash from around his waist. He wrapped it around his mouth and nose and tied the ends before he wrapped the reins around his fist and looked inside. He nearly retched at the sight and the smell.

Ian looked down at the first wagon and saw Miley vomiting. When he straightened, his face was stark white and drawn into a mask of horrified disbelief. He disappeared around the back of the wagon. When he returned, there was a shovel in his hand.

"I don't see the drunken guide, Calston, among them."

"Nae, and you will'na. One set of tracks leads away from the wagons. I suspect the bastard left them as soon as they sickened," Ian said grimly.

"It ain't right for men and women to die alone in

their own filth. Same as murder to me," Miley said grimly. "He could've come back to McTavish Plain for help."

"Aye, he could." Ian said, "But he dinna. He let them die alone. I found this in Clarence Wilson's hand." He held out a piece of paper. "Looks like he wrote a letter to their kin back in St. Louis when he knew the end was near."

"I'll see it gets to Belle Fourche next mail run," Miley said. "Let's get these folks buried and those pitiful animals back to town."

"Aye. There is not enough wood for coffins; we will have to wrap them in sheets and bury them deep," Ian said grimly.

Hours later, with the gaunt oxen plodding in front of them, Ian and Miley left fifteen graves and three wagons behind in the dusky wash of sunset.

They had said a prayer over the graves that included a plea that Calston have a taste of divine retribution.

Jack paced back and forth along the bank. The river shimmered in the sunlight, a ribbon of liquid that meandered in a westerly direction.

Toward Susan's brat—the pot of gold at the end of the rainbow.

But he was without funds once again. Nobody in any of the gambling parlors in this little town was going to play a hand of cards with a man who just got out of jail. Even if they were inclined, the sheriff had made it plain: leave by sundown or else go back in the lockup.

Jack didn't want to find out what that threat entailed, so here he was at the river, hoping to find a sheep to fleece for enough money to buy a horse.

"Coming through." The words were spoken at the moment Jack was rudely shoved from behind. He turned, ready to verbally flay the hide of the miscreant until his gaze fell upon three stout stevedores. Each one was tall and broad as his dim-witted brother-in-law, Roamer. And they looked tough as rawhide.

"Move aside," one wearing a red-and-white knitted cap growled while he shifted the weight of an oaken cask and prepared to stack it like cordwood into a flat-bottomed boat moored at the dock.

"What have you got there?" Jack asked as the barrels were stacked, six deep and four high along both sides. The waterline slid higher on the planking with each cask.

"Whiskey. Bound for upriver," the man answered over his shoulder. "Always need more whiskey upriver. Settlers and forts go through barrels of the stuff."

"Do you need another hand?" Jack heard himself ask.

"Ha. You don't look like you know hard work." The man straightened and grinned. "Those hands of yours are white and soft as a woman's."

"I don't, but I do know cards, and where there's whiskey there is usually a card game. If you stake me we could split fifty-fifty."

"Why would I want such a small split?" the man asked with a toothy grin. "I could go to a game and keep all my own winnings."

"True. How about seventy-five–twenty-five?" Jack gave the man his most charming smile.

"Make it ninety-ten in my favor and you can ride

the river with us. But if you try to cheat me I'll cut out your liver and throw you to the turtles." His hand moved smoothly to the butt of a wide knife at his waist. "And I know how to do it—done it before. Make no mistake; I am not a man to make idle threats."

Jack grinned, though he was seething behind the smile. Once again he was being forced to bargain with men that were beneath him. Because of his father and grandmother, he was being forced to consort with the scum of humanity when he should be ordering them around.

"Sure," Jack said. "I'll keep my word, and maybe we can have a friendly game of cards to pass the time."

"I hope I don't regret this. There is something I don't like about the gleam in your eye."

Jack scrambled aboard before he could change his mind. The filthy whiskey boat was a far cry from the elegant sailing ship he intended to take to Paris, but at least he was moving again—heading in the general direction that Roamer was supposed to have gone. At least he was on the trail, following the clues one by one.

And I will find him, if it's the last thing I do, Jack swore to himself as the boat moved out into the current.

Mattie woke in a panic, with her heart pounding in her chest and a sense of terror sweeping over her—disoriented and unsure of what had happened. She had not intended to fall into an exhausted sleep. But her mouth was dry and her brain cottony, so she knew she had slept—soundly and long.

"Scout?" She swung her feet to the floor and tried to stand, but her knees were liquidy and she swayed.

Strong hands reached out and steadied her, making the room stop shifting like quicksand beneath her feet.

"Mattie, hold on," Roamer's deep voice washed over her. "Take a moment, Mattie."

"Scout . . . I have to see to Scout." Groggy from sleep and her own ebbing strength and too much worry, she tried in vain to push his hands off her shoulders.

She felt so weak and Roamer was so strong. She wanted to fold herself into that strength but didn't dare let herself, for fear of what she would say and do.

"Shhh, he is resting quiet. His fever is down and he took some broth. Now it's time for you to rest a bit yourself."

Mattie stopped struggling and looked up at Roamer. "Is he really better? His fever is broken?"

"He is better. He feels no warmer than you and me. You were right, Mattie. You saved that boy by making him take liquid whether he liked it or not." He smiled. "There are not words enough to say thank you." He reached out and grabbed a wayward strand of her tousled hair. Gently, almost reverently, he put it behind her ear. "I can never repay you."

Mattie managed to smile. Roamer was looking at her as if she were wonderful; the sensation was the closest thing to heaven she had ever known. But the look in his eyes was enough to put her already taut nerves on the thin side of frayed. It would take only one wrong word and she would collapse into tears.

"I didn't do it to be repaid. I love Scout and I . . ."

She swallowed hard and tried to get control of herself. They had spent so much time alone together, and her feeling for him was growing stronger every day.

She nearly blurted out her feelings—nearly blurted out the truth. The only thing that kept her from telling him about her lie was the fear of what would happen to Lottie and Addie. It was too much of a risk, especially since Addie was now pregnant. She needed Ian and his love, not his suspicion and anger. And certainly not since she was the one who had to be talked into the whole crazy scheme in the first place.

"You must be hungry." Roamer gently stroked his fingers down her cheek. Without meaning to, she leaned into his fingers. He cupped her cheek, not speaking, just holding her face in his wide, rough hand. It was warm and fit just right.

Oh, she wanted to be touched in that way—wanted to touch him. But she couldn't take her own happiness at her sister's expense.

With a Herculean effort, Mattie shook off the feeling of contentment. She lifted her head, stiffened her spine, and moved away from Roamer's caress.

It was the hardest thing she had ever done.

"What time is it?" Mattie blinked and looked toward the window. There was nothing but darkness beyond the edge of the curtain.

"Middle of the night." He watched her for a moment as if he were considering saying more. Then he gave her that wondrous smile.

"Can you eat? I can scramble up some eggs, Mattie. I ain't the best cook, but breakfast I can manage without burning down the house."

"You must be tired yourself, Roamer; I can find something." She started to stand, but her knees seemed as wobbly as a newborn lamb's. She staggered against Roamer's chest.

His arms came around her.

"Oh, Matilda." His raspy voice sent chills running over her arms. He placed his smooth, dry lips against her forehead. "Matilda, my sweet Matilda. Can't you let me do for you?"

"Roamer," she sighed. And then, against all odds, against her judgment and resolve, against the fear she felt for her sisters, she tilted her head and offered herself.

That was all the invitation he needed, and she knew it. Deep in the darkest corner of her soul she knew she was tempting him, tempting herself to disaster.

But she was too far gone in exhaustion and heartache to care.

He obliged her by pulling her into a passionate embrace. The kiss had all the power and urgency of a lightning bolt. All the moments of self-doubt, of swearing that nothing like this could happen again, simply evaporated from Mattie's mind. Suddenly her concerns about her sister's security, and her own foolish, naive dreams of poetry and chaste love vanished. She became a creature of wanton desire, and the object of that yearning was Roamer Tresh.

Roamer felt the warmth and sensual pull of Mattie's lips, and he didn't care about her low-down husband or his own lost soul or its everlasting damnation. At this moment all he cared about was the honey-sweet sensation of having her in his arms, the salvation of not being alone in a cruel world, and the joy that Scout was out of danger. All of these wondrous emotions swirled through him as he held her.

She was a soft weight against him. When she inhaled, her ample bosom rose and fell, her breath no more than a sweet, gentle gust that made his pulse quicken and his heart pound. He wanted her in a way that he had never wanted another woman. If he could have crawled inside her, he would have done so. It was the most humbling and powerful experience he had ever known—wanting to be so near another person that he wished they could meld their souls in some mystical way, to join forever and beyond.

His hands and body moved without conscious thought. His loins ground against her; his fingers plucked at the buttons on her clothing.

He wanted to free her, to touch her, to have her.

"I hate corsets," he grumbled, the deep sound of his voice making Mattie smile.

"I do too," she agreed in a breathy voice that had never been hers before. "But I am not wearing one, Roamer."

As if to prove her words to his own doubting mind, his hands skimmed over her ribs, cupping the soft bulk of her breasts.

"Oh, Mattie, I can feel the heat of you through this cloth. Your body is so soft and warm."

"I know, but it's still too much between my flesh and yours. Take it off. Undress me, Roamer."

And he did.

The sheer fabric and lace were nothing against the power of his big, strong hands. In a heartbeat she was naked but for her drawers. Cool air and a man's eyes were foreign to her body. She felt exposed and bare, as if taking off her clothes had also stripped back the layers of deceit that covered her soul.

"Oh, Matilda, I never saw anything so perfect in my life." He cupped each breast in his palm. Mattie leaned into his hands, wanting him to do more than just kiss her. Wanting to know what lay at the end of the path of passion.

"Hold me tighter," she moaned. She had always been naturally curious, and since her glimpse of Roamer's body, she had been obsessed with *knowing* him.

His hands tightened on her breasts, squeezing and kneading in a gentle, demanding way that made her lower belly thrill with excitement. Her muscles drew taut and she felt her body leaning toward him.

"I've been dreaming of this," Mattie said in a seductive voice that slid over his skin.

"So have I," Roamer admitted.

And then it was too late. For they both had given up their sanity. In that moment when she gazed into his eyes and he saw the smoldering haze of her own passion, Roamer knew it didn't matter. The laws of man and God were conveniently forgotten as he allowed himself to think only of loving Mattie.

Roamer pressed his palms against her body. Slowly, sensuously, they sculpted the small of her waist, the flare of her hips. Then, gently he laid her back onto his bed and shed his own clothes.

When he climbed above her he was mad with lust. Her skin was like satin, the air still and quiet. The sheets were cool against his fevered flesh, but that was not enough to quench the inferno raging in his blood.

He burned for Mattie, ached for her, could not wait to bury himself deep inside her. He took her face in his hands and kissed her again.

"Ah, Mattie, you are lovely." Roamer wanted to know her secrets. He wanted to know what would make her writhe and moan, how to bring her pleasure.

"Sweetheart, you are a man's dream." He nuzzled her ears, her neck, suckled at her breast until she arched up against him like a kitten. He took her hand in his and brought the palm to his lips. He kissed the tender center of her hand, licked it, then one by one began to suckle the tips of her fingers. . . . Until his tongue encountered the cool, rigid ring of gold on her fourth finger.

Roamer stiffened. He drew back and looked at Mattie, all soft and hot and willing. Then he looked at the ring on her hand—the ring that made her another man's wife.

"I can't do this," Roamer groaned. And though it took more strength than he had, and cost him in ways he never thought possible, he pulled himself from her. "I can't drag you down into the gutter with me, Mattie. God knows I want to, but I can't."

Mattie lay on the bed, shaking, trembling with unslaked lust and shame. Then she raised her arms to him and said, "I want to be with you, Roamer."

"Oh, Mattie, do you know what you are asking?"

"Yes, Roamer, I know and I understand what we risk. I don't care. I want you to love me—come love me till morning comes."

Ten

Just as time had slowed when Scout was near death, now it accelerated to a pace that made the minutes speed by until Mattie felt dizzy. It seemed as if the sun would be upon them in the blink of an eye.

Roamer feathered kisses down Mattie's breasts and over her ribs. She moaned and turned her head from side to side, arching upward, trying to meet his mouth, his body. Every breath he took seemed to promise delight, fulfillment . . . love.

"Easy, honey, let it happen slow," he purred as he sipped at the soft flesh below her naval.

"Roamer, I—I need—," she gasped, trying to understand the gallop of her heart, the throb of that place between her legs.

"Mattie, I know what you need. I need it too."

She wanted him to slide his hand over her and stop the throbbing hunger inside her.

"Roamer—"

"I know, Mattie." And he did know.

He put his hand on her mound and with the thick, callused heel of his hand applied gentle pressure and began to rub her in wide, sensuous circles.

"Ohhh," Mattie moaned.

The sensation was like being hit by lightning. Every nerve in Mattie's body tingled, but it was not enough.

She wanted more.

She had to have more of what only Roamer could give.

Mattie, like any girl who grew up in a farming community, knew the ways of reproduction. And after glimpsing—no—after drinking in the image of Roamer's naked body, she had a pretty good idea of what should take place, but the getting there was driving her half mad with unslaked desire.

Couldn't he hurry?

"Oh, honey you are so hot," Roamer murmured as he continued to rub gently, just barely grazing over that part of her that pulsated with need.

"Roamer, I shall lose my mind," she whimpered. "You must do *something.*"

"Go ahead, darlin', lose your mind. We will lose our minds and our souls together," he said, and with one smooth motion he covered her body and entered her.

There was a flash of searing hot pain as his bigness filled her, stretched her wider than she imagined. Mattie's body stiffened, recoiled, tried to shrink back from him, but it was impossible. For as one set of her muscles shied from his body, another pulled him in and caressed him.

Within a moment or two the pain subsided to a dull throb. Mattie was still unaccustomed to the tight stretch. He was big—Lord, she knew just how big; she had seen the proof with her own eyes. But now he was *bigger*—and hard.

He kissed her breasts and fondled her lower parts with one hand, and though she was sure it could not happen, Mattie began to relax. She began to enjoy what he was doing.

Soon the pain in her lower regions was forgotten entirely. A whole new set of feelings invaded her loins. Roamer was inside her, moving slowly and tenderly, and her body was matching those movements.

A coil of something taut and wild began to tighten inside Mattie's middle. She wasn't sure what was supposed to happen, but then Roamer stiffened, cried out, and thrust hard into her.

For long moments she felt him, tense, rigid, almost strained. And then his body relaxed. His head dipped to her shoulder. He kissed her collarbone.

Mattie lay there, still feeling the unslaked hunger in her body. Part of her wanted Roamer to keep doing what he was doing. She felt as if a great mystery, a great and wondrous satisfaction, was just beyond her reach. She was itchy, impatient, and unsatisfied. A wild thought entered her head: *Is that all there is to it?*

The moon was a fat pearl in the night sky. They had traveled the meandering Missouri River as the whiskey boat slid northwest. When the current was strongest, they hired mules and teamsters that plied their trade on the banks to help pull the load.

Whiskey had been traded at a little burg that someone jokingly called Kansas City, and at every tent city, immigrant camp, and fort along the way.

At night they took turns sleeping under the little canvas tarp at one end of the boat. During the day, their meals were cooked in a battered iron brazier that sat on three squat legs.

And Jack counted the days and the miles that brought him closer to his goal.

Over the past week Jack had been careful. He had played like a fool, letting everyone lose and then win back their money. Whenever they stopped, he found a game on shore and asked questions about travelers and what lay beyond.

He had also worked harder than ever before in his life. He looked at the broken blisters across the pads of his fingers and silently cursed the crew of the whiskey boat. Most of the rest of the crew were sprawled out across the open deck in varying degrees of drunkenness tonight. Some were snoring; others were still pulling on their jugs. With it so hot and muggy inside the little tent, they had tapped a cask of whiskey and indulged. It wouldn't be long until they were all out for the night.

"And then I am putting a knife in their ribs, emptying their pockets, and tossing their filthy, worthless carcasses overboard," Jack murmured to himself.

In another hour or so it would be Jack's boat—his whiskey and his money. There would be no more dawdling, no more delays. And he would take no more orders from ignorant bullies.

At the last stop on the river, his sly questioning had finally hit pay dirt. One of the outfitters remembered Roamer and a toddling child. But even better than that, he remembered where they were headed.

It was only a matter of time before Jack found the town far to the north called McTavish Plain.

Mattie dared not touch Roamer. In fact, as they went about caring for Scout—who was regaining his strength and color—she barely even allowed herself so much as a quick glance at Roamer.

She didn't need to look at him to be filled with his presence. The air fairly crackled with awareness of him.

When Roamer took a deep breath, she found herself hanging on it. If he frowned, she asked herself why.

The invisible connection between them had intensified, strengthened. Now it was almost painful to be around him, but excruciatingly lonely to be away from him.

Her hands itched to touch him. Her lips hungered to feel the sweet, masculine pressure of his mouth, the searing explorations of his tongue. And her body betrayed her in a million small ways every time he came into the same room. Her breasts felt full and tender when he was near. There was a heat in her womb that ached and throbbed.

Then there was her guilt.

On the night when she welcomed Roamer's touch and then found herself strangely dissatisfied, he had seemed to reach some elusive pinnacle that she had not achieved.

What had she expected?

His kisses were magical. His touch was searing. Perhaps that was exactly all there was and ever would be.

Then why did her body still crave *something?* Some touch, some release? Or were there differences in the act of love for men and for women?

Questions and guilt hammered at her heart and soul. Each time she looked at Roamer she caught the unmistakable glint of shame in his eyes as well. That only made her feel worse. He was suffering because of her—because of her lie.

She had lied about being married. It was a small lie—a lie that was not supposed to hurt anyone—and yet it was hurting Roamer and it was killing her. The one small, insignificant lie caused Roamer to chastise himself for caring for and lying with someone he thought was a married woman.

Mattie shook herself. She needed to get beyond this tangle. Roamer was not what she had planned for herself. He was not lettered or genteel, but he was intelligent and romantic. He was not free to lavish attention on her alone because he was raising Scout. But that was one of the aspects of his personality she found the most appealing—his ability to care for a small boy.

He and Scout were in her thoughts, in her dreams and in her heart. She wanted what she knew she should not have, and could not have if she was going to keep suspicion from her sisters.

Did Roamer feel this same bittersweet discomfort? Was she the kind of woman he didn't want to be with? Was he, like her, afraid that a simple look or touch would lead to reckless passion—a passion that could ruin all their lives?

"Did you notice Scout took a little more broth today?" Mattie said to Roamer's broad back while she cleared up the supper dishes. Something so mundane as eating a meal together had taken on an almost mystical significance for her. She savored each moment, knowing that it would soon end and she would return to her lonely, unfulfilled life, and that Roamer would resume writing letters to the matrimonial agency.

"Yes, I noticed Scout is getting stronger. And I think there is a bit of color to his cheeks," he said without looking at her. "And you, Mattie, are you feeling well?"

"I'm fine. A little tired."

"Yes, I can see how you would be." He kept his back to her to avoid looking at her while he spoke. "You have worked hard tending him."

"I think it's time I went home—for good."

Roamer spun around and stared, slack-jawed. His expression was a mixture of pain and . . . *relief?*

"Do you have to go?" His voice was soft.

"If I stay much longer there will be talk." Mattie replied, afraid to admit if she stayed they would do what they had done again.

"Nobody would dare say a word in my hearing," Roamer said fiercely. He had not moved his feet or raised his hands to touch her. And though he was unmoving, there was nothing truly still about him. His eyes, lit by an inner fire, flicked hungrily across her face. His fingers flexed; the muscles in his lean, square jaw ticked.

"It is time I left, Roamer. Under the circumstances it would be better for both of us," she said softly. "I have—"

"I know. You have a husband," he interrupted. His voice was loud and harsh. "A man you never speak of. A man who is not here. A man that I . . . *hate.*"

"Oh, Roamer, you are so wrong." Mattie rushed toward him before she caught herself.

Lottie's and Addie's images swam before her eyes. She could not tell him.

"Wrong, am I?" His lips curled in a sardonic sneer. "I thought I was wrong about Susan too, but in the end I was not."

"I—I don't understand." Mattie wanted to touch

him. She wanted to smooth the lines of worry from his face. The hours he had spent at Scout's bedside had taken a heavy toll on him. He was still handsome and strong, but there was a poignancy and a vulnerability in his eyes that ripped and clawed at Mattie's heart. She longed to pull him to her breast and give him the comfort of her body.

"My sister was mistreated by her husband. And so, I think, are you, Matilda."

The words hit harder than his hammer on the anvil. Mattie gasped and brought her hand to her lips. Now she knew what angry beast ate at Roamer day and night. He thought she was married to a horrible man who treated her badly, whom she never spoke of because there was nothing good to say.

And it was all because of her damnable lie.

Mattie walked across the street, headed for her own home. The sun was shining and the songbirds flitted in the nearby meadow where Ian's spring lambs gamboled and played. Bees buzzed industriously at the blackberry vines that climbed the fence around the meadow.

But there was a cloud of sorrow over McTavish Plain, and it wasn't just in Mattie's heart. The town was unnaturally quiet, still observing an unspoken mourning for the fifteen graves and three empty wagons somewhere on the lonely prairie.

Ian and Miley had told the story of how the guide had left all the settlers to die alone and untended, then left their bodies unburied. Several of the men said he should be hunted down and strung up. They considered his crime tantamount to murder because the entire wagon train might have had a chance at life if they had not been abandoned without anyone to care for them.

"No, lads," Ian had said softly. "The good Lord has a way of balancing the scales against those who hurt their fellow man."

Though Mattie held the guide responsible as well, a part of her hoped that it was not true, for right now she felt the scales were tipped against her.

She had sinned. She had lied to Ian, lied to the town, and lied to Roamer. She had lain with him, given her virginity, all the while allowing him to believe that he was an adulterer taking another man's wife.

Now, with his heartfelt admission that he thought Samuel Smith, her fictitious husband, beat her, another measure of guilt settled upon her shoulders.

She was a liar. She was a blackhearted sinner.

She told herself it was one little, white lie—a small thing. But now the finest man she had ever known was being consumed with hatred and jealousy against someone who didn't exist, while his own guilt weighed upon his soul.

"Oh, I wish I had stayed in Gothenburg," Mattie said miserably as she opened the door and stepped inside her tidy little house.

She stood for a moment at the threshold and looked around.

Rows of precious books lined a pine shelf on one wall in her front parlor. Her comfortable rocker sat between the window and the side table with the kerosene lamp—a location designed to give her light to read by at any hour of the day or night. Her kitchen was neat, her bedroom feminine and virginal.

It was everything she had always wanted. She had risked everything for this cottage and her independent life. It was the reason for all her deception.

But now all it seemed to signify was a lonely, silent life full of sorrow, ever since she had let her heart be stolen by a child and a mountain of a man.

She wanted to see the floor sullied by the dust tracked in on a man's boots. She wanted the mess and clutter of a small boy's treasures. She wanted frogs and snakes and insects kept in wide-mouthed jars.

Mattie wanted to see pots on the boil and a dry sink full of dirty dishes while she struggled to learn Addie's cooking technique. She wanted shirts to mend and socks to darn.

And after a night of passion she wanted rumpled sheets and a bed that spoke of love shared between a man and a woman.

She wanted Roamer Tresh and Scout in her cottage and in her life.

"Oh, Ian, Mattie looks so unhappy." Addie glanced up from her knitting. The fine wool from their own sheep was being spun and knitted into baby clothes for the winter. But even that joyful task had not kept her mind off her sister.

Addie had done as Ian asked and stayed home for weeks, but today the draw of sunshine and the need to hear the latest gossip had lured her to town. She had spent many wonderful hours with Gus and Gert. They had told her how sick Scout had been and how horrible the carnage at the wagon train had been.

Gert wept when she described Miley's face when he got home.

Addie made a mental note to have a reckoning with Ian for lying to her about how bad it had been and the toll it had taken. Her crazy husband would do anything to keep her from worry, and although it was sweet and wonderful, it was also maddening.

Now her prime concern was Mattie. Gert and Gus had noticed how melancholy she was. Lottie agreed.

Something was going to have to be done.

"I went by the schoolhouse," Lottie said. "At first I thought it was just because Scout had been so ill. You know how Mattie swore she would never have children, but I swan, Addie, you'd think that boy was hers. But there is something else bothering her—something important."

"Roamer is also suffering in silence, if Gus is to be believed."

"I think I need to have a talk with Ian about this," Addie had said and set her course for home.

Now she sat with her knitting, wanting to bring up the subject of Roamer and Mattie.

"I hear that Roamer and Mattie are not studying together any more," Ian said abruptly.

"Oh, Ian, do you think—" Addie didn't finish.

"They are in love, Adelaide, in love and trapped by that damnable foolish lie your sisters wrangled you into," Ian said, staring into the fire. Though spring had come, the stone house still held a bit of chill when the sun went down. Four hound puppies were sprawled beside his stocking-covered feet.

"Ian, sometimes I blame you for Mattie's unhappiness."

"What? Me? But how could you blame me, lass?"

Ian sat bolt upright. Two of the pups staggered to their feet, growling at the unseen menace that had upset their master. "You canna be serious. If there is any sorrow in your sister's life it is due to her own wicked lie."

"It was my lie too, Ian." Addie said softly.

His manner softened a little. "Aye, Adelaide, 'twas your lie as well, but I know you were persuaded to go along. I have watched Mattie and Lottie sailing through their days, smiling like cats in cream when they look at you. They think they fooled me and the whole town and that all it cost was you being forced to wed. If Mattie now has to contend with what her lie has done, then 'tis high time."

"Ian, you can't mean that," Addie said in some shock. "Are you trying to punish my sisters?"

"Nay, not punish . . . not exactly punishment, though 'tis not a bad idea." His gaze slid away sheepishly.

Addie stood up. She was just beginning to see the slight swell to her belly beneath the waistband of her comfortable housedress. Ian's eyes followed her and she saw the glow of love within them.

"Will you do *something,* Ian?"

"Not for them, but for you I will go to town tomorrow and see if I can't find some way to ease your sister's unhappiness."

She leaned down and kissed his forehead. "Thank you."

"Ah, 'tis no way to properly thank a dutiful husband." He pulled her down on his lap and claimed her mouth, slipping his hand beneath her skirt and up her thigh.

"Then Ian, I suggest you do your duty."

* * *

"Well, lad, 'tis certainly good to see you back on your feet," Ian chucked Scout under the chin. He sat on a stool near the open door of the smithy while Roamer worked.

Scout was as thin as a rail and had dark spots under his eyes, but he still had a quick smile and a twinkle in his eyes.

"Uncle Roamer won't let me go back to school yet," Scout said with a frown. He had a slate and was slowly, laboriously forming his letters while the tip of his tongue was poking out one side of his mouth.

"Mrs. Smith says to work on my handwriting while I am waiting to get stronger. She says if I can write well, I won't have missed a thing."

"Good advice. My sister-in-law is a wise woman." Ian did not miss the way Roamer flinched each time Mattie was mentioned. Or that the hammer was coming down on the cooling metal with more and more force with each successive blow. Ian smiled to himself. Roamer acted like a man in love.

"Roamer, how are you coming with the wife search?" Ian said abruptly, taking an inordinate amount of pleasure when Ian's blow missed the iron and skidded off the side of the anvil with a harsh metallic screech and a shower of sparks.

"I haven't received a single reply," Roamer answered sullenly, his focus on the glowing metal at his forge.

"I canna understand why," Ian said, rubbing his chin thoughtfully. Scout squirmed on the upturned keg he was using for a seat when Ian's eyes lingered on him.

"Surely Mrs. Smith has given you the benefit of her experience."

The hammer once again missed its mark. "Maybe I am still not charming or romantic enough to win a woman's heart. Maybe I need more lessons in how to be romantic." The bitter note in Roamer's voice nearly made Ian change his mind about his latest plan.

Nearly, but not quite. Addie wanted something done, and he was going to give her what she wanted no matter what.

"I am going to Belle Fourche tomorrow with Miley. I think you should come with us. Perhaps you can find a woman there," Ian said.

"What? Tomorrow?" Roamer's eyes were wide. "But I can't leave Scout."

"Oh, dinna I tell you? I stopped by Mattie's place on my way here. She said she'd be happy to watch the lad while you are gone finding him a new mother."

Eleven

Mattie bit the inside of her lip while she paced the schoolhouse floor. The children had gone home more than an hour ago, and yet here she was. It was as if she were unable to leave the security of the schoolhouse. But for the first time in her memory the books of poetry and other people's words on paper did not offer her any solace.

Her heart was breaking in two.

Ian and Roamer were bringing Scout to her house early tomorrow morning. And then they were riding to Belle Fourche to find Roamer a wife.

A wife.

"Oh, Lord, why does it hurt so much?" Mattie pressed her palm against the hollow ache just below her left breast. The raw void opened wider, painful and cold each time she thought of Roamer and another woman.

Another woman in his arms, his bed . . . his heart.

Her throat was tight. She wanted to weep; she wanted to yell. She wanted to rush to the smithy and tell Roamer the truth. In fact, Mattie had gone so far as to sit down and make a list of the reasons why she should do so.

She looked down at the paper on her desk.

The first good reason was Scout. The child did need a mother and she loved him. In spite of all her plans, in spite of never wanting children, there it was.

She loved Scout.

Then there was Roamer himself.

Each time he was near, she experienced a longing so fierce it buckled her knees. He made her feel a wide range of emotions and she wanted to explore every one of them. She wanted to today, tomorrow, and forever.

Mattie wanted him.

But then she thought of Addie. She was carrying Ian's child now. How would he react if he learned his wife and her sisters had lied to become part of his charter town?

And even if Ian forgave Addie for the child's sake, what would happen to Lottie? Or to Roamer or Scout for that matter? Ian wouldn't just let Mattie and Roamer get married and set up house together after the entire population learned of the lie.

Lottie had worked hard to become successful with her dressmaking. Mattie remembered when Lottie was still a girl, when she had been wild and free. Learning to sew perfect, small stitches had been her punishment for a hundred adolescent sins.

Now their sins were black and ugly. Ian would never forgive them. How could he? And he would never allow Roamer and Mattie to remain as a constant reminder to the town that his rules had been flaunted, that Mattie had lied.

They would have to leave at the very least. Scout would be uprooted. Roamer would have to turn his back on a thriving business and start over with nothing.

How could a man as prideful as Roamer do that? How could Mattie ask him to?

"There is no way out. No way at all." She wrung her hands. She was alone in her misery. She couldn't talk to Lottie or Addie about this. They couldn't know how unhappy she was, because they would try to help and would only make it worse.

But Mattie did have the Lord. She opened the desk drawer and pulled out the big, much-dog-eared Holy Bible. She used it in conjunction with the primers as a reading tool for the children, frequently letting them memorize verses to use at Sunday worship.

She flipped up the stiff tooled-leather cover and let the pages fall where they might. Then she picked it up and began to read.

> "I am my beloved's, and his desire is toward me. Set me as a seal upon thine heart, as a seal upon thine arm: for love is strong as death: jealousy is cruel as the grave."

Mattie raised her head. She thought of Roamer's hatred and jealousy of her pretend husband, and of how she felt about the nameless woman Roamer was soon to marry.

Jealous.

> "Many waters cannot quench love, neither can the floods drown it. Make haste, my beloved, and be thou like to a roe or to a young hart upon the mountains of spices."

One fat tear plopped onto the page. Mattie rubbed it off before it could ruin the print by making the ink run. She looked for comfort in the book but she only found more pain.

"Love is strong as death, jealousy is cruel as the grave," she sniffed. "And when Roamer brings home another woman to be his wife I will know how cold and bitter that grave truly is. Because I am already jealous of the woman who will have what I cannot."

Jack hunkered down and scooped up the tepid, gritty water into his mouth. He was sick of being dirty and sleeping on the ground, of eating cold biscuits and nearly rancid bacon as a steady diet. But he was close, so close now that he could practically taste the sweetness of victory as he sucked the muddy water between his lips.

He had been riding alone for days now and had never even seen another person. It was eerie to be alone on so vast a prairie with none but his horse for company.

"Where ya headed, pilgrim?" The slurred question brought Jack to his feet, his hand going to the pistol he had purchased before he tied up the whiskey boat and headed north on horseback.

"Who is that?" Jack spun around, startled. His gun was still holstered.

"Whoa, pilgrim, ain't no call to get techy." The man lifted his hands.

Jack could not make specific details of the man's features while he was silhouetted against the red-gold ball of the sun. He flipped the rawhide thong off the gun and wrapped his fingers around the grip.

"Show yourself," he said as he slid the gun free.

An odorous apparition staggered from the shade of

a cleft rock. Jack grimaced and held his breath. He had never encountered such a stench on anything living. He gagged, barely suppressing the urge to vomit.

"Where ya headed?" The question came again and with it a gust of foul breath. Behind the stinking creature was a worn and thin saddle horse.

"McTavish Plain," Jack said, never taking his finger from the trigger. It was reassuring to have the weight of the gun in his hand.

"I been there. . . . I can guide yer if yer got enough whiskey and victuals." The man slurred his words. "I know the whole damned town."

"Well, if you aren't lying to me we might be able to come to some arrangement," Jack said with a smile. "Because I need to know about some people living in McTavish Plain."

Mattie was standing at her front door with her arm looped around Scout's shoulder. She felt his shoulder bones sharp and angular. The boy needed fattening up since his illness.

He glanced up at her. He was gnawing on his bottom lip, looking every inch as unhappy as she felt.

She would like to be the one to feed him and care for him, but it was not to be. Ian and his damnable rules were going to make sure it wasn't she who washed his clothes, cooked his meals and worried over him.

It was going to be some other woman.

"I canna say for sure when we will be back, Mattie, but likely Roamer can find a wife in two days' time." Ian smiled. "Since he has no real particulars except that she can cook and clean and care for him and the lad, it should be an easy task."

"Take your time," Mattie managed to croak out. "A decision like that shouldn't be rushed." Her gaze was on Roamer.

"She is right about that. A man shouldn't rush these things," Miley agreed. He had his hat in his hand, turning it nervously in his fingers. He toed a bit of dirt with his boot.

" 'Tis true, but Roamer has run out of town," Ian said with a shrug.

Is he so coldhearted? Mattie found herself thinking. Surely Addie could not love a man who had no more feeling than that.

Roamer, beside him on his horse, shot Ian a dark look but remained silent. Mattie could tell he was not happy by the stiff set of his broad shoulders and the hard glint in his green eyes.

Was Ian forcing him?

But of course he was. Just like Addie had been forced.

If Roamer wanted to remain in McTavish Plain and provide a good, solid home for Scout, then he had to marry to appease the town. Ian and a few others had met at the church and voted. They had decided for the good of Scout and the community that he needed a wife—now.

And he had received no replies from any of his letters.

"Ian, I wouldn't mind helping Roamer with his Heart and Hand letters for a while longer," Mattie blurted out, feeling a rush of panic at the thought of losing him. "Then he wouldn't have to make this trip so soon after Scout's illness. We could wait a while longer. Perhaps they were just not romantic enough. We could try harder. I wouldn't mind."

Both Scout and Roamer stiffened, hope shining in their eyes like stars in a black velvet sky.

But Ian shook his head. "Nay, if the letters have gotten no response by now, then I dinna think they will. You did your best to teach Roamer how to woo. Sometimes lessons take and sometimes they don't. 'Tis time for the man to bring a wife home so the lad will have a woman's influence. We canna wait any longer for a Heart and Hand woman to answer."

Both Roamer and Scout seemed to shrink from the inside. Misery was telegraphed through Mattie's arm. Roamer—big, muscled, powerful Roamer—slumped in his saddle like a man defeated. She wanted to comfort them both, to prepare hot tea and feed them Addie's cinnamon buns. She wanted to tell them that she would be the only woman in both their lives, but her tongue was still, held by the cold iron of her own stupid, selfish lie.

Mattie simply could not risk the fate and security of her beloved sisters for her own happiness. No matter that it felt as if her heart had been torn open and her soul was rent in two. She had to be strong. There were Lottie and Addie and an innocent child to consider.

"Good-bye, Mattie. Good-bye, lad." Ian paused for a moment, his hard gaze going from Roamer to Mattie. Then with a smile and a wink he said, "Roamer should be marrying very soon now, I ken. Once a man is faced with the inevitable decision, he usually picks the right path."

"It must be nice to be so very confident, Ian," Mattie said, noting the bitterness in her own voice.

Ian studied her for a long minute before he turned.

And without another word, he rode off toward Belle Fourche with Miley at his sidc. Roamcr was a pace or two behind, as if his horse were as reluctant as he was to leave McTavish Plain. At the edge of town he stopped and turned.

Across the expanse, Mattie felt his eyes upon her. For one mad moment she nearly ran to him, begging him to stay. But before her feet would move, he rode away to catch up with Ian and Miley.

It was like death. She couldn't breathe. A heavy weight settled in her breast and it had a name: sorrow.

Mattie and Scout stood watching until Roamer was little more than a speck on the far horizon. She wanted to cry; she wanted to run after him, but all she could do was stand and watch him ride out of her life. Forever.

"Come on, Scout, let's go have a cup of tea and read some poetry," Mattie said, trying to ignore the painful breaking of her own heart. "And I have some fresh bread and butter. I think we could both use some."

"Do you think he'll find one?" Scout asked, his eyes still focused on the now invisible riders, his feet unmoving.

"What?"

"A wife," Scout said softly. "Do you think it will be easy like Mr. Ian said? Do you think the next time we see Uncle Roamer he will have a wife?"

"He has to, Scout; for all our sakes, he has to."

"Are you sure that's him?" Jack asked from his perch on the rough, splintery wagon seat. He had sold his horse, and by cheating at a hand of poker in a tent town, he had acquired a sturdy team and well-worn wagon. It was all part of his plan.

A wagon would be really easy to hide a body in.

Jack had watched Roamer and two other men ride out of town at first light. The boy who stood watching Roamer was about the right age to be Susan's brat, but Jack needed to be sure. He certainly didn't want to waste time with some sniveling kid only to find it wasn't the right boy. He needed Judson Maravel and none other.

"You have to be sure before I make my move," he told Calston. "I can't be snatching the wrong brat. Are you positive?"

"I'm sure . . . well, leastways, pretty sure. Little bastard hung 'round the wagon train asking questions and annoying me until we pulled out. I heard him say his name was Scout—the big fella's name is Tresh. He's the blacksmith."

Jack frowned. "I am not looking for Roamer's spawn, you inebriated fool. I am looking for a child with the last name of Maravel."

"You never said so 'afore now. You said you was looking for a kid about this high who lived with his uncle who was a blacksmith in McTavish Plain. Well, that kid lives with the blacksmith in McTavish Plain," Calston growled. "What is that word knee-brated mean anyway? Are you bad-mouthing me?"

"It means you drink too much, you ignorant cretin," Jack sighed. "Listen, I don't want to kidnap some other brat and then have the law after me. I *have* to know if that kid is Judson Maravel."

"Told you they call him Scout. Law'll be after you anyway you take that boy or any boy, to my way of thinkin'. This ain't Mexico, where you can jest go snatchin' kids," Calston said sullenly.

"You are as thick as mud. A man can't be charged with kidnapping his own son. The boy I am looking for, Judson Walker Maravel, is my son—or so his mother claimed," Jack snapped.

"If'n he is your son, why is he with that Tresh fella?"

"Never mind. All I need from you is that you be certain before we take him. I can't afford to waste any time on the wrong boy."

Jack watched the boy called Scout skipping beside the rather plain young woman. She had brown hair and a brown calico frock. And sturdy brown shoes. It seemed everything about her was brown.

"A plain, little brown wren. Just what I would expect in this dusty town." Jack heaved a sigh, thinking of the future, when he would be surrounded by exciting women with soft, red lips and dewy flesh. They would call his name with a French accent and do things to him no proper woman would think of doing.

And I will be their favorite, he promised himself. *Just as soon as I find Susan's brat and get him back to St. Louis.*

The boy ran ahead and then whirled to pull a face at the wren who followed.

"Scout Maravel, you scamp!" the woman laughed. "Just for that you are going to do your letters again. And I won't let you stop until your hand is as fine as mine."

A smile broke across Jack's face.

Maravel. She called him Scout Maravel.

The child was Susan's brat. No doubt Roamer had

given him the quaint sobriquet of Scout, though Jack thought it was very stupid.

But it doesn't matter anymore. He is the one. And come nightfall he'll be trussed up and headed back to St. Louis. Won't old Judge Mills be shocked? Jack grinned, thinking of the pleasure he was going to get by surprising the old fool. He thought Jack was whipped.

But I am not. And when I have the money my dear, stupid grandmother willed to the little bastard in my control, I will pitch him into the Missouri River. Nobody will be the wiser and the money would be mine. As it should've been all along.

Jack spent the day in McTavish Plain, trying not to attract attention to himself. It wasn't easy. Everyone in town was nosy and acted friendly, but he was not fooled. Jack knew they shoved out their hands and plastered on a wide smile just to find out what he was up to.

Nobody was *really* nice. He knew that when a man was smiling at him it was more than likely he was aiming to stick a knife into Jack's liver or slip an extra ace into the deck.

Several men came by to question him, casting a suspicious eye to the tarp across the back of the wagon. Luckily the stench of alcohol and Calston's unwashed body was strong enough to discourage any close-up inspection. Even with the tarp lashed tight over him while he slept off his latest binge, the odor was overpowering and a wonderful deterrent to getting near.

Once Jack realized he had been noticed and could be identified, he decided to brass it out. He had marched straight into the mercantile. He bought a pickle and stood by the cracker barrel, listening to the boring town gossip until afternoon shadows were reaching across the street.

It galled him to find that Roamer was well liked and had a prosperous business. A man on the run shouldn't be so lucky.

Jack wondered how it was that Roamer was even using his own name since he had killed a man. He wondered why no bounty hunter had ever come to collect the reward on him. But he could not very well ask without having someone wonder how he knew Roamer. So Jack ate his pickle and listened to the sad little stories of the people who lived in the town.

Roamer, he learned, had gone to Belle Fourche for several days on some mysterious mission that nobody was willing to speak of. It was odd, because when the subject came up they all looked like their last coin had been spent.

Jack could only hope the errand was costing Roamer dearly. It would only be justice after all if he had been found out. Maybe the two men he rode with were lawmen and they were taking him in for the bounty. That would be sweet.

In the afternoon Jack heard the clamor of children in the street. Only then did he leave the mercantile. He hid by the privy and watched each child. Some went to the mercantile and bought a penny stick of horehound candy; others scampered toward their homes. But the boy called Scout once again stayed with the little brown wren inside the schoolhouse.

Maybe an hour later, the wren and the brat finally appeared at the schoolhouse door. They went to a house with frilly curtains in the window.

Jack glanced impatiently up at the sun. It would be dark soon—dark enough to snatch a kid on his way to the outhouse. And if that drunken fool Calston kept up his end, they should be far away before anybody even noticed.

"Let me see your letters, Scout." Mattie leaned over his shoulder, smiling at the scent of sunshine and mountain air that clung to his clothes.

"They are still not as good as yours." Scout tilted his slate so she could have a good look.

"Nonsense. I'll bet even my own sisters would be hard-pressed to know I didn't write this. Actually it reminds me a bit of Addie's hand." She ruffled his thick, pale hair.

He smiled at her. "Really?"

"Really," Mattie grinned. "Now that you are done, I wonder if I could impose on you to help me? It's a big job, and I need somebody strong and brave."

Scout puffed out his chest and set the slate aside. "I can do it." He pulled himself up to his maximum height.

"I have a feisty little bantam hen that has gotten out of the coop. She goes to roost in that little tree near my privy. If we could catch her up and put her back in, she might not end up being some owl's supper tonight."

Scout laughed. "That doesn't need anybody brave. Shoot, I can catch her out of that little tree in nothin' flat. It ain't much taller'n me. I can skin up the trunk quicker'n lightning."

"Are you sure?" Mattie frowned as if truly concerned. "You know you have been sick—"

"You can depend on me," Scout interrupted.

"Good. You go on out. I'll get my shawl from the parlor and meet you at the coop."

"Yes, ma'am," Scout said over his shoulder as he fearlessly ran outside into the darkness.

Jack snugged up against the side of the house. There was no moon tonight, but his eyes had adjusted and he could make out the dark shapes of houses, privies and barns in the gray velvet of the darkness. His plan was foolproof; as long as Calston didn't pass out but managed to get the fire going at the other end of town in time, there should be nothing and nobody to stop them.

Now Jack had only to wait. Sooner or later the call of nature would bring the brat out to the privy.

And there Jack would be waiting.

The back door opened, a golden arc of light spiking into the darkness. The boy dashed outside.

Jack hunkered down and held his breath. His fingers twitched on the gunnysack he was holding. A smile plucked at the edges of his mouth. He wouldn't have to wait any longer. He would give the kid a few minutes and then he would nab him.

Mattie wrapped her shawl around her shoulders. It was silly of her, but going to the privy at night always made the small hairs on the nape of her neck prickle. She felt a little foolish that she needed a light when Scout had dashed outside without a single qualm.

Feeling a maternal tug for the boy that would soon be some other woman's son, she fetched a lantern. Once it was lit, she turned the wick down low and stepped out the front door. She would intercept Scout at the side of the house.

A strange, muffled yelp and a dull thudding sound

made her stomach clench. Had he fallen from the tree?

Fear for his safety clutched at her heart.

"Scout?" She held her skirts in one hand and the lantern in the other as she ran toward the faint noise. Expecting to find Scout on the ground, Mattie was stunned when the glow of the lantern revealed a man. He had a gunnysack in his hand and he was grappling with Scout.

"Let him go!" Mattie shouted.

"Miss Mattie, help!" The boy was kicking and fighting for all he was worth. "Go get help."

The man's hand came down hard and suddenly Scout was silent. No more kicking, no more flailing of arms. His body went limp as a rag.

"Dear Lord, Scout! You've killed him!" Mattie swung the lantern like a club.

The man ducked, still holding Scout like a rag doll in one hand. But in the process the light arced across his face, giving her a good look at his features.

"Who are you?" Mattie cried. "You are not from McTavish Plain. Who are you and what do you want with Scout?"

"It grieves me that you saw my face," the man said coldly.

He dropped Scout like a bag of grain and knocked the lantern from her hand. The flame guttered and went out, the scent of kerosene filling the air as the chimney shattered on the ground.

"Scout?" Mattie went to her knees and groped her way toward Scout's motionless body, but the man stepped in front of her and blocked her path. He was more frightening in the dark, when she could only hear his cruel, flat words.

"I am taking him—taking back what is mine."

"You cannot take him. The law—"

"Will do nothing. I am that child's father. Legally and morally I can do anything I want with him."

"We'll see what the town says about this." Mattie stood up and opened her mouth to scream. Before she could get a sound out, a golden glow suddenly filled the night at the opposite end of town. There was a tremendous whoosh, and suddenly flames leaped high into the dark night sky.

"As you can see, dear lady, the town has eminent concerns of their own right now. The fate of one boy and one woman is indeed a small concern when they will be battling to save their homes and businesses."

His voice was like velvet when he addressed her as *dear lady.* She remembered what Roamer had said about Susan's husband—how he was a sweet-talking man. Her stomach clenched at the thought of what that really meant.

"You don't know the men of McTavish Plain, Mr. Maravel. They will come. As soon as I call, they *will* come."

The conflagration was growing, filling the night sky with a dusky orange glow. Shouts and the sounds of a town working to save itself filled the night. Mattie would have to scream very, very loud indeed.

"It is unfortunate that you have seen me and can provide a description, and it is even more unfortunate that you know who I am; but since you call me "Mr. Maravel," I can see that Roamer has been telling you stories of his past. I want to be fast away before anyone, including that big ox Roamer, hears of what has happened. I had planned on simply taking the boy and leaving, but now—"

"You'll never get away with it." She turned toward the fire, ready to shriek her lungs out.

"Ah, once again, my dear, I must disagree."

A crushing pain at the back of her neck brought her to her knees. Stars danced in Mattie's head against a black background, and she felt herself falling into a deep pit.

Twelve

The sun was blazing down, turning the insides of Mattie's eyelids to a sickening crimson, making her stomach roil and toss. Her tongue was swollen, thick and dry. A pulsing pain filled the back of her head. When she took a deep breath, a sickening wave of pain and nausea flowed over her. She tried to move but, weighted and trussed up, was unable to. She lay flat and still, taking inventory of her body. Nothing seemed to hurt more or less than any other part. Her wrists and arms were tight and cramped from the bonds.

Slowly she opened her eyes, bracing herself for the worst as she tried to figure out where she was and what had happened.

She was lying flat on her back, but the noise and the cloud-dotted sky moving over her head told her she was in a wagon bed. The clink and creak of leather harness and rigging was like wind chimes as they rolled along over uneven ground.

"Miss Mattie? Are you awake?" Scout whispered near her ear.

"Mmmm." Relief swamped her. She offered up a prayer of thanks to God that the boy was alive and able to speak.

"What happened to us?" he asked, his young voice cracking with fear.

It came back to Mattie in a blazing, painful rush. The man—Scout's father—had been trying to take him. Mattie was going to get help, but all she remembered was blinding pain and then nothing until this moment.

He must have knocked her out.

"I—" Her lips were so dry, her throat so parched, that it took two attempts to get the words out. "We were taken, Scout. Taken from McTavish Plain. Do you remember a man grabbing you?"

"Ah, dear lady, you are risen." The syrupy-smooth voice rippled over Mattie's skin like dry sand before Scout could answer. "Not any the worse for wear, I see."

"Where are you taking us?" Mattie gritted her teeth against the pain and tried to sound strong. Inside she was quaking with fear. She could not see Maravel from her position, and she was glad of it.

"Peculiar you should ask that, dear lady. You were going to be abandoned at the first opportune moment, but I have discovered, most happily for my circumstance I admit, that the boy is easily handled when he fears threats upon your person. He has been very tractable all morning. So you see, fair lady, I was not intending to take *you* anywhere. If you have any complaints about your accommodation on this journey, you take it up with young Judson there."

"My name is Scout."

"Not to put too fine a point on it, boy, but it is not. You are Judson Walker Maravel. That coarse brute Roamer may have changed your name to make it easier to run from the law, but you are indeed Judson Walker Maravel."

Run from the law? Mattie swallowed hard and tried to think of everything Roamer had told her, but each word that came from this man's mouth was perfectly pronounced and so full of poison that he robbed her of the ability to think. He was learned, charming, and the vilest snake she had ever encountered.

For the first time in her memory, Mattie was truly terrified.

"My uncle Roamer never ran from anything in his life. You can't be my father," Scout said with complete conviction.

"I said the very same thing to your mother, but she assured me it was so. And as to the conduct of your sainted uncle, he killed a man with his bare hands. Did he tell you about that?"

Cruel laughter edged with genuine merriment washed over Mattie. She remembered what Roamer had said about taking a man's life. Was this person speaking more truth than lie? Was Roamer running from the law? Had he settled in McTavish Plain to begin anew, far from a long-ago crime? She couldn't believe it of Roamer.

"I don't believe you," Scout said fiercely with all the conviction of a trusting child. "My uncle never ran from anything in his life, especially not the law."

"Leave the boy alone. Stop taunting him," Mattie shouted as she struggled helplessly against her bonds, seeing nothing but the sky above.

"Little filly's got some scrap to 'er," someone else said in a voice that was vaguely familiar. It took a moment or two for Mattie to remember where and when she had heard that voice. She shuddered when she finally placed the drunken, murderous guide, Calston.

"Lemme have 'er when yer done with her. You don't need her to get the money on the boy."

"I will give some thought to your request, Calston; I will surely give that some thought."

Mattie closed her eyes. She was doomed, but perhaps she could find a way to see Scout free. Calston and Jack Maravel would think nothing of killing her, but evidently Scout was important to them. But why?

Money. Her sluggish brain processed the information. There was some way Jack could have money by taking Scout. He had hinted at it, Calston spoke of it. Scout meant nothing but money to his horrible father.

Ian had been watching Roamer fidget and frown for the better part of an hour. Miley had long since given up trying to draw him into conversation. If the blacksmith's jaw got any tighter, he wouldn't be able to pry his teeth apart with a stick. Love did terrible things to a lad.

The trio had been moving at a pace a lame man could have bested. Every so often, Ian would make some remark about Roamer's as-yet-unknown bride, and a flash of fury would ignite in Roamer's green eyes. It turned to barely suppressed rage when Miley speculated about the mysterious bride-to-be's hair, eyes, or figure.

"Another hour should put us into Belle Fourche," Ian said cheerfully. He wondered just how much would Roamer take before he realized he was in love with Mattie, and then did something about it.

"I suppose so," Roamer said sullenly.

"First thing I am going to do is get a drink and a steak," Miley quipped. "God love her, Gert is a fine woman, but she ain't much of a cook."

"Funny how that is," Ian said with a grin. "Mattie is not much of a hand in the kitchen, either, but it dinna seem to matter, since her seafaring husband just stays out at sea."

Roamer's tawny brows were knit into one angry slash over his eyes. "What kind of a man marries and then leaves his wife?"

"Maybe one who wants to have a long, peaceful life," Miley guffawed.

Roamer did not laugh.

"After you fill your belly we must get this letter in my pocket to someone so it can go on to St. Louis," Ian said somberly, his entire mood changing as he remembered the graves of the settlers. "The kinfolk of that doomed wagon train will be hungry for news."

"Whatever you say, Ian." Roamer stared at the trail and the shimmering creek, a small tributary of the Missouri, that ran beside them.

"Then we can see 'bout finding you a lassie."

Roamer acted as if he hadn't heard. "What do you suppose Mattie and Scout are doing about now?"

Ian opened his mouth to speak, but the sound of running horses coming hard and fast behind them caused him to snap his mouth shut. He slid the rifle from the leather-fringed scabbard beneath his leg in one quick movement. Roamer did the same as they all wheeled their mounts around.

"Ian! Roamer!" John Holcomb was on Gert's fastest horse. The animal was heavily lathered from being ridden hard and long. "You've got to come back right away."

"What has happened? Is it Adelaide?" Ian's heart clenched with pain at the thought. "Is it the bairn?"

"No, Addie is fine. Someone burned down the ice shed last night—"

"You didn't need to ride out to tell us that," Miley said, holstering his gun. "What has happened to bring you here, near ruining Gert's favorite horse?"

"Scout and Mattie are missing as well."

"What do you mean, 'missing?' " Roamer felt the blood leave his face. Icy fear pooled in the pit of his belly.

"We fought the fire until it reached the layers of straw and ice and put itself out. Gert noticed first that nobody had seen Mattie or Scout since school let out. The house was just like they had walked off, but there was a broken lantern in the yard and signs of . . . a struggle. We formed a search party and Gus rode to the Salish, thinking it might've been one of them."

Miley grimaced. "No indian would take Scout and Mattie."

"No. At sunrise we found the wagon tracks leading out of town."

"And?" Roamer asked.

"There was a stranger seen in town earlier in the day. He asked a lot of questions—about you, Roamer. He had a wagon. A big, heavy, stinking thing it was. I kind of thought he might have been a buffalo-bone collector, but he seemed too slick and citified for that."

"Get on with it, man," Ian growled.

"We found deep tracks that matched his wheels heading out of town—going south."

"What did the man look like?" Roamer's voice was tight and raw.

"Dressed fancy, but a bit travel stained. He had a tongue smooth as warmed honey and a right slick way about himself. The kind of fella you might call a lady's man. Like I say, Roamer, he was real interested in the town blacksmith."

A lethal stillness came over Roamer as his past rose up before him like the grim reaper. "Jackson Maravel," Roamer whispered. "The son of a bitch has found us."

"You know who took Mattie and Scout?" Miley asked.

"I do. I have been expecting the sorry bastard to show up for more than five years. In fact, I wonder what took him so damned long."

Roamer turned his horse. "I have to go after them."

"Whoa, wait a minute; we'll organize some men from the town," Miley said, trying to cut Roamer off.

"No. I can't wait. I have to go now."

"Then I will be goin' with you. Adelaide would'na like me letting you go off alone for her sister."

Roamer stared at Ian as if he had sprouted two heads. "You can't go with me. You have a wife at home with a child on the way. Besides, this isn't your fight."

Ian eyed Roamer for a moment, the muscle in his jaw jumping. "What you say is true about Adelaide and the bairn, but I canna say I like it, Roamer."

"Give me that letter for those folks who had kin on the wagon train. If I know Jack Maravel, he'll make a run for St. Louis, where his family and money are. I will see this gets to the right people after I get Mattie and Scout back."

Ian dug the letter from his buckskins and handed

it to Roamer. "Find them, Roamer. Find them and bring them back."

"I don't like the water." Scout planted his feet on the bank in a manner that made Mattie's heart lurch. He looked so much like Roamer, it was difficult for her to keep her sorrowful tears at bay.

"You will learn to like it or your friend will be taking a swim—a long one-way swim," Jack threatened.

They had come to an overgrown spot where a flat-bottomed boat was pulled up into the marshy ground. There was a ramshackle building where varmint traps and whiskey were sold; a bone-thin hound snoozed on the porch; and a man in faded, dirt-stained clothes was cleaning a line of fish.

Mattie had hoped she might enlist the help of the man wearing a badger-pelt cap but when she saw Jack Maravel give him a keg of whiskey she changed her mind. It would be little more than leaping out of the frying pan and into the fire to leave Maravel for this man who looked at her with an evil glint in his eye.

Jack unhitched the horses from the wagon and handed them over to the badger-capped man. When he returned, Scout stepped in front of him.

"I am not going," Scout pronounced. "I don't like being in the water."

"Well now, you are not *in* the water—yet. But if you open your sassy mouth another time, I promise you, boy, your lady friend will be," Jack said with a smile that was all teeth and evil menace. "I will tie her hands and feet, weight her with rocks, and toss her in. So don't push me."

Mattie saw Scout falter, but only for a moment.

Then, true to form, the boy Roamer had raised him to be said, "If you toss her in I'll jump right in after her. And then you'll have to swim to catch me."

They stood glaring at each other on the muddy banks of the Missouri River, while the disgusting, smelly, perpetually drunk Calston chuckled. Mattie nearly lost what little was in her stomach each time he came near her. He had leaned over her last night and whispered vile things to her.

"Fine. I'll see that the lady is safe and dry," Jack finally snapped. "For now, but don't push too much, boy, or I may start pushing back—and I guarantee you will not like the result."

"And I want you to leave her hands untied, and feed her. She hasn't eaten all day," Scout said boldly, putting his small fists at his waist and spreading his slender legs a bit.

Jack's eyes narrowed down to predatory slits, and Mattie was reminded of what Roamer had told her about Jackson Maravel. If he would beat his wife, he would think nothing of hitting Scout.

"I'll let her cook something as soon as we are out in the middle of the river."

Scout glanced at Mattie. "I won't leave you, Scout, you have my word upon it," she said.

"And a lady never breaks her word, boy, so if you will be so kind as to come aboard, St. Louis is beckoning. But let me give you fair warning: I need you in one piece—for now—but don't nettle me too much or you may see a side of me you don't like."

"That won't be hard; I don't like you now," Scout said defiantly as he hopped into the boat beside Mattie.

Jackson laughed as he untied the boat and pushed it out into the slow current. "The feeling is mutual."

Roamer rode with ghosts at his side. Susan's spirit was on his right, and the man he had killed was on his left. And while his sister's ghost brought him strength and determination to find Scout and Mattie, the specter of his victim taunted and tore at his confidence and manhood.

Each mile was torture as he went over every detail of his past and how he had failed to keep his sister safe. He could not forget the bruises, the pain in her eyes, or how he had allowed himself to believe her stories of falling down or walking into a door.

"I can't fail Scout and Mattie the way I failed you, Susan."

But the ghost of the man—Harry Malone had been his name—mocked Roamer and laughed. He was a specter of Roamer's shortcomings, of every lost dream and failed chance.

"You made a vow, Roamer Tresh, to never raise your hand against any man, and that includes Laughing Jack Maravel. You have failed; you have failed *again.* Because you can't kill again. Your sorry soul will not allow it, so Mattie and Scout are lost."

"No. I won't fail. I will find a way to save them and keep my vow."

But the hollow laughter of the specter rang in his ear as surely as if the man were flesh and blood. Guilt and fear ate at Roamer's confidence, sapped his strength, and threatened to defeat him.

He fought the urge to give up, thinking of Scout and Mattie and how much he loved them.

Roamer was sure Jack Maravel was heading for St. Louis, but traveling with a heavy wagon and captives would make his journey slow.

So Roamer headed cross-country, veering away from the Missouri River in an effort to make time. If he rode hard, slept little, and luck was with him, he would be waiting in St. Louis when Laughing Jack Maravel arrived.

A full day into travel, Roamer headed straight south. It was his intention to bisect the wagon tracks John Holcomb had spoken of, though he was fairly sure he knew where Jack was going.

For years Roamer had been afraid that Scout's grandmother would want the boy brought back to St. Louis to live in wealth and security, and he feared as much now. But even if she had decided to exert some control over Susan's child, the old woman would have sent an army of men armed with law books in one hand and guns in the other—not her wastrel son that she had no use for.

No. This was the work of Laughing Jack Maravel, and he was working alone.

"And since the bastard denied Scout from the moment he heard Susan was carrying a child, the only reason he would want him now is because of money."

Money. It gnawed at Roamer's gut to think of the two people he loved in danger over something as fleeting as wealth. He put his boot heels to his horse's belly and rode hard, his heart pounding like the echo of hooves as he offered up a prayer for the safety of those he loved.

* * *

Mile after mile Roamer pushed his horse until the animal could go no farther. The night was dark and moonless as he yanked off the saddle and rubbed the horse down with a handful of leaves stripped from a nearby bush. Then he ate the biscuit and bacon Ian had stuffed in his saddlebag before they parted. Roamer stared unseeing at the twinkling stars overhead until sleep took him.

The dream was upon him with a shiver. He was back in St. Louis. The waterfront saloon had been full when Roamer found Harry Malone. And if he lived to be one hundred, Roamer would never forget the look on the man's face when he pushed his way through the crowded room and yanked him out of the chair by his shirtfront.

"I am Susan Maravel's brother."

"Yea?" Harry had said with starch, but his face was whiter than the sheet they had covered Susan's body with.

"She died this afternoon. The beating you gave her killed her." Even through the red haze of his rage Roamer had heard the silence descend. The hardest sharpie and most jaded floozy had reacted to the fact that Harry Malone, waterfront tough, had beaten a woman to death.

Then Roamer drew back his fist—his right fist. The fist and arm he used to strike iron all day, the arm that was so thick he frequently shredded the sleeves of his shirts when he flexed his muscles. The forearm that was so corded with bulk that his veins popped up when he moved his wrist and hand.

Roamer drew his arm back and put in it every ounce of strength and rage within him when he hit Harry on the chin.

The sound of bone breaking was loud in the silent room. The blood that came from Harry's ears dripped and pooled beneath his feet as Roamer continued to hold him, held him long after the realization that he had driven Harry's shattered jawbone through his brain.

Roamer held the lifeless man while the crowd erupted into shouts and cries of terror and justice. He held him until the sheriff came and hit him over the head with the butt end of a Peacemaker.

Roamer woke, shaken and alone on the prairie. He was fighting off unseen demons while he tried to clear his mind. In the east, a pinkish gray light was sliding over the horizon.

"Sorry, old boy, but we have to push on," Roamer apologized as he saddled the horse and rode off.

"We are out of fresh water," Mattie said at sunrise on the third day.

Jack Maravel roused himself from his position by the tiller. She was amazed at how little he slept—if he slept at all. The man was not human. She watched him stretch, catlike, and remembered everything Roamer had said about Susan.

Mattie could see how a young, impressionable woman could be attracted to a man like Jack Maravel. His features were even, almost classical. He had a wide, sculpted forehead, dark brows, a slender, patrician nose. His chin was even graced with the merest hint of a cleft. He was by most standards a handsome man.

Until Mattie looked in his eyes.

Jack Maravel's eyes were cold and dark as the river

water. Each glance was calculating as a viper's, and just as deadly.

She shivered under his gaze.

"Well, now, we must have fresh water." He gave her a smile that put her in mind of a snake-oil salesman.

"And we are almost out of food, too. I assume you don't intend to starve Scout." She glanced at the boy who slept with his head in her lap. Her heart swelled with love for him.

Jack smiled at her. "You are right there. I want to keep that boy hale and hearty . . . for now."

"But you know, little lady, I just can't bring myself to trust you." Jack tilted his head and gave her his full attention. "If I stop at any town near the river, I just have this nagging feeling that you will try to get away. You might even cause enough ruckus that someone might believe you and try to stop me."

Calston made a growling noise from his pallet by the half-dozen kegs of whiskey. "Don't need water. Drink whiskey."

"What a tedious man," Jack Maravel sighed. "Now what was I saying? Oh yes, to take on supplies could be a risky proposition. I will have to ponder this dilemma."

"And in the meantime?" Mattie asked.

Jack shrugged, causing the dirty lace on his shirt-sleeve to hike up. "Either drink whiskey or go thirsty."

Thirteen

The Missouri shimmered like a gossamer ribbon as it snaked and rolled by. Out in the middle, where the water was deep and swirled in treacherous eddies, it was dotted with islands where wild berries and scrub oak grew in abundance.

Roamer stopped to water his horse at midday. The horse drank long and noisily, pushing his nose deep into the cool water.

"I have got to find another mount," Roamer grumbled, patting the animal's neck affectionately. The horse had given all he had, and Roamer feared he was close to blowing his heart if they kept the grueling pace much longer.

Roamer knelt and filled his canteen and then mounted up. He had pushed his own body and mind beyond exhaustion. Coherent thought was now a futile effort. He was running on willpower alone.

He reined his horse away from the Missouri River. He had no choice but to find a town on the trail and do some horse trading.

YANKTON, the crooked, gray-weathered sign proclaimed. Roamer saw little other sign of habitation except for the crisscrossing of deep rutted wagon tracks in the worn trail. A nagging worry that he had not yet intersected Jackson's trail because he was going the wrong direction nibbled at the edges of his mind.

Surely he wasn't wrong about Maravel's destination. He could not be wrong about that lowlife's motive.

"The only reason he would want Scout is money," Roamer growled. And the Maravel money was at the end of the trail in St. Louis.

Roamer's numb, sleep-deprived mind clouded with old memories. Sights and sounds he had ignored for years now refused to be pushed aside, for he was too exhausted to bury them in the recesses of his memory.

He remembered the last time he had been in St. Louis. Judge Mills had looked almost sympathetic when the bailiffs dragged Roamer in, cuffed and shackled, his vision blurred from the wound he received when he had been arrested.

For days Roamer had sat mute, listening to the testimony of every cardsharp, whore, and drifter that had been in the saloon to witness his deed. A part of him had been sickened to know he was capable of such mindless carnage; the other part didn't care.

Roamer found it hard to care about anything except the towheaded baby, Susan's child, who sat beside Mrs. Maravel, tended by a servant.

Jack Maravel's mother was a stern woman, seamed and wrinkled from a long life of hard opinions and bitter disappointments. She was dressed in quietly understated elegance, a string of jet beads at her wrinkled throat.

Roamer could not forget that she had cut Jackson off without a cent when he married Susan, a girl beneath the Maravels' lofty social and economic station in St. Louis society.

That loss of easy income for Jack was partially responsible for Susan's death—Susan's murder.

Harry would have had his damned money if old Mrs. Maravel had continued to open her purse to Jackson like she had done all his life, buying his way out of trouble, turning a blind eye to his misdeeds. Treating Jack as if he were better than men who earned their way by muscle and sweat had given him a distorted view of life.

His mother shared the blame for Susan's death. Roamer had fixed his eyes hard upon her and willed her to know what he thought of her and her accursed family.

You killed my sister just as surely as Harry and Laughing Jack Maravel. The thought drummed in his mind hour after hour.

And remarkably, one single tear had threaded its way down her lined face. She had pinched her thin lips even tighter and given Roamer one curt nod as if she agreed. In that moment, he had found it in his heart to forgive her. In that moment, he knew he had found an ally.

Day after day Mrs. Maravel had come to the hot, airless courthouse with Susan's child and a black servant. The toddler looked lost—bewildered—as he sat next to the stern woman who was his grandmother and the kindly servant who saw to his needs.

And the trial for Roamer's life marched on through the hot, dry days. He wondered if the road to hell was as parched as St. Louis was that ill-omened summer.

Roamer had sat in sickened silence as the town physician, Doc Reed, told in graphic detail how the force of Roamer's fist had shattered jawbone and cartilage and ultimately driven slivers of the man's own bone through his brain.

"Could just any man do that?" The Prosecutor had asked mildly.

"Oh, no. Only a man with extraordinary size and strength."

"Like a man who earns his living as a blacksmith?"

"Yes, a man who has used hammer and iron day after day would surely have the strength."

"Like Roamer Tresh."

Roamer had nearly retched as he stared in silence at his hands.

It was in that moment that Roamer begged God for one more chance. Roamer wanted to take Susan's child away from St. Louis, to a place where he would not be tainted by his mother's death or his father's reputation or even Roamer's reckless deeds. He wanted to make amends for his crime by providing his nephew with love and a proper home. Roamer prayed endlessly and promised God he would never again raise his hand in anger if he could have that chance.

Now Mattie's and Scout's lives hung in the balance. Could Roamer keep that sacred vow and save them? It was a question he dared not dwell upon, because the answer left him shaking with doubt.

"You can't mean to leave us on this island," Mattie said as she stepped out into the marsh prairie grass. Several ducks and other birds took wing at the sound of her voice. Overhead a slender crane cut through the air like an arrow.

"I can't take you to town, so this is the next best thing," Jack said cheerfully. "At least you have privacy."

"It's chilly. Give us a blanket." She hugged Scout to her while he glared at Jack. The boy had become quiet, but she knew his mind was racing, trying to find a way out of their trap.

"No. But I will leave you a lantern, in case you are afraid of the dark," Jack laughed and pushed the flat-bottomed boat back into the current. With Calston poling and Jack on the tiller, they soon slipped away on the muddy water, out of sight behind water grass, reeds, and cattails that swayed in a graceful dance.

"Well, Scout, at least we are away from them."

He tipped his head up and looked at Mattie. "Can we swim it?" He nodded toward the Missouri River.

Mattie stared unseeing at the water for a moment, foolish hope warring with good sense. "No. We can't risk it; the current is too strong."

"I hate him. I don't care if he is my father; I hate him."

Mattie could not bring herself to chastise the child for his honesty. For the first time in her life she had met someone who had not a speck of good in him. She hated Jack Maravel, but she also feared him—feared what he might do to Scout if angered.

"Let's see if we can build us a fire. I feel damp to my bones after so long on this river." She tried to sound cheerful, though she was cold and miserable. A fire might buoy her spirits as well as dry out her damp clothes.

Mattie and Scout fed the driest sticks and grass they could find into the little fire, but they continued to get more smoke than heat. Being on an island, and a small one at that, everything was damp. The pitiful finger of smoke choked their lungs more than it served to warm their bodies.

"Maybe if we yell real loud someone will hear," Scout suggested, coughing and wiping at his smoke-filled eyes.

Not wanting to dash his hopes, Mattie agreed. They stood at the edge of the water and shouted, whistled, and screamed until their throats were so raw that they sounded like spring peepers.

"Nobody is near enough to hear us," Scout finally said, sitting down.

"Who knows how far we are from a town?" Mattie sat down beside him and gently moved a strand of pale hair from his eyes. "We'll be all right, Scout. I promise you. I will find some way to see you set free when we reach St. Louis. It will be different then, there will be people and law. Jack Maravel can't keep you from Roamer; you can depend upon that."

"He is my father," Scout said in a whisper that was all misery and pain. "How could I have a father like him?"

"You listen to me." Mattie tilted Scout's face up and touched the tip of his nose with her finger. "You are more like Roamer than Jack Maravel. Just because he gave you life, Jack Maravel has not given you his outlook on life; that has all come from Roamer. He is the finest man I have ever known."

"You love him, don't you?" Scout said softly.

"Whether I do or I don't is of no consequence. When he returns to McTavish Plain he will be married to someone else." Mattie held Scout close and stared at the smoldering wood. "But none of that matters now. Keeping you safe and getting you back with your uncle is all that matters." Mattie swiped at the smoke. Surely that smoke was causing the tears in her eyes.

Roamer once again found himself meandering along the wagon-rutted trail that snaked beside the river. Off in the distance above the trees that lined the bank at the water's edge, a thin tendril of smoke rose. His gaze lingered on the gray line wending its way upward. It was an odd place to see smoke . . . unless it was coming from the islands that sprang up in the river. Still, it was strange.

Was someone in trouble? He pulled up, considering riding over, to see if he could offer assistance. But then he thought of Mattie and Scout. They would be afraid—they might even be hurt. His mind rebelled at the thought of Laughing Jack touching either one of them, but he remembered Susan and knew with cold dread that Jack Maravel was quite capable of hurting them—and more.

A long-forgotten vision of Susan with a black eye flashed in Roamer's mind. Then Susan with a split lip. Susan with her arm bandaged.

"Why did I ever believe her feeble explanations?" Roamer roared into the silence of the day. "Why?"

The smoke on the horizon was forgotten as Roamer put his heels to the horse and thundered away from the Missouri River toward Yankton.

Roamer was surprised to find that Yankton was enough of a town to have a sheriff and a whorehouse. Today both were bustling with activity. Rough-looking mountain men and scruffy saddle tramps were either waiting to get into the bordello or digging their heels in to keep from being tossed into one of the cells made of riveted flat-iron bars. In order to have a jail like that, the town had to have a smithy.

He spotted the smoke before he saw the forge. Roamer rode in the direction of the steady ring and ping of the hammer falling on steel.

"Morning," he said as he dismounted, his body stiff and awkward after so long in the saddle, his eyes feeling raw and gritty.

"Mornin'." The blacksmith was the color of soot, his eyes and teeth flashing white in his dusky skin. He wore a pair of overalls that strained across his broad chest. His bare arms glistened with sweat from the heat of the forge. "Your mount looks done in." The comment was made with the unmistakable tone of disapproval.

"He has given me all he can." Roamer patted the horse's neck. "I was hoping you might have another to trade. I have to travel hard but I don't want to kill the horse," Roamer said wearily.

A glimmer of approval flashed in the man's dark eyes. The blacksmith used his tongs to put the iron in the coals. As he turned, Roamer saw a crisscross of angry raised scars on his wide back. The thickest welts were the color of a bruised plum.

He might be free now, but the man would forever carry the marks of having been a slave once. This wasn't the first black man Roamer had seen with scars like that. As the unrest in the South grew and talk of secession fueled the conflict more and more, slaves were coming west—to freedom.

"Name's Dodger. I have a pot of coffee boiling," the blacksmith said.

"Coffee would be fine, real fine."

"I also have a big stallion out back I would be willing to trade, but I have to warn you, he's no angel."

"I don't need nice, Dodger, but I do need speed. I have to get to St. Louis as fast as I can."

"You running from trouble?" The man asked, narrowing his eyes. He poured out two cups of thick, dark liquid.

"*To* it. A woman and a boy I care about were . . . taken."

Dodger's eyes once more narrowed to slits. "By force?"

"Yes." The weight of his helplessness rested like a yoke upon Roamer's neck. But he refused to give into despair—he could not do that to Scout and Mattie.

"I got no truck with them that takes folks—bounty hunters and such. Ought to be flogged, the lot of them. I'll trade you the horse and toss in some grain and victuals."

Roamer sipped the coffee, barely hearing Dodger's deep, melodic voice. "It should be easy to find a slick-talking man with a woman and boy," he said as much to himself as to Dodger. "How many men are traveling fast and hard with a young woman and a towheaded boy? How many roads can there be to St. Louis?"

Feeling a little stronger after Dodger's coffee and a plate of cornpone slathered in molasses, Roamer transferred his saddle, rifle, and bedroll to the stallion called Lucifer. The horse watched him warily, as if he were waiting to bite a chunk out of his side at the first opportunity.

"I thank you, Dodger. You've been a mighty big help."

" 'Afore you ride out you should go to the saloon

and ask about. If this man is as slick as you say and fancies himself to be a sharp with a deck of cards, it could be he sat in on a game. Those in this town like to gamble."

Roamer nodded gravely. "You're right, Dodger. And that is something I should've done before. My mind is not working." Roamer dragged his hand across his face warily.

"I'll pack some more grain and check Lucifer's shoes. He'll be ready for you."

Roamer paused for a moment, staring at the big, powerful black stallion. "Lucifer is a fitting name for him, considering I am after a devil of a man."

Roamer rolled his shoulders to loosen the tension across the back of his neck and walked across the street toward the saloon. He elbowed his way through the crowd and shoved himself into a group that had gathered to bet on a cockfight. Roamer had no urge to watch bloodsport of any kind, but he was wedged tight on every side, obliged to inch his way through.

He looked up absently and froze. Laughing Jack Maravel, carrying a keg of whiskey on one shoulder, was threading his way around the edge of the mob.

"Maravel!" Roamer bellowed, causing a second of silence to grip the jeering crowd. "You bastard! Where are they?"

Laughing Jack turned and stared at Roamer. The color drained from his face, blanching him to the hue of the worn lace at his cuffs. He dropped the keg, the staves shattering, whiskey running into the dirty street.

Jack found Calston getting the last of the supplies, paid for with the last kegs of whiskey from the boat.

"Come on," Jack said, jerking him along.

Calston's lips rolled back in an expression that was as wild as his odor. "What's wrong with you? Why're you in such an all-fired hurry?"

"Shh." Jack shoved the brown-paper-wrapped salt pork into Calston's poke bag. "Take this and those canteens of water to the boat."

"What've you been up to? You act like the law's on your tail."

"If you don't hurry, the law may very well be on my tail and yours as well. I doubt you want to be answering a lot of questions either, now do you, Calston?"

It took Roamer precious minutes to disengage himself from the press of men. When he was free he ran after Jack, his mind a blur of fury and hatred—and hope.

He rounded a corner and saw the cuff of Maravel's fine striped trousers disappearing behind another building. It was like chasing a rat through a stack of grain bags.

Thoughts of what Roamer would do to Jack filled his mind. He was enraged, reckless. So when he rounded another corner he was not ready for what met him at chest level.

"Nice thing about Sam Colt," Jack said with a smile, training the gun on Roamer and pulling back the hammer with a soft click. "He can cut a man down to size. Even a giant like you won't stand up to a lead slug in the heart."

The gun jumped in Jack's hand, the scent of gunpowder filling the air as Roamer fell.

* * *

Darkness came to the little island on a carpet of mist. Scout snuggled close to Mattie, his teeth clacking together as they shivered in the cold. It was summer, but the darkness and the moisture of the night made the pair cold as the grave. The sound of crickets and frogs was a steady chorus. Occasionally something slapped the water out on the river.

Mattie didn't think they could get any colder . . . until it began to rain. A slow drizzle soaked their clothes, then their flesh. Soon Mattie was holding a shivering Scout close, trying in vain to warm him.

She thought of his recent brush with death, and a panic unlike any she had ever known gripped her. She shook, but not from cold. Fear became a tangible thing, an iron fist that squeezed her heart and threatened to force the air from her lungs.

It was cowardice, she knew. Cowardice and the inevitable loss of hope. She could not give into it. She could not allow Scout to know she was this close to giving up hope that Roamer would find them.

"I'm scared," Scout whispered.

She wondered if he felt her terror. "I am too, Scout," she admitted in a soft voice. "But you know what?"

"What?"

"I am not going to let that horrible Calston or Jack Maravel know it. I am frightened right down to my bones, but I am going to act like I am enjoying myself, as if this were as exciting as a picnic. And do you know why, Scout?"

"No ma'am, why?"

"Because Calston and Jack Maravel are bullies. They like to see people frightened; it gives them power and I refuse to give them any more power.

And when your uncle Roamer comes to find you, he will be proud of you for being strong."

"He will be proud of you too, Mrs. Smith."

"I hope so, Scout." Mattie swallowed hard. Would Roamer be proud, or would he hate her for not keeping Scout safe? He had left the child in her care, trusting her to do what was best, and she had failed miserably.

For a moment Mattie was lost in her own misery. She felt Scout stiffen in her arms and raised her head, listening, but the river had gone silent. Not a peep or croak or comforting, watery sound could be heard beyond the marsh grass and cattails. With her free hand she lifted the lantern, their pitiful fire having long since guttered and died. There in the waxy glow the tall grass and spindly limbs of the island trees parted.

"Ah, there you are. Did you miss me?" Calston smiled like a wolf who has cornered a lamb. "I bet you missed me."

There was no sign of Jack Maravel. Mattie leaned near to Scout's ear and whispered, "No matter what you hear, I want you to run. Find out where Calston left the boat if you can. If Maravel is not in it, take it and go. If he is in it, then hide. Hide so he can't find you."

"I won't leave—"

"Do as I say, Scout. Save yourself." Mattie stood up and smoothed the front of her dress. "Oh, yes, Mr. Calston. I did miss you. It was awfully lonely out here."

Scout stood motionless for one minute, staring at Mattie. Then, as if he understood, he plunged past Calston into the thick growth of grass and shrubs. Mattie heard the sound of breaking twigs as he vanished.

"Here now, wait a minute," Calston said, whirling. "Li'l bastard." He floundered in the tall grass, half drunk and unable to get his body to do his bidding with any speed.

Mattie picked up the lantern and brought it down on Calston's wet head. The smell of kerosene was a welcome scent as the liquid covered his hair, clothes, and body, masking his hideous odor. He staggered and fell to his knees. She jumped over him, running in the same direction that Scout took.

"Please, Lord, please let the boat be empty," Mattie prayed as she ran, stumbling on her skirts as they whipped around her ankles, gripping her, threatening to bring her down.

In the dark the island seemed to grow, becoming larger with each fearful step. Her petticoat caught on twigs and branches. Twice she heard the fabric rip. She didn't care. All she cared about was finding Scout—if God willed it, in the boat. Then they could escape, it didn't matter where. They could float where the river took them; at least they would be safe.

As she ran, she prayed a singsong litany that Calston and Jack had had a falling out, that the wicked man had met with disaster—that he had fallen in the water and drowned.

With each yard of ground she covered, her heart rose in hope. Maybe Calston had killed Jack for some offense. Maybe he had met with a rattler, or someone he had cheated at cards had been a little faster, a little more lethal. Suddenly she crashed through the veil of greenery and felt the water lap over her ankles.

"Here is our own dear lady now," Jack said smoothly, the blade he held at Scout's throat flashing in the dull glow from the lantern that sat on deck. "And she seems to be in a hurry to get going, so I think we had best oblige her."

"Run, Miss Mattie," Scout yelled.

"I wouldn't," Jack said coldly. "I won't kill him, but I can bleed him a little. It isn't pleasant, but only rarely is it fatal."

Mattie remembered Roamer and the stark pain in his face when he spoke of Susan and what Jack Maravel had put her through. He would not hesitate to hurt Scout to gain her compliance.

Mattie lifted her skirts and climbed aboard the flat-bottomed boat, mud sucking at her shoe as she pulled it from the water. She had barely stepped aboard when Calston broke through the undergrowth.

"You little bitch, you'll pay. I'll use you hard and then I am goin' kill you slow."

"Calston, you have no gentility. I think it is time to lighten my load. I know you will understand my position in this matter because you would do the same if it were reversed. Good-bye, Calston," Jack said with a smile. He took a pistol from the waist of his trousers and calmly pulled the trigger.

Calston grabbed at his chest. He fell facedown into the water as the boat bobbed away from the island and the current took it.

"Now, then, we should be off. Next stop, St. Louis," Jack said cheerfully as he slid the gun into the holster. "No more interruptions."

Fourteen

Roamer came to consciousness with a wrenching pain in his side.

"Here now, lay back or I'll have to hit you." Dodger looked at him with a mixture of amusement and concern. "Can't have you thrashing about."

Roamer looked around in confusion. He was in a small room, sparsely furnished but clean and airy. "Jack Maravel. Where is he?"

"If you mean the fool that shot you, he got clean away. Headed to the river. Sheriff said he lit out of here on a flat-bottomed whiskey boat. He the one you are chasing?"

"A boat? No wonder I never found his tracks." Roamer tried to rise and once again Dodger shoved him back on the straw-filled mattress. He stared at the black man's face in surprise. "It's not often I meet a man that can keep me down."

"It's not often I meet a man I'd trouble for," Dodger quipped. "Now lay back and let the bleeding stop. You'll be on your way in an hour or two I 'spect. Bullet went clean through and doesn't seemed to have nicked any bone. I'll bind you tight; you'll live."

An hour or two. It was too much time to waste. Jack

could be a long way toward St. Louis in an hour or two. "I can't waste an hour or two."

"Oh, I 'spect you can. You'll be wanting to talk to the man we fished out of the water."

"What man is that?"

"Won't give his name but he says he was shot by Laughing Jack Maravel. Claims he knows all about the woman and the boy you are looking for."

An hour later Roamer was at the jail, staring at the man on the cot.

"His name is Calston. He left fifteen people to die all alone and then didn't even have the decency to bury them," Roamer said flatly.

"Sounds like a cheat and a liar. I am not sure I'd believe anything he has to say," the sheriff advised as he picked his nails clean with a rattlesnake fang.

"You're right. Why should I believe anything you say, Calston?"

"Cause I got this here hole in me. Jack Maravel tried to kill me cause I was trying to help that boy and woman escape."

"Just tell me where he is headed," Roamer said coldly, stepping forward. His shoulder hurt like the blazes and it sickened him to have to deal with a monster like Calston, but for Mattie and Scout he would do it—he would do anything.

"Well, now maybe if you put in a good word with the sheriff here I might be able to remember." Calston looked sly as a fox as he eased himself back on his bunk. "You were quick enough to tell the law about that wagon train; will you be as quick to talk up to save that boy?"

Roamer's belly burned with hatred and anger. "I don't need your information, Calston. I know where Jack Maravel is going."

Calston sat up fast. His eyes were narrowed down to evil-looking slits. "You're bluffing."

"No, I am not. Jack Maravel is bound to be headed to St. Louis."

Calston leaped to his feet. "But how did you know? Jack said you didn't know the old lady died! He said you didn't know about the will and leaving everything to that boy—" Suddenly Calston's face contorted. "You tricky bastard. You didn't know."

"Not about the will and Mrs. Maravel, no. But thanks to you I do now." Roamer turned on his heel and headed for Lucifer. If the horse was what Dodger claimed and if Judge Mills was still alive and if the old man would listen, perhaps Roamer stood a chance.

Mattie took the loss of Calston with mixed emotions. On the one hand she was happy to have the filthy lecher gone. But on the other it marked well the desperate lengths Jack Maravel was willing to go to in getting Scout to St. Louis with the least amount of resistance and annoyance.

But why? How could he hope to get money by taking Scout to St. Louis?

"What scheme are you involved in? How can taking Scout to St. Louis put money in your pocket?" She heard herself ask.

Maravel looked up from his position at the tiller. He stared at her for a moment and then flashed his slick smile.

"I see no reason not to tell you, dear lady. Young Judson Walker Maravel is as wealthy as Midas."

"My name is Scout."

Laughing Jack's smile evaporated. Quicker than a striking snake, he left the tiller and backhanded the boy. Scout fell to the rough plank deck, a trickle of blood coming from each nostril. He glared down at Scout with calculated fury blazing in his eyes.

"You are Judson Walker Maravel! If anyone asks you better remember that, boy. Or I will beat that name into you, by God, I will."

"Don't you touch him again." Mattie shoved her body between them. For an instant she was transported back in time to the day she thought Roamer was going to take the barber strop to Scout.

How foolish I was, her heart cried. The look in Jack Maravel's eyes was cold and flat and devoid of pity, but Roamer's green eyes had been filled with shock, surprise, and even a little humor when she accused him.

"I have warned you repeatedly not to have a sassy mouth with me," Jack said to Scout, though it was Mattie he looked at. "Don't push me or you won't be alive much past the point I drag your worthless hide in front of that pious Judge Mills."

"I can't wait until Roamer gets hold of you," Mattie whispered. "He'll kill you with his bare hands."

"Dead men aren't much of a threat, my dear." Jack returned to the tiller, lounging against it as if he hadn't a care in the world.

"What do you mean?" Mattie felt a cold, leaden weight in her belly.

"Oh, didn't I tell you, dear lady? I shot Roamer Tresh in that one-horse town where we got supplies. And if there is any justice in the world he is as dead as good old Calston by now."

"You lie."

"Do I? Well, you can't be sure, can you, my dear?"

Jack raised one brow in an expression of amused cruelty. "Maybe it is a lie, and maybe it's the truth. The trouble is, you won't know and your doubts won't let you think of anything else. Quite a quandary, isn't it?"

Mattie slid nearer to Scout. She cradled his head in her lap and pretended not to notice when he began to cry. The sound of her own breaking heart and Jack Maravel's cruel laughter rang across the shimmering water.

"Scout, I will find a way to help you." Mattie whispered as she stroked Scout's hair. He slept, head in her lap as usual, the mottling bruise across his cheek and lip a constant reminder of Jack's black heart.

"You can do nothing, madam. The boy is my son," Jack said with cold authority.

Mattie had not realized she spoke so loud, or that Jack was listening. "If Scout is truly your son, then you should have some feeling for him. A father should want the best for his child. The boy deserves the best."

"Well, ma'am, most of us deserve better than we get in this life," Jack said with a laugh. "Take me, for instance. I should've been a hero."

"A hero?" Mattie was willing to let him talk if it might provide her with some diversion, some way of getting him off-guard. Perhaps she could simply shove him in the water; then she could hit him on the head. . . .

"You will hardly credit it, but I went to West Point," Jack said with a chuckle. "Of course it had nothing to do with me and everything to do with Andrew Jackson Maravel, may he rot in hell."

"I assume that was your father."

"You assume correctly, and a colder bastard never drew breath."

"What happened to you? How could anyone be so lacking in humanity?"

"Perhaps it was my upbringing." Jack said with a yawn. "Obviously you have no grasp of the enormity of what it is to know that one is a complete disappointment to his progenitor."

"I think you wallow in self-pity. You are unhappy and you are taking your misery out on an innocent child."

"Ah, my dear, that is family tradition. The fine old name of Maravel has long been associated with wastrels and unfortunate children."

"What are you talking about?" Mattie asked in frustration. The more Jack talked, the less she understood. He played the villain and the victim by turns. She hated him for abusing Scout and for lying about shooting Roamer.

But is it a lie? Her heart cried out.

"I am the son my father wrought. I am the result of a lifetime of never measuring up. He hounded me throughout my childhood and berated me when I was sent down from West Point." Jack shook his head as if bewildered. "Then he insisted I marry and give him an heir. I did exactly as he wished, but he cut me off without a dime."

"He disinherited you for marrying Scout's mother?" Mattie could not believe so much misery had arisen from one marriage.

"Yes. I mean just because I married the most unsuitable, fresh-faced, uneducated, unsophisticated farm girl I could find, and just because she was increasing in an embarrassingly short space of time, I ask you: Was that any reason to cut me off?" Jack looked as if he actually expected Mattie to commiserate with his circumstance.

"You married Susan to spite your family?" Mattie said in a gasp of shocked outrage. Her life had been spent in dreams of a romantic, intellectual marriage. In her naivete, she had not known that people like Jack existed.

"Absolutely," Jack grinned, his teeth flashing in the moonlight.

"You never loved her?"

"Not for a single moment, though her virginal tears were a diversion for a time."

Mattie thought of the loving way Roamer had touched her. Their coupling had been mystical, enchanted. Jack, however, spoke of such an act in a way that made Mattie mourn for what Susan must have endured—for the shame and degradation she must have felt each time he touched her.

"You are vile."

"Absolutely rotten to my core, madam. And if blood runs true, then the boy will be the same shining example to the name of Maravel."

"Never. Roamer will never let Scout turn out like you," she hissed.

Jack shrugged. "Time and blood will tell. I mean, we all make mistakes, miscalculations that cost us. Take me, for instance. I never expected my father to die before he changed his will back to my favor, but he did."

Jack fell silent then, staring out at the ribbon of moonlight that shimmered in a gold-and-silver ribbon on the Missouri.

Mattie watched the jeweled water slide by, her own past mistakes swirling before her eyes. She was not sinless either. She had lied about being married for her own gain, her own purposes. And right now Roamer was being forced to marry to stay in McTavish Plain.

It was as if God had taken notice of Mattie's foolish little lie and decided to show her all the aspects of her sin and what it meant to lie about something as blessed and sacred as marriage.

Every person that had married for some reason other than love had met with tragedy or had some terrible calamity befall them.

Had Roamer found someone? Was he now returning to McTavish Plain to find that Mattie had failed to keep Scout safe? Or was Jack telling the truth? Had he shot Roamer?

"Oh, please, God, don't let him be dead," she prayed softly with her hand on Scout's soft cheek. "Even if he hates me, please, please let him live."

Roamer was barely conscious of the passing miles. Only when he encountered a trapper or found himself in some little settlement did his mind mark the passage of time.

Lucifer was all Dodger claimed and more. The horse traveled in a ground-eating gait and never tired, never slacked. He was meaner than sin but stronger than any horse Roamer had ever ridden. Before the sun was even up, Roamer would saddle up and ride hard until he found himself in a settlement. Then he would stop and inquire about anyone seeing a man traveling the river with a pretty woman and a towheaded boy. They had to put into shore for supplies just as Jack had done the last time. Roamer was hoping that he would find them at one of those stops.

Today Roamer found himself in a rough community called Pikestown. He let Lucifer have his head. The horse went straight to the town trough and buried his nose, drinking deep and long while Roamer looked around.

The town was a ramshackle collection of tents and tepees—a place where white and Indian came to trade and barter. But this town was different than most in the number of soldiers crowding the street. Blue uniforms decorated every doorway.

The fractious stallion snorted and tossed his head as Roamer maneuvered through the throng of wagons and troops. He finally managed to find a vacant spot at a hitching post, tying Lucifer beside a number of horses wearing government saddles and brands. Within seconds Lucifer had tried to bite one and kick another.

"What is going on?" Roamer asked a half-grown boy without shoes who was watching a trio of soldiers loading a wagon.

"Soldiers are headin' east, leaving all the forts hereabouts."

"Why?"

"Ain't you heard? There's goin' to be a fight. My grandpa says war is coming. It's been like this since we got word that Union troops got Fort Henry." The boy stood taller and puffed out his slender chest. "First chance I get, I am joinin' up."

Roamer shoved his way into the saloon, needing something to cut the dust from the back of his throat before he began asking questions. He was too tired and too edgy to care much about war. All he could think about was Mattie and Scout at the mercy of Laughing Jack Maravel. When he finally reached the center of the bar, he found himself smack dab in the middle of a heated debate.

"Them damn Southerners got no call to be trying to split the states," one man said with a slur that let Roamer know he had been pulling on a jug.

"Ah, you don't know what you're talking about," a bluff man with a generous girth said. The slow drawl to his voice marked him as a man of the South. "Northern states got no right to tell Southern states what to do. We need slaves to run our farms and plantations."

Roamer ordered a shot of whiskey and tossed it back. He motioned for the barkeep to come nearer so he could be heard over the din of voices.

"Have you seen a man traveling with a woman and a boy? They were in a whiskey boat, last I heard. Would've been wanting supplies, but the man likes a hand of five card stud."

The barkeep didn't answer; his eyes were flicking to a spot behind Roamer. The small hairs on Roamer's neck prickled. He turned and found himself staring at the man who had been espousing pro-union sentiments.

"Yer one of the damned stinkin' bounty hunters, ain't ye?"

"No, I am not." Roamer turned back to the bar. "Have you seen them? The boy is about this high, with pale hair." Roamer flattened his palm and estimated Scout's height. "The woman is real pretty, honey-colored hair—"

"Yer got no call to turn your back on me, you damned stinking manhunter. Turn around."

Roamer felt a hand clamp onto his shoulder. "Stinking bounty hunter, trying to drag them poor darkies back to slavery. It ain't right and we ain't goin' to stand for it."

"I am not a bounty hunter—" Roamer began.

"Yer looking for a man, a woman, and a boy. I call that shameful and sounds like bounty hunting to me."

"The woman and boy I am looking for are—"

The man swung wildly, his fist grazing off Roamer's chin. The blow was nothing, a trifling matter, but it was all the crowd needed to ignite into a mob. Fists flew, bottles broke, splintered furniture was used as cudgels. Roamer found himself in the middle of a brawl, but he did not fist his hands. He took several punches to the stomach and one to the nose, and all the while he repeated his vow over and over in his head.

I will never strike another man.

The gunshot froze everyone in an awkward tableau. The scent of gunpowder, sweat, and fear mingled in the tight, close quarters of the saloon.

Blue uniforms began to break through the edges of the crowd. Each soldier held a rifle at the ready. The look in their eyes gave no doubt as to their intentions.

"I warned you boys about this," said a man with a fair amount of gold braid on his blue coat. "Now each and every one of you will cool his temper overnight in the stockade."

"No!" Roamer bellowed. "I can't stay here."

The soldier turned and gave Roamer one quick, assessing glance. "You'll stay or I'll shoot you where you stand. This town is under martial law."

Fifteen

Scout was sick. He hung his head over the side of the boat and retched. Mattie tore off a strip of her petticoat and used it to wash his face.

"We have to stop and let him rest. He has been ill recently. The people that hired Calston had cholera; Scout nearly died," Mattie pleaded.

Jack paled a bit and stilled his hand on the tiller. "Cholera?"

"Yes. All of the train died. Did you know that? Did you know what kind of a man Calston was?" Mattie tossed the dangling, uncombed hair from her face and glared at Jack. "Of course you are the same kind of man, so I suppose it doesn't matter."

"I am not like Calston," Jack said in a deadly soft tone. "I am a gentleman. I am educated, and I resent you comparing me to that filthy savage."

Mattie wanted to jump for joy. At last she had found a way to reach Jack Maravel. All she had to do was insult his vanity and he responded.

"If you wish me to believe you are not exactly like Calston, I am afraid you will have to prove it." Mattie met Jack's eyes. "Stop the boat. Let Scout rest and regain his strength. Besides, if you have really killed Roamer as you say, you have no reason to be running as if the devil himself were nipping at your heels—or was it a lie?"

"Eat a little more of this broth, Scout." Mattie spooned the hot liquid into a tin cup and handed it to Scout. Evidently, she had goaded Jack Maravel sufficiently, because he had not only stopped and tied the boat to a cottonwood sapling but had built a proper camp and provided blankets and some tins of meat for Scout.

Mattie was pleased to see some color returning to the boy's pale cheeks, but her heart was breaking. Her bravado about Jack having lied about shooting Roamer was only bluff. In a private corner of her heart she was grieving. If Jack was willing to stop, then there was more than an even chance he had told the truth.

He had run into Roamer and had shot him. *Roamer could be dead.*

No. No, I won't believe it, she told herself. *I can't let myself believe it. Roamer is alive. He is coming. He is coming to rescue Scout."*

But deep inside, Mattie was quaking with fear and doubt. She needed to be strong, but her faith was weakening. And she hated to come to God with prayers when she had committed so many sins; her soul was black with them—small sins, piled one upon the other until the stain was dark and foul. She had lied to get what she wanted. She had given her body to Roamer while letting him think she was another man's wife.

Everything Mattie had done for her own selfish pleasure had come around to hurt someone. She was wicked and sinful and, she realized with a jolt, she was years older than she had been at the start of spring.

Matilda Green, romantic little fool, had met life and it had aged her.

"How did you wind up in that ridiculous little town?" Jack sat opposite Mattie with the campfire between them. He had a cup of coffee in his hand and the glitter of speculation in his eyes.

"I *wanted* to go to McTavish Plain; I didn't *wind up* there." Mattie shifted her position and tugged her tattered brown calico tighter about her knees. Though she was fully covered and even had a blanket draped over her shoulders to ward off the chill, something in Jack's gaze made her want to be invisible.

"The boy calls you Mrs. Smith from time to time. Are you a widow?"

Once again the lie appeared like a sword over her head. Mattie glanced away. "No. My husband is at sea."

"Ah, so you are a widow of sorts." Jack gave her his slickest smile and her stomach roiled. "Are you very lonely, Mattie? I hope you will give me leave to call you Mattie."

Mattie swallowed hard. Once again the folly of her youth had come to mock her. Here was an educated man with smooth manners. No doubt if he had access to a tailor and a barber, he would be perfectly dressed and impeccably groomed.

Jack Maravel was just exactly the image of the man Mattie had spun girlish dreams about. And without doubt he was the most hideous and repulsive creature she could imagine.

She longed for Roamer's honest face, his deep

green eyes. But most of all she craved the wonder of his touch, the way she felt safe and cherished in his presence.

"This trip doesn't have to be completely unpleasant," Jack was saying. "I am sure we can come to some arrangement that would be beneficial to us both. After we arrive in St. Louis our circumstances will change . . . dramatically."

"How?"

"As I told you, Judson Walker Maravel is the heir to a substantial fortune. Point of fact, it is *my* fortune. I intend to see that mistake rectified quickly. A few papers duly signed and filed, and it will all be in my control. I will be a rich man, Mattie."

Mattie tossed another log on the fire, feeling a little more secure when it caught and the flames leaped high into the air, obliterating Jack's features into shadows.

"What do you intend to do with Scout once you are finished with him?" Mattie asked, suddenly emboldened by the anonymity afforded by the fire.

The silence was thick with something tangible . . . something evil.

"What would you say, dear Mattie, if I said that boy's fate may well depend upon you, and how willing you are to accommodate me?"

The cell Roamer was locked in was hot and sticky. No air circulated through the small barred window. The stockade was built of sturdy timber and the chinks were closed tight with daub. It was built to last and to keep the elements from the gunpowder that sat in kegs around the room. It was not built to provide comfort on any level for the men who were now locked inside.

"What're you pacing for?" asked a man stretched out on a straw palette, his face obscured by a soft brimmed hat. Until this moment Roamer had not given much notice to anyone sharing his confinement.

"I can't be still."

"What'd you do to get locked up?" The question came softly.

"Somebody thought I was a bounty hunter."

At that the hat was grasped by a long-fingered hand and slid downward, revealing a pair of silvery-gray eyes under black brows. "You a sympathizer?"

"A what?" Roamer asked impatiently, still pacing the width of the room.

"A man with leanings toward the Southern states?"

"No. I don't care one way or the other. I took a vow not to fight," Roamer said absently, his mind on Mattie and Scout.

"Lots of men think they won't or can't fight, but I wonder what you'd do if your back was up against it."

Roamer stopped and stared at the stranger. Those eyes, liquid and pale as fish scales, seemed to bore right through him.

"What do you mean?"

"If your way of life, your home and your family, were threatened, I think you'd fight right enough." The man stared at Roamer for another minute before he laid his head down and slid the hat back into place. "Yep, I imagine if something or someone you really cared about were in jeopardy you'd manage to forget your vow quick-like."

Roamer stared at the prone figure as the words ran like a litany in his head.

Would he? Could he put aside his vow in order to save Scout and Mattie? At times he wasn't so sure anymore.

The days on the river would have been pleasant for Mattie if she and Scout had been alone. He was not mortally ill, but he had a slight warmth to his cheeks and a dry cough—a result, no doubt, of the dampness of the boat and their time on that accursed island.

Jack Maravel had decided to turn charming toward Mattie—an event she could have done without. Now he found every excuse to fetch and carry for her. He seized every opportunity to grasp her fingers, to compliment her, to show he was a literate and charming man.

Mattie knew she looked like a wild woman, but she was loath to do anything to improve her appearance, lest Jack think she was doing it for his benefit. Each morning she waited until he left their small camp to go relieve himself, and then while he was occupied she would race to the river to wash herself and heed the call of nature. It was like a subtle game of cat and mouse between them. Today she walked with a bucket of water, pondering how long this trip would continue.

"Oh, dear Mattie, don't carry that bucket of water, it's far too heavy for you."

Mattie whirled to find Jack right behind her. He had come upon her silent as an Indian.

"Nonsense. I carry my own water at home." She raised her chin and pulled herself to her maximum height.

"Ah, yes, the seafaring husband is never close at hand, is he?" Jack reached out. She shrank back, nearly stumbling over her skirts with the heavy bucket. "Easy, dear Mattie, I was only going to get this." His long fingers flicked toward her temple and came back with a bit of marsh grass in his fingers. "It was tangled in your hair."

Jack watched her with the glimmer of speculation in his eyes. "I have a small comb you could use—for your hair, I mean. I know what value pretty women put on their appearance."

"Well, I have never made the mistake of thinking myself pretty, so there is no need, but thank you," Mattie said stiffly, turning with the heavy bucket and making her way toward the camp. "I have no care for the way I look, only that I can see Scout cured of his cough and fever."

"Yes, you do that, Mattie, my little brown wren. You keep the boy healthy . . . for me."

Jack's laughter rippled over the dew-kissed river grass, ruining the morning, flushing water birds into the sky.

By noon Scout had taken a line to try and catch a fish, and there was Jack again, watching Mattie like a tabby watches a mouse.

"Why don't you come sit by me and talk awhile, Mattic?" Jack said suddenly.

Mattic was shocked again to find him close enough for her to feel his breath upon her neck.

She tried to sidestep him, but he grasped her arms. She tried to pull away, but he was stronger than he appeared.

"Don't be timid, Mattie, dear. I am a generous and experienced lover. I have had no complaints."

Jack's cocky smile flashed. "There is no need for this journey to be so . . . *tedious.* We can give each other pleasure." He yanked her close and covered her mouth with his. His lips were cool and hard. They gave no thrill, no comfort to her. She felt his tongue dart out, but she kept her own mouth tightly shut against it.

Finally Jack lifted his head. There was a feral gleam in his eye. "Relax, Mattie, you can learn to enjoy my kisses." He bent his head, but before he could kiss her again she turned violently the other way.

"I—I am a married woman!" she blurted in shocked outrage. "How can you even *suggest* such a vile thing?"

Jack did not release his grip, but he tilted his head and regarded her seriously. "You are not even a tiny bit tempted?"

The tone of his voice made Mattie speculate that he had rarely if ever been spurned by a woman, married or otherwise.

"Not in the least." Mattie tucked in her chin and gave him what she hoped was a withering stare.

"I can scarcely believe it. A virtuous woman." Jack's fingers relaxed until she was free. "Can it truly be? If so, then I have seen one of God's true wonders." He turned and walked away, shaking his head as if completely baffled.

Mattie rubbed at her arms and thought of Roamer. Was he dead? She prayed he was alive, even if he was now wedded to another—as long as he was alive.

Roamer had counted the hours spent in the stockade with each beat of his heart. Now he was once again free, released by the stern blue-coated soldier.

"Take my advice," the solider said, returning his knife and belongings, including the rifle and scabbard from his saddle. "Steer clear of any debate about this question of states' rights. The country is a powder keg right now."

"Believe me, I intend to," Roamer said, gathering his reins and mounting Lucifer. "All I care about is getting to St. Louis as fast as I can."

The soldier nodded and Roamer wheeled away. Wind burned his eyes and whipped Lucifer's mane into his face.

Faster, faster . . .

He had to get to St. Louis and find Judge Mills. Convincing the old man that a murderer was the best person to raise Scout was Roamer's only hope.

"We are leaving today." Jack's voice caused Mattie to drop the frying pan she was cleaning at the river's edge. The heavy iron embedded in the mud, dirtier than when she began.

"But Scout—"

"Is quite well enough as you know, dear Mattie." Jack gave her a crooked grin. She wondered how many women had found that particular smile and expression charming and disarming.

"There is no need to delay any longer. The boy's cough is gone, and I trust I have proven my claim about Roamer by allowing you to have this leisurely rest. Surely you don't still think I was lying about shooting him."

Jack Maravel said this in the same smooth, easy way that most men would discuss the year's crops or the mild summer weather. Mattie wondered how anyone could be so *broken*.

She retrieved the frying pan and rose to her feet. "I will never believe you, Jack. If Roamer was dead I would know it. I would feel it in my heart."

For a moment Jack's face went blank and then it contorted, twisting into an ugly grimace. "You love him?"

"I never said so." Mattie tried not to blush under Jack's incredulous gaze. "You know I have a husband. I have told you so many times."

"By God, you do! You love that big, clumsy, uneducated ox."

"How dare you call him that! Roamer is the kindest, most honorable man I have ever known," Mattie blurted.

"And your husband—where does he figure into this pretty tableau of admiration, Mattie?"

She could not answer, but she did manage to stare unflinching while Jack's eyes skimmed her from head to foot.

"I should've known. A little brown wren like you would pick a man like Roamer. So tell me, virtuous Mattie, have you succumbed to your feminine emotions? Have you shared his bed? Or is this a 'pure' love unrequited and bittersweet?" Jack loosed a sharp bark of laughter. "This is rich, by God. Rich indeed. I almost regret killing him." He reached out and took Mattie's chin roughly between his thumb and forefinger. "I would love taking you and having him watch. It would be *so* delightful. And even though he is gone, I may take you still."

"You wouldn't dare," Mattie said fiercely.

"Ah, but I would. And you know what, Mattie? The

more you struggled and the more you screamed, the better I would like it. Yes, I think when we reach St. Louis tomorrow I will have to contrive a place for us . . . somewhere private."

Mattie jerked herself free. Jack walked off chuckling softly to himself. Mattie saw Scout's pale hair shining above the tops of cattails. How much had he heard?

"I will kill him," Scout said calmly as he stared at Jack's back. "If he puts his hands on you again, I will have to kill him."

Mattie sucked in a shocked breath. There was nothing childlike about Scout now, his expression was cold and deadly—too much like Jack's.

"No, Scout. You mustn't even think that way." She pulled the boy near and ran her fingers through the soft silk of his hair. "That is not a burden I would want you to carry all your life. Jack will get what is coming to him."

"Do you think so?" Scout looked up, reflecting the sky in his pale eyes. A flock of ducks flew low overhead, landing with a splash along the edge of an island in the middle of the river.

"I am certain of it." Mattie was prepared to do what she would not let Scout consider. She had stolen one of the knives that had been aboard the whiskey boat for cutting line and hemp rope. She had sharpened it on river stones until it held a lethal edge. "People who do wrong things always get what they deserve."

"Always?"

"Mmm." She stroked his pale hair and thought of her own mistakes.

"I have to tell you something, Miss Mattie."

"What?"

"When I took the letters to John Holcomb to send to Belle Fourche—"

"Yes?"

"I climbed in the back window and got them back out of the pouch. I stuffed them down the privy. That was why no woman ever answered Uncle Roamer's letters."

"Oh, Scout." Mattie felt the choke of tears.

"I didn't want a mail-order mother. I wanted you." He wrapped his arms around her knees and squeezed her tight. "I always wanted you."

Mattie made her own silent vow then. "I will do what needs to be done, Scout. Now go to sleep and don't worry anymore." Mattie folded her fingers around the knife in her skirt pocket. It was in her mind to lure Jack to her bed and then slit his throat.

Sixteen

Lucifer's shod hooves rang on the planks of the ferryboat with all the force of Roamer's hammer on the anvil.

"Easy, easy." Roamer stroked his neck, but the stallion was still wild-eyed and uneasy. He had no liking for the deck that swayed gently beneath his hooves. He shook and splayed out his legs trying to achieve some balance, but it was not to be had as the ferry skimmed over the water toward St. Louis.

Roamer had hardly slept since being released from the stockade. And by the grace of God the big horse had managed to find more within himself when more was needed. They had covered a good bit of ground in a small space of time.

"Grain, a good rubbing, and a softly bedded stall will be yours, my friend," Roamer promised softly. God willing, he would be able to find Judge Mills. *And I pray he will listen to me. Everything depends upon him.*

The house was stately, solid, and spoke of money and position. Roamer looked down at his dusty boots and travel-stained clothes with misgivings.

He stopped at the wrought-iron gate outside the

large brick house and slapped at his trousers with his hat. Little puffs of dust wafted into the air.

"Well, I guess I look the part," he said with a shake of his head. His hair was beyond long now. It hung in heavy strands around his face. He had bathed at the stable where he left Lucifer, but he did not dare take the time to find a barber.

"Scout and Mattie need me," he said to himself and reached down to open the gate. On silent, well-oiled hinges it swung open. Roamer strode up the herringbone walk and lifted the heavy knocker.

Within moments the door swung open. A black man with white hair looked Roamer up and down with one almost imperceptible flicker of his catlike eyes.

"Yes sir?"

"I need to speak with Judge Mills," Roamer said.

"The Judge sees no one without an appointment. Perhaps you'd like to leave your name and come back—"

"No. I must see him now. I *will* see him now." Roamer put one boot on the threshold, blocking the big oak door.

"I am sorry—"

"Who is it, Albert?" a deep voice asked from somewhere inside the forbidden interior of the house.

Roamer put his palm on the door. Though his strength was no match against Roamer's, Albert braced himself, holding the heavy carved door for a moment before he stepped aside and let it swing inward, spilling sunshine across a highly polished marble floor.

"Do you remember me, Judge Mills? I am Roamer Tresh."

"Ah, yes, I remember. I presided at your trial when you were convicted of murder."

"I never expected you to show up in St. Louis," Judge Mills said sternly over a glass of port. Roamer noted that the man was still sharp-eyed and agile, though he had taken on the somewhat bent appearance of a man well on in years.

"I had no choice in the matter," Roamer said.

Was *he* also older, with lines of worry etched deeply into his face? Would Mattie see a change in him? "It is a matter of life and death. You are the only one I could think of to help me . . . and Susan's child."

"Well, now," Judge Mills smiled. "This sounds like the beginnings of a good story. Since I retired I rarely hear good stories." He turned to his servant. "Albert, since our guest won't have a glass of port, bring coffee. Are you certain you would not like something stronger, Roamer?"

"No, sir. Coffee would be fine."

"And some bread and that fine hickory-smoked ham that Marjorie fixed for us last night. You suppose there is some of that in the larder, Albert?"

"Yessir, there surely is."

"Fine, fine. Bring us coffee and bread and some thick slices of Marjorie's ham and put a couple of hunks of her molasses cake on the tray as well." Judge Mills glanced at Roamer. "Are you hungry, Roamer?"

Roamer opened his mouth, but Judge Mills raised his hand to silence him. Albert was still standing there—waiting, it appeared, for any other last-minute things the Judge might want.

"Course you're hungry. A man your size can always eat. So we will eat and you will tell me this story of yours."

"I am anxious to, sir, but before I do I must go deliver a letter." Roamer patted the pocket where he kept the settlers' letter to their kinfolk.

"A letter, you say? Why, surely we can see that done without you going yourself, Roamer. Albert, don't we have a boy that can take a letter round?"

"Yessir, we do. I can fetch up Toby. He can run it to wherever it needs to be delivered."

"Who is your letter to, Roamer?" Judge Mills eyes sparkled with interest.

"To the relatives of a wagon train that came through the territory." Roamer pulled the letter free. "All of the settlers died of cholera. I promised I would see it delivered."

"Cholera . . . bad, very bad. All dead you say?"

"Dead and left for the buzzards."

"Bad business all round." Judge Mills reached out for the letter. "I am sure the family will be most relieved to get this letter—knowing is much more merciful than not." Judge Mills scanned the address before he handed it to Albert. "See Toby takes this right away, Albert, and then bring our lunch. I am sure Roamer is starving, and I am most anxious to hear his story."

An hour or so later, with the remains of lunch on the silver tray between them, Judge Mills leaned back, tented his fingers, and stared at his fine, pressed-tin ceiling.

"So, Laughing Jack has finally decided to claim his child," Judge Mills commented in a mild voice that made Roamer's blood run cold. The man's lack of emotion was unnerving.

"His grandmother is probably turning over in her grave. That was all Rebekah ever wanted from Jackson—that he take responsibility. Trouble was, she went about trying to teach him in the wrong way," Judge Mills sighed and let his chair come forward. He looked Roamer straight in the face. "But I suspect that means little to you."

"Frankly, sir, all I care about is saving Scout and Mattie Smith. I know what Jack Maravel is capable of."

"Yes, I suppose you do know more than most would." Judge Mills watched Roamer with speculation sparkling in his eyes. "Yes, I suspect you most certainly do." Suddenly he smiled. "I am glad you came to me, Roamer. And it looks as if fate is on the side of the angels in this case. I have no doubt you did manage to reach St. Louis before Jack, or he would already have come here to my door making claims and demands upon the estate."

"Can you be sure?"

"Oh, yes, I think we may be confident of it. The last time I saw Jack was when I read Rebekah's will. He was shocked—a bit more than shocked—to hear Rebekah's wishes." The Judge chuckled. "Yes, it would be in character for Jackson to think that producing a boy and claiming it is Susan's child would be enough to change the situation."

"But Scout *is* Susan's child," Roamer said.

"Ah, yes, there is that." Judge Mills stared off at the wall of books for a moment.

"Do you doubt what I am telling you?" Roamer was growing angry. He had come for help, not to be doubted.

"No, no." Judge Mills waved his thickly veined hand in the air. "I don't doubt you at all. But Roamer, there are some things I have often wished you knew about the past—about your case."

"Such as?" Roamer's gut was twisting with impatience. The Judge was not an easy man to read.

"I am retired now as you know, but most of my life I was a judge. And as a judge my responsibility was to the law alone."

Judge Mills rose stiffly from his chair. He walked to the window and pulled back the thin, lacy curtain, staring out at the traffic going by in fashionable surreys and buggies. The window was open and the sound of hooves on paving stones was a steady sound.

"I wonder if you can imagine what it is like to have to sit and listen to the crimes of a man who is beneath contempt."

Roamer swallowed hard. The judge was putting into words the same feelings he had for himself.

He had killed a man. It was the burden he carried through life for having set himself up to be judge, jury, and executioner.

"Day after day I sat mute, required by my position to be silent. I wanted to speak out, Roamer," Judge Mills spoke softly. "I wanted to cry out that justice was not being served, and the blindfold should've been lifted from the lady's eyes so she could truly see the monster who was guilty."

Roamer stood up. "You aren't saying anything I haven't said to myself each day, Judge. I have to live with what I did."

Judge Mills frowned and waved his hand in a gesture of impatience. "Let me finish, Roamer. One thing I got used to on the bench—and still enjoy—is being able to have my say without interruption. I expect to be able to do that in my own home."

Roamer fell into a miserable silence of respect. He stared at his dusty, cracked boots. He would listen to what the judge had to say, because it was all true.

"I sat and listened to the evidence surrounding what you did, and all I could think of was that it should've been Laughing Jack Maravel on trial. He should've been indicted for his cruelty to your sister. He should've been scorned for his callous disregard for his son. And he should've been held responsible for the death of the man you killed."

The air escaped from Roamer's lungs. "I thought—"

"You thought that since you couldn't forgive yourself that nobody else would either. I understand what you did and why you did it, Roamer. And it is about time you stopped wearing a hair shirt over it."

Roamer slumped into the chair. "How can I?"

"You are human. You took no pleasure in what happened, I saw that and the jury saw that. You killed because you were consumed with grief over Susan. That was why I commuted your sentence and persuaded Rebekah to let you take Susan's child. Jackson was the reason for your vengeance; Jackson is the reason for much of the misery I have seen. It galls me that he has remained untouched by his crimes." The judge raised a hoary brow. "And never forget, the man you executed had killed your sister. An eye for an eye, eh?"

Judge Mills walked to Roamer and placed his hand on his shoulder. "And I think it is about time that he paid. What do you say, son? Will you accept the hospitality of my home and help me see Laughing Jack get his dues?"

"What do you mean?"

"I believe I have thought of a way to see young

Judson Walker Maravel and his fortune safe from Jack forever."

"I don't care about the money. I care about Scout and Mattie."

"I believe we can save your lady friend as well. With a little cunning and luck, we can bring Jackson to his knees and neutralize the threat of him ever bothering you or the child again. And no matter how you feel about it, Roamer, the boy is wealthy beyond belief. It is his birthright, and to be blunt, you have no right to make decisions about it."

"I suppose you are right. Susan wanted what was the child's due."

"How about it, Roamer? Will you become my confederate? Will you be willing to play a little charade to see justice done?"

"I would do anything for Scout and Mattie," Roamer said softly.

"Yes, I do believe you would," Judge Mills said thoughtfully.

Mattie's heart fluttered with excitement. A couple of hours ago the current had changed, pulling stronger and in a slightly different direction. The current of the Missouri spilled into the channel of the mighty Mississippi with an unmistakable force, and the river grew wider, stronger, and more vital. The little boat was now being shoved at twice its previous speed. The shore was farther away now as they swung in a more southerly direction. It was not long before Mattie could hear voices and the clamor of activity on the unseen banks.

They were nearly in St. Louis.

Perhaps she would take Scout and simply run for it. Somebody would help; this was a civilized place.

"Scout, stay near me," she whispered as the flat-bottomed boat broke through the morning fog. The shore was coming nearer. She could see beefy stevedores loading and unloading cargo. There were dray wagons and bales of goods sitting on the dock.

And people! People meant safety.

But suddenly the whiskey boat veered away, passing the dock and the rows of small craft moored like corks. Mattie looked around wildly. There was nothing she could do, but she nearly wept when the men on the shore grew smaller and smaller.

"Ah, disappointed are you, Mattie?" Jack chuckled. "I thought you might be. But I am no fool. We will go a bit farther down, where the wharf is not so genteel. That way if I have to put a knife in your ribs, there will be few who will care."

Jack managed to set the boat on a course that put it next to a crooked dock trailing streamers of green moss. The weathered gray structure didn't look trustworthy; in fact, it was canted at a treacherous angle.

"Careful, Scout," she warned as she gathered her skirts and prepared to climb up the ladder after him. The structure creaked and groaned beneath her weight. She could feel the give and squish of the moss beneath her shoes.

"Ah, not so fast," Jack said as he grabbed her arm, jerking her back down. In one smooth motion he had her arm behind her back. When he raised it a pain shot through Mattie's shoulder, making her gasp.

"I just want you to know what it feels like, Mattie." He smiled and let her see the glitter of a knife blade in his hand. "Judson, if you get any ideas about running away or calling out for help, your friend will be dead."

Scout narrowed his eyes and clenched his fists. His small body shook with pent-up rage. "My name is Scout. And I hate you."

"Ah, like father like son, I suppose. I hated my father as well," Jack said with a snort. "Seems to be a family tradition. Now step aside and wait for us to come up."

"Where are you taking us?" Mattie said through teeth gritted against the pain as she climbed, careful not to let her foot slip, lest she impale herself on Jack's knife.

"There's a place I know where the boy and I can clean up, get some proper clothing. After all, he cannot go claiming his inheritance looking like some backwoods hayseed."

"Claim his inheritance?" Mattie repeated. "That is what you are planning?"

"Yes, Judson Walker Maravel will claim it and then sign it all over to me."

Seventeen

"Laughing Jack, you are a crazy man to return here to St. Louis with empty pockets. You still have enemies here, *oui?*"

The knife the Frenchman flashed while cleaning his teeth made Jack's look like a toothpick. Mattie hoped they would break into an argument and simply kill each other so she and Scout could run, but Jack smiled at the man. He still kept her arm behind her back and her body before him like a shield.

"Pierre, my old friend. I came here because I know you are first, last, and always a businessman. I know you have a nose for profit and aren't too particular how you get it."

"Oui, a businessman who likes to see a profit—that I am. *N'est ce-pas?"*

"Profit, *oui*—yes. I am going to be a rich man, profit like you cannot imagine."

"Ah, *mon ami,* you have told me the same sad tale since I know you," Pierre laughed.

"This time it is true. Do you know who this child is?" Jack nodded toward Scout.

"Non, n'importe." Pierre twirled the wicked blade in his hand as if bored by the company and the conversation.

"Ah, but it is important, Pierre. This boy is the goose that lays the golden eggs. He is the key to a fortune—my fortune."

"Bah, you are whining again about your lost fortune." Pierre raised his hands in a Gallic gesture of disgust. "No more, Laughing Jack, I have heard this enough."

"Pierre, this is the heir to the Maravel money," Jack snapped. "This is Susan's child."

Mattie did not miss the fact that Jack rarely if ever referred to Scout as his son.

Pierre narrowed his eyes and studied Scout. *"Non.* The son of the poor murder—" His words trailed off and he coughed as if embarrassed to have said so much in front of Scout. Then a slow, feral smile appeared beneath his grotesque waxed mustache. "What will be my share, *mon ami?* And what do I have to do to earn it?"

"One quarter, Pierre. I will sign over one full quarter for rooms, a suitable wardrobe, and your promise to keep an eye on this woman until all our business is concluded in St. Louis," Jack said with a satisfied grin.

"She is *tres jolie.* Watching her would be no problem, eh?"

Mattie swallowed hard as Jack gave her arm one more vicious tug. "She will be no trouble—will you, Mattie?"

"No trouble," Mattie grated out.

"Then we are agreed. Now give me a room with a good, sturdy lock, Pierre, so we can send a message to my grandmother's old friend the judge. And send a boy round to run to the nearest tailor."

* * *

Even though Mattie and Scout were still prisoners, they were being treated very well while under the Frenchman Pierre's watchful eye. He had given her and Scout adjoining rooms over the gambling palace. Once she adjusted to the loud music from below and the clomp of boots on the stairs when one of the soiled doves brought a man up, it wasn't so bad.

Pierre had sent a tub and many buckets of hot water, even providing hard milled soap from Paris and thick toweling.

First Mattie had soaped Scout and scrubbed him until he was pink, ignoring his pleas for privacy and his embarrassment at being bathed by her. She laughed aloud as she thought of his reaction to the new wardrobe.

"Now that you are clean, let's see what has been brought for you, my fine sir."

"No. I don't want anything from him," Scout said stubbornly, plucking at the frayed cuffs of his worn trousers. He had insisted on returning to his dirty clothes after his bath. At the time, Mattie preferred to see him eat, so she had not argued with him. But now he was clean and fed, and his appearance needed attention.

"Scout, we are in the city. And people dress according to their station in life in the city."

"I don't care." He stuck out his bottom lip in a pout.

"But *when* we are able to escape, we don't want to make it easy for Jack and Pierre to find us because we look like paupers running through the street, do we?"

Scout tilted his head and squinted his eyes. "I guess it would be easy enough to point me out in a crowd, wouldn't it?" He wiggled his toes.

"There is an awful lot of them," Scout said, feeling the weight of what Mattie handed him.

"I suspect it is a full suit. Jack Maravel has his reasons for seeing you fitted out in the best fashion of the day. Now take these clothes and see what you can do with them." Mattie handed him a bundle. "Or do I need to dress you?"

"Miss Mattie!" he said, and he dashed off to his own room.

He soon emerged looking like a proper boy. Then after a bit of bread and milk, also courtesy of Pierre, Scout fell asleep on the bed in the connecting room.

Mattie was sure the child was on the verge of complete exhaustion. He had not eaten or rested well since they were taken. Even if they were prisoners here in this den of ill repute, she was grateful for a place for Scout to rest.

Now Mattie had decided to indulge herself in a bit of stolen comfort in Scout's leftover bath. Slowly, by degrees, she was ridding herself of the feel of the river and Jack's hands upon her flesh. Her hair had been soaped and rinsed twice. At last she felt less contaminated.

The water was cooling rapidly. Finally. it was to the point she must get out or risk becoming ill with lung fever. If she sickened, what would happen to Scout? How could she help him?

She stepped out and wrapped one of the generous towels about her body. Mattie peeked into the other room to see that Scout was still sleeping.

A knock on the door brought her whirling around. They were locked in, but she had felt too insecure with that arrangement, so she had modified the door somewhat.

"Who is it?" she asked, stepping nearer.

"It is Pierre, *mon cher.* I have come to see if there is anything else you may desire, *n'est ce-pas?*"

Mattie stood, unable to decide. It was obvious Pierre had more heart than Laughing Jack Maravel, but how much more? His eyes didn't have the cold flat glimmer of a murderer, but how far could she trust him? Could she hope to enlist his help when Jack had dangled a fortune before him?

She glanced at Scout. An innocent child being used by an unscrupulous man. Then she looked back at the door.

If there was even a glimmer of a chance, she had to take it. And there was always a possibility that Pierre could be swayed by the promise of more money from Scout than Jack was offering.

"Just a moment." Mattie looked about the room. She had no clothes to put on but her worn, dirty calico and tattered petticoat. Her stockings had so many holes, she could have passed them off for lacework. She just couldn't put those filthy rags on again.

With a small snort of annoyance, she yanked the faded quilted coverlet from the bed and wrapped it around herself until she looked like an exotic Eastern woman. Then she went and dragged the chair from its position under the door handle.

"Come in."

She heard the clink of the lock being turned from the outside. Pierre opened the door. "Ah, *chere,* what a pity to lock such a pretty woman away."

"I feel safe with the door locked. I have taken to putting a chair beneath the knob on this side," Mattie said without moving.

Pierre laughed. "I thought as much. You are a cautious female. Your couture is most, how you say? Attractive." Pierre nearly salivated as his eyes skimmed over Mattie's body. She was grateful for the quilt, which covered her completely from neck to toe.

"Was there something you needed?" she asked.

"Needed? *Non,* I have brought the clothing that Jack requested for the boy, and something else too, *oui?* I cannot stomach seeing a pretty woman in rags. It is . . . how you say? Disgusting. It was *bon chance* that you appear to be the same size as one of my . . . friends."

His hesitation and the expression that flitted across Pierre's face made Mattie blush. She was quite sure the clothing she was being given belonged to one of the women of easy virtue that occupied the other rooms on this floor. But when she glanced at her own pitiful, worn frock, she was able to put that thought aside.

"Thank you," she said, still not moving. "I am most grateful."

"Ah, you do not trust Pierre," he said with a wink. "That is *comme il faut* . . . how you say? As it should be. I am not an honorable man, *cheri.* Once I might have been, but that was long ago." He snapped his fingers and a young girl of no more than twelve darted forward. Mattie had not noticed her standing behind Pierre in the doorway until now.

The girl's arms were full of beautifully colored fabrics. She darted past Pierre and deposited everything in a heap on the bed. Then she flitted away like a wisp of smoke.

"I will leave you to dress; I know how much women like the feel of fine lace against their bodies." Once more his eyes skimmed over her. "If you need Pierre—for anything—do not hesitate to ask, *cher.*"

Mattie shut the door and waited. After what seemed a long time, she heard the key turn firmly in the lock. She dragged the chair over and wedged it beneath the knob. She heard the rich sound of baritone laughter outside the door.

"Ah, I like you, *cher.* You possess the *esprit present*—the quick mind. I am happy, for you will need it to deal with Laughing Jack Maravel."

The sound of Pierre's footsteps, heavy and even, proceeded down the hall to the stairs. Only when there had been no sound outside the door for a good ten minutes did Mattie turn to see what her new wardrobe consisted of.

She spread out the garters, the chemise, the layers of ruffled and taped petticoat, and finally the corset. Mattie never knew women's small clothes and personal undergarments could be made from such *scandalous* materials.

Wisps of lace and black satin appeared in places and in ways that she had never dreamed they could be put, rolled, sewn, or tucked.

And the cut! Each item of personal clothing was more daring, more revealing than anything she had ever worn, let alone imagined. It took a moment of steeling herself before she shed her quilt and began to dress. When she had them on, she swallowed hard. Her body was different inside those suggestive, silken items. Mattie *felt* different, and in the back of her mind a little voice once again cried out for Roamer.

Would he like this? Would his fingers itch to untie the laces? Would his hands wish to skim her new curves, to explore the places revealed by the crafty lace? She closed her eyes and could almost feel his hot, moist tongue playing at the scandalously low-cut top of her chemise.

A single tear threaded its way down her cheek.

She had managed to keep her desperation at bay while they were on the river. But now in St. Louis, she was afraid—afraid that Jack had killed Roamer. Because if there was still breath in his body, wouldn't he have come to rescue them by now?

"You look different," Scout said, his nose wrinkled, his tone doubtful. "You smell different, too."

Mattie laughed. "Why, Scout Maravel, I do believe you have developed some diplomacy on this little adventure of ours."

"Dip—what?" he said, looking at Mattie with his head tilted.

"Diplomacy. That is what you just used when you said I smelled different rather than saying that I no longer stink like fish and sweat and brackish water. You are growing up. Now tell me the truth. Do I look truly awful?"

Scout looked Mattie up and down. "It isn't *awful*, but it's . . . an awful lot of flowers and everything."

"I agree," Mattie said, looking down at the garish cabbage roses that decorated the entire skirt of the frock. The fabric was fine, rouge-colored silk, and the craftsmanship was excellent—nearly as good a hand as Lottie's had sewn this gown. The tucked seaming down the front was elegant and even and molded Mattie almost as much as the daring corset beneath. It was a pretty dress; there were simply too many embellishments on it. Mattie examined the roses and found they were not sewn by the same hand. They looked as if they had been added hastily at a later time.

"Come here, Scout, and help me," Mattie said as

she broke the threads holding a rose. "Let's take all these off and see what we've got."

Scout obliged by going to his knees and dutifully plucking flowers from the skirt. Within moments there was a cloth bouquet on the bare plank floor.

"Now what do you think?" Mattie asked, turning in a circle.

"The bottom looks fine, but the top is still funny," Scout said.

Mattie looked down at her bodice. Three rows of ruched material followed the contour of the scooped neckline. It made her bosom look inches larger than it really was, and her waist even smaller than it was nipped in by the corset.

"Perhaps if it is not sewn too tightly . . ." She grasped one end of the fabric and tugged. To her relief, the ruching fell away, revealing a smooth, clean view of the excellent silk with the fine princess seaming that ran all the way to the waist.

"Now you look just fine," Scout said, tipping back on his haunches. "You look pretty enough to be getting married, Miss Mattie."

His words made Mattie flush. She had lied for such a long time that the lie had soured in her mouth. Little Scout had had the courage to tell her of his theft of Roamer's letters of proposal. Did *she* have the courage to tell him the truth?

"Scout, there is something I think you should know. It is about my husband—"

The sound of heavy boots on the stairs preceded a knock on the door. "Get ready in there." It was Laughing Jack. "I am taking the boy for a while."

The key clicked in the lock. Mattie held her

breath—and Scout—as the door rattled. But the chair beneath the handle held.

"He isn't going anywhere with you."

"Don't be silly, I am only taking him to the barber."

"No, I won't open it."

"I am going to give you three seconds, Mattie. And if this door isn't open I am to get an ax and chop my way in."

"You better do it, Miss Mattie," Scout said solemnly.

"But, Scout—"

"Do it."

Slowly she released her hold on the boy's shoulders. She slid the chair away. Immediately the door crashed inward, hitting the wall with a bounce.

"You shouldn't have done that, Mattie." Jack slapped her hard across the face. She sprawled on the floor. "Now don't try anything like that again or you will find out just how unpleasant I can be."

"I have not eaten so well in a long time," Roamer told Judge Mills, scooting his chair back to give his belly a bit of room. The older man sat at the far end of a table that was big enough to dance upon. He raised his crystal glass of liqueur.

"Shall we share a toast, Roamer?"

"I have little to be toasting about, sir. The last week or so has been hell, and I still ain't sure that Scout and Mattie are safe."

"Ah, then let us toast to our future success in finding out." Judge Mills smiled. "Take heart, Roamer. You did the right thing by coming to me. I have put men out throughout the city. I am owed any number of favors by people of every ilk. I suspect that by morning we shall have news of the child and your lady friend."

Reluctantly Roamer lifted his glass and sipped. "Thank you, Judge."

"No, thank you for being brave enough to put your trust in me. What you have done is no small thing, sir. It would have been easy to believe the worst of me and of humanity after all you have been through."

Roamer barely tasted the liquor or heard the judge's words as the expensive drink slid down his throat. "I just want Scout and Mattie safe. Once I get them, I am never letting them go—either of them—no matter what the cost to me or anybody else."

"Then to your future, Roamer. May you have what you desire most, and may I see Jackson Maravel brought to his greedy knees."

When Roamer climbed the stairs to the third floor, he found that one of Judge Mills's silent servants had come before him to turn back the bedcovers and open a window for air and ventilation.

He stood just inside the door and surveyed his room. There was a huge wardrobe, a washstand and side table with a chamber pot on the shelf.

He could want for nothing. And yet he was restless, loath to put his head on the soft pillow when he did not know if Mattie and Scout were all right.

Were they cold? Hungry? In pain?

Questions swirled through his mind while he slowly tugged off his dusty boots. He walked to the window, lifted the sheer gossamer aside, and looked down on a tree-lined boulevard. The scent of lilac and honeysuckle from the walled garden below perfumed the evening air, but Roamer found no joy in the tranquil scene.

Day and night, all he thought about was Mattie and Scout. His longtime guilt over killing a man had been replaced by bone-grinding worry.

And suddenly, as he stared out into the twilight, it hit him. He didn't care about the long-ago death of Harry Malone. Just as the judge said, it was not intentional—it had happened because of Susan's death.

It was old news.

A strange lifting of tension seemed to envelop Roamer. Suddenly, after so many years of carrying the burden of guilt and regret, he felt *free.*

"And I am ready to do whatever is needed to get Scout and Mattie away from Jack."

He flexed his hands and looked at them.

"Even if it means using these."

Though he was sure he would not, sleep found Roamer almost immediately.

Memories of the past melded with events from the present.

He saw himself throwing the fatal blow, the blood coming from the man's ears. But the dead man changed and became Ian McTavish. He laughed and told Roamer he had to marry or leave town. Then, in Roamer's tortured nightmare a fire sprang up, and in the center of the conflagration were Mattie and Scout crying out for Roamer to save them. He woke shaking and drenched in a cold, clammy sweat.

Dear Lord, where are they? Please, if you have any mercy, let me at least know they are safe . . . please. Roamer lay there until the pink rays of morn found their way between the window curtains. If they didn't get word soon, he was going to go looking for Jack himself.

"Roamer? Are you up?" Judge Mills's knock brought Roamer to his feet. He tugged on his trousers and went barefoot to the door.

"Ah, I am glad I found you before you were dressed. Albert has a few things I thought you might have need of." The Judge spoke over his shoulder. "Put them in the wardrobe, Albert."

Roamer started to protest, but his words died in the back of his throat when the butler scooted past him with boxes, bundles, and a look that invited no comment.

"I have good news, Roamer—exceptionally good news. I have received a message from one of my many contacts. The boy has been seen."

"Where?" Roamer asked as he snatched up his boots. He had tugged one on and was hopping to the door before the judge blocked his way.

"No, no. Wait a minute." Judge Mills held up his hand. "If you go blundering out there now, you could ruin everything. We must contrive a plan, Roamer."

"Judge, I don't care—"

"Do you care about keeping them safe?"

His words froze Roamer. "Of course I do. I wouldn't do anything to put them in more danger."

"Then trust me, Roamer. For now, it appcars they arc bcing carcd for and arc quitc comfortablc. Jackson had the boy at a barber, getting his hair trimmed. He and the child were followed. I have it on good authority that they are being fed, clothed, and given every comfort."

"For now?"

"Well, we both know Jackson is an unpredictable

sort, but I have a spy in place. A *spy*—I kind of like the sound of that word." The judge chuckled, seeming to lose himself in thought. Then suddenly he sobered and came back to himself. "Please dress, shave, and join me for breakfast. We must put our heads together. I have a vague notion, but we need a bit more help. It is important that you agree, Roamer, because the ultimate outcome may depend upon how good you are at playacting."

Eighteen

Roamer left off the fancy neckwear that came with the rig the judge had sent to his room. He shoved his arms into the coat, amazed that they did not bind and that the coat lay smooth across the width of his shoulders. He had never dressed in a suit that fit his bulky shoulders and thick thighs so well. The pants were of fine gabardine, and the shirt was not simple homespun but of the softest cotton, with fine cuffs and a pin-tucked placket down the front, held closed with mother-of-pearl buttons that shimmered.

"Excellent fit, if I may say, sir," Albert said, brushing his hands across the shoulders, smoothing the cloth to complete perfection.

"How—?" Roamer was amazed by the clothes. They clung as if made to order, and he had never owned a made-to-order suit of clothes in his life.

"The judge has a way of sizing up a man," Albert said softly. "He asked his tailor to do this up special in double time for you."

"I don't like owing any man. A suit of clothes like this did not come cheap," Roamer frowned.

"You are almost as prideful as the judge himself," Albert said with a lift of his white brows. "He said you'd not be happy about them and would likely kick up a fuss about the cost."

"Oh, he did, did he?" Roamer asked.

Albert's face remained impassive. "Yes, sir, he did. The judge said to tell you this makes things nearer to equal. He likes for things to be equitable. That is a word he uses often: equitable. He says what happened to you and your sister was not in the least equitable, and he intends to see accounts settled up proper." Albert looked Roamer straight in the eye.

"I hope you will allow him to do these things, sir. He is not a young man. I would like to think he can go to glory with a clear mind and heart."

Roamer looked at his reflection in the oval shaving mirror that sat on the stacked chest of drawers. It went against his grain to be given anything.

He glanced at Albert. He was not a young man either; the weight of worry was etched into his dark face. Roamer couldn't help grin at the man.

"For now, Albert. I will accept his hospitality and generosity for now."

"I can't ask any more of you than that, sir. And thank you. 'Sides, the judge has a plan. And he told me, sir, that part of his plan is making you look like a man who has come into wealth and property, and you surely do look like that, sir, you surely do."

A few moments later Roamer entered the sun-flooded dining room to find the judge smiling at him from the end of that huge table. Once again it was laid out as if half a dozen men were going to be sitting down to eat instead of just two.

"Ah, Roamer, I see my tailor worked magic with my feeble estimation of your size." The judge shook a white linen napkin.

"Thank you, Judge, but I intend to pay you for the

suit," Roamer said. He did not miss Albert's annoyed glance.

"Nonsense. We have more important things to discuss and worry about. And you must look your part if we are to catch Jackson in our trap."

Before Roamer could ask for details, the judge nodded and a flurry of activity ensued around the table. Silent girls in starched white aprons went about pulling silver lids away to reveal eggs, bacon, fat sausages, and griddle cakes.

"Eat, and we will work on our plan. I have had another report. The boy and your friend are fine, even if their lodgings are a bit colorful. Jack is busy getting them fed and clothed—for their appearance here, I would suspect." The judge chuckled. "But we will be ready for him. Yes, we will."

"About this plan of yours—" Roamer began, but the sound of the heavy knocker on the front door froze the words in the back of his throat. He half rose, his gaze going to the entryway. "Is it him?"

"No, no; relax, Roamer. I should've told you that I will get word before Jack makes his appearance. Sit down, Roamer, and relax. Enjoy your meal."

Roamer did sit, but he was not relaxed. In fact, the calmer the Judge became the more agitated Roamer felt. How could he be so unruffled?

Within moments the old servant Albert returned. He stood stiffly and said, "Sir, there are visitors for Mr. Roamer."

"But nobody knows I'm here . . . unless Jack has found out."

"No, Jackson does not know you are here, but evidently somebody does," the judge said looking at Roamer. "Shall we find out who? Show them in, Albert."

Roamer frowned, his palms flat on his thighs. Who could it be if not Jack? Not even Ian knew that Roamer was here.

A round-faced man and a small boy walked into the dining room. At the sight of the food-laden table, both of them snatched off their hats. The child had pale, flaxen hair and was of an age with Scout. Just seeing him made Roamer's heart contract painfully.

"Oh, forgive us; we didn't mean to interrupt your meal. We can return later at a better time." The man turned, but the judge stood up.

"Nonsense. We have enough for everyone. Nothing aids my digestion nearly as much as good conversation over breakfast."

The man hesitated, his gaze flicking from Roamer to the judge to the table. "If you are sure."

"Of course." The judge sat back down and motioned for them to do the same. The boy ended up sitting on Roamer's right, near enough to touch. "Albert, bring cups and plates. Now introduce yourself."

"Thank you, thank you," the man began. "I am John Gathings. This is my grandson, Noah."

"Welcome. I'm Judge Mills. This my guest, Roamer Tresh."

"Ah, so you are the man we came to see. You brought the letter from—" John's voice cracked and broke. He could not go on.

Roamer nodded. Now he understood. These were some of the relatives of Clarence Wilson. "I am sorry about your loss. We were all saddened by what happened to your kin."

The man's head lowered as the weight of his pain bore down on him. For a moment he sat, silent and nearly broken, then looked up.

"It means a lot—to know they had somebody see to

them proper for the burying and all. And we thank you for bringing the letter. Just knowing eases my missus's mind."

"It was little enough to do," Roamer said awkwardly. He was unaccustomed to so much *thanking*. He started the morning needing to thank the judge, and now before he even had a proper cup of coffee, a stranger was thanking *him*. It was uncomfortable for a man who spent most of his time with horses or at the forge.

"If there is anything we can do. *Anything*. I am not a rich man but I do all right. I don't know what your circumstances are, but money is not all I am offering. Any service I or my kin can do you, just ask."

Roamer lifted his hand in protest, but for some strange reason he set it lightly on the boy's head and ruffled his hair. His thoughts were on Scout.

"I want nothing from you, Mr. Gathings."

Judge Mills cleared his throat. "Don't be so hasty, Roamer. I insist you all eat first. My cook is a temperamental woman, and if this food goes to waste there is no telling the agonies I will have to endure. Then, afterward I have a favor to ask in Roamer's stead, and I hope you will agree, Mr. Gathings. It is a matter of some importance."

They sat and ate in silence. Now and again Roamer saw Judge Mills watching the child with quiet speculation in his canny eyes, and he wondered what scheme the judge had arranged. At every sound and movement, Roamer found himself looking at the entryway, half expecting Jack to arrive.

But he didn't. The meal went on uninterrupted while the worry and strain inside Roamer drew tighter and tighter until he was almost ready to explode.

It was a heavy weight on his heart to sit here and eat with a child so near to Scout's age and coloring. Finally

Roamer could stand no more. He stood up, tossing his napkin on the plate of untouched food.

"Judge, I can't wait any longer. I must go find Scout," Roamer suddenly blurted out.

"I wondered how long you would be able to hold yourself in. But Roamer, before you go running off half-cocked, please hear me out. I do have a plan, and if Mr. Gathings meant what he said about doing anything for you, then I know it will work. I was planning on hiring someone from the stage, but if this fine young gentleman can do a fair bit of playacting, then we have all we need right here to put an end to Jackson's foolishness."

Roamer frowned at the judge. "Just what have you got in mind?"

"Sit down and I will tell you; I will tell you all. It is nothing illegal in the strictest sense of the word, and it will finally settle accounts."

They all went into the study and seated themselves while the judge went to his big chair behind his desk.

"I have given this problem a lot of thought, Roamer. As much as it galls me, Jackson Maravel has a legal claim to his son."

"In a pig's eye! Then I will see him dead and buried. That should settle his legal claim once and for all." Roamer was half out of his chair before the judge calmly raised a hand.

"Now, now, I didn't say he was going to get the child, but only that by strictly legal definition he has a rightful claim—not a moral claim but a legal claim. There is a difference, Roamer."

"So what are you saying? I will not see that boy go to a blackhearted bastard like Laughing Jack."

Mr. Gathings looked both curious and confused.

"Should we leave? I feel as if we are interrupting private business—"

"No. I need your help, Mr. Gathings—your help and the help of your fine young grandson there."

"To do what?" he asked softly. "I don't hold with violence and chicanery."

"Nor do I, and you have my word that in this case justice is going to be served. Did you know, Mr. Gathings, that the guide who left your family has traveled in the company of the man we speak of?" Judge Mills looked sincere and serene.

"No, I did not. But as you well know, that changes everything in my mind. My family and I will be pleased to help you."

The judge smiled. "I thought as much."

"Speak plain, Judge. Tell us all what you are planning," Roamer said impatiently.

"The way I see it, your problem lies in finding a way to get Jack to give up the boy. The only way he will do that is if the boy has no monetary value."

"But you said that Scout is the rightful heir to the Maravel fortune."

"Ah, yes, Scout . . . Scout Maravel. *Judson Walker* Maravel is the rightful heir."

"But they are one and the same," Roamer said, rubbing a spot at his temple that had begun to throb.

"But how do we know that? How do *I* know that? How does anyone here in St. Louis know for a fact that the child presently being held in a certain waterfront bordello is really Judson Walker Maravel?" the judge said with a sly smile. "In fact, does anybody but you and your lady friend know for certain who that child really is?"

"I am finally seeing the way your mind works, Judge," Roamer said, shaking his head in amazement.

"Yes?" Judge Mills grinned.

"All I can say is that I am glad you are not my enemy."

Mattie stared out the window at the street below. The same scruffy man she had seen all day was still loitering on the corner. Now the sun was beginning to set behind tall trees and buildings. She could see the glow of his cheroot grow brighter.

There was another man, even more disreputable-looking, down on the next corner. They had been there, watching in turns the window where she now stood, as they had since the day Pierre had given her the dress.

Since Jack had returned with Scout, she and the boy had been mercifully left alone. She had no mirror, but the way Scout looked at her cheek told her that there must be a hideous bruise.

She lightly touched her fingers to her cheek and winced at the pain. Jack Maravel was a monster. She had to find a way to get Scout away from him.

A knock on the door brought Mattie around. It was too early for dinner. She walked to the center of the room, where she and Scout listened to the lock being opened. Since Jack's outburst she had stopped putting the chair in front of the door. She expected Pierre, but her heart dropped.

"Ah, this is a pretty picture. The dutiful schoolmarm and her student." Jackson Maravel smiled. He had transformed himself, at least on the outside. Now he was dressed in a fine white shirt, an elegant dove gray vest, and a fine black frock coat. His boots were so new, Mattie could see the candlelight reflected in them. His hair had been trimmed and he sported a neatly clipped mustache.

"Well, you cleaned up rather well, boy," he said, stepping into the room, locking the door, and dropping the key into his watch pocket. "Don't you think so, dear Mattie? Don't you think the boy looks rather nice in that suit of clothes?"

"It itches," Scout said sullenly, running his finger around the inside of his collar.

"Then you will be happy to hear that you won't have to endure them for much longer." Jack smiled widely.

"What are you planning?" Mattie shoved Scout behind her and lifted her chin. "I will not let you hurt him."

"Ah, these feminine histrionics are so tedious. I am not going to hurt him. Quite the contrary, my dear Mattie. Tomorrow we will be taking a short journey."

"Where are we going?" she asked, her mind a whir. If she could escape . . .

"No, no, dear. *We*, as in the boy and I. You are not going anywhere—just yet. Tomorrow it will be the pair of us, the boy and myself. We are paying a little visit to an old friend. Tomorrow we are going to see my grandmother's solicitor."

"And then? What do you plan to do with him?" Mattie's voice had risen in panic.

"I haven't quite decided. In fact"—Jack stepped closer and used his index finger to lift Mattie's chin, turning her face this way and that, examining the mark—"his fate and yours may depend entirely on how nice you are to me, Mattie. Think about it. Tomorrow when I return, things will be different. I will no longer need the boy in such good condition, if you get my meaning." He dipped his head and tried to kiss her.

Mattie twisted her head away. "You are an animal."

"There is an old saw, Mattie. Something about talking sweetly in case one has to eat one's words." Jack's eyes were hard, glittering with malice. "You would do well to remember that, Mattie."

"Roamer, come and have a drink." Judge Mills strode through the library and poured the liquor himself—something he usually let Albert do.

"Why? What has happened?" Roamer clenched and unclenched his hands at his thighs.

"Here, drink this. It will steady your nerves." Judge Mills thrust a cut-glass jigger into Roamer's hands. He tossed his own drink back and set the empty glass down with a clink.

"Ready yourself, Roamer. Noah is coming tonight. He will sleep here and practice what he needs to do."

"Do you mean—?"

"Yes, Laughing Jack Maravel is about to play his hand. He has sent word that tomorrow morning he wishes to have a conversation with me—a legal conversation," Judge Mills said with a grin. "I suspect he is feeling very good tonight, probably indulging himself in all his vices. But Jackson doesn't believe other men know how to play cards and bluff as well as he does. Now he will learn what it feels like when the deck has been stacked and all the cards shaved."

Nineteen

The long afternoon had been endless. Roamer had prowled his room until he nearly wore the nap off the beautiful Aubusson rug. He finally had come outside to the garden, listening to the crickets, katydids, and frogs. And beyond the walled-in garden were the sounds of the bustling city on the river.

Soon, Mattie, soon you and Scout will be safe. I promise you that.

He wasn't allowing himself to think much further, but during his long search and the time he had been with Judge Mills, he had come to a decision.

He didn't care about Mattie's erstwhile husband, or her marriage vows, or Ian McTavish's town. Once he had Scout and Mattie with him again, he was keeping them, if they had to go to the mountains beyond the north territories to do it.

I love her and I am going to be with her—forever, he vowed to himself. Roamer sat with his palms on his knees, feeling the heat and dampness of his own sweat through the gabardine trousers.

His mind was a flurry of fury, doubts, and fear.

What if this did not work? What if Jack wasn't as predictable as Judge Mills thought he was?

Anything could go wrong.

Roamer wanted to get his hands on Jack and take care of him in a direct, expedient fashion.

"Steady, Roamer. It won't be long now." Judge Mills sat behind his desk, looking calm, stern, and completely confident. When the heavy door knocker echoed through the house, Roamer clenched his fingers into his own flesh. He had a moment of panic.

He had been a fool to let the judge concoct this crazy scheme. He should just get Jack and beat him within an inch of his life. Then he would see what was worth more to the bastard, money or his life.

"Sir, the young gentleman has arrived," Albert said.

"Well, bring him in, bring him in." Judge Mills grinned widely.

Roamer turned to see Noah Gathings, dressed in his Sunday best. The boy looked as calm and assured as the judge.

"Are you ready?"

"Yes sir," Noah said, seating himself in a chair to the right of Roamer.

"You know your part?"

"Yes sir. I've been practicing like you told me."

"Fine, just fine. Now we will have a fine dinner and wait for the fly to wander into our trap, eh?" Judge Mills chuckled, and a spot of color came into his papery cheeks. "I expect we will have visitors quite early in the morning."

Roamer could barely swallow his coffee. There was a lump in his throat composed of cold fury and searing impatience.

"Are you going to be able to do this, Roamer?"

Judge Mills looked worried for the first time. "If you bolt up, grab him, and beat him senseless . . ." Judge Mills lifted his hands in a gesture of helplessness. "Well, everything will be lost. And speaking to you as a man of the law, you will have handed Jackson the fortune and condemned Susan's child to a life in his hands."

"I would never let Scout be hurt."

"If you can't control your rage, I can predict that Jackson will swear out charges. You will be arrested. Your past record will be brought up. There will be nothing to stand between Scout and Jackson."

"I won't let that happen," Roamer said between clenched teeth.

"Then wipe that frown off your face. Look happy, content, and smug. Everything—*everything* depends on bluffing our way through this."

Roamer nodded stiffly. He could do it. He *had* to do it, for Scout and Mattie.

They didn't have to wait long. Within the quarter hour, the knocker sounded against the thick wooden door. As Albert went to the door, Judge Mills winked at Noah.

"Remember," he whispered, tapping his index finger at the side of his nose. "I am depending upon you, lad."

Roamer went into the library and took a seat near the door. Noah sat across the room, nearer Judge Mills's desk. The judge was behind the desk and everyone was ready to play his part.

When Jack and Scout walked in, Roamer felt his heart give a little kick before it dropped to his feet. Laughing Jack looked slick as a snake-oil salesman.

Scout looked taller—thinner—sad and defiant in a way that hurt Roamer deeply.

"Judge, we have some business to discuss," Jack said with a stiff smile.

"I'll just bet you do," Roamer said, taking pleasure at Jack's surprise when he spun around and saw Roamer sitting in the same room. The color leached from his face. Scout grinned and started to take a step toward Roamer, but Jack's hand came down hard on his shoulder, his fingers biting into flesh.

"Stay right where you are. Remember what I said about your friend," Jack said softly. Immediately Scout stilled. It cut Roamer to the quick to see how Jackson controlled the situation.

"I thought—" Jack began.

"What? That I was dead? That your aim was better?" Roamer growled. "It was little more than a scratch, but I remember it, Jack, and intend to repay you in kind."

"Not while I have Susan's brat, you won't," Jack laughed. "In fact, I believe I am holding all the cards."

A wash of red flooded Roamer's vision, but he remembered the judge's warning. Roamer wanted to bolt from his chair in the shadows by the heavy velvet curtains. But he saw Judge Mills's warning glance and managed to restrain himself, trying to appear unconcerned. He wanted to kill Jack Maravel, and just maybe he would; but right now he had a part to play.

It took every ounce of control he could muster, but Roamer smiled and said, "Oh, I hardly think so, Jack. In fact, I think you have played your top card—and it isn't enough."

"What brings you here, Jackson?" Judge Mills asked impatiently.

"I am here to get a few details straightened out." Jack frowned, as if trying to re-gather his concentration. His bravado had slipped a bit and Roamer saw it.

"What details? We concluded our business at your grandmother's grave, as far as I know." The judge leaned back and cast a lazy gaze Jack's way.

"This is Susan's child." He shoved Scout forward, talking fast as if in a hurry to get things done. "I am his legal guardian. I want the power of attorney put in my name; I want the use of the house and all the property." Jack was smiling widely now. "And I want the cash and jewels—all of them. Now."

Judge Mills sat staring at Jack for a few minutes. Then he leaned forward and speared Jack with a glare. "What kind of a confidence game are you trying to pull, Jackson?"

"No game, Judge." Jack smiled again. "Legally I will have control of everything."

"You come in here out of the blue, trying to foist this boy off as being Susan's child? What kind of a fool do you take me for?"

"It is the truth."

"That is the most pitiful thing I have ever heard, Jackson. I knew you were a desperate man, but this takes the cake."

"What are you talking about?" Jack's lip pulled back in an ugly sneer. "This is Susan's child. This is Judson Walker Maravel." Jack jerked Scout forward again. "Look at him."

Roamer was about to lose what little control he had

left, but Noah quickly stood up and walked toward Jack, putting himself between Roamer and Jack.

Noah tilted his chin. "I am sorry, sir, but that is not possible. Because I am Judson Walker Maravel. This is my Uncle Roamer. We have come to visit the judge and claim my inheritance."

The look on Jack's face was worth nearly every moment of worry that Roamer had endured. He saw horror, disbelief, and finally anger.

"No. Oh, no. You are not going to screw me out of my inheritance. Not this time." Jack shoved Noah from his path. "*This* is Judson Walker Maravel. Go ahead, boy, tell him your name."

Scout pulled himself up and looked Judge Mills straight in the eye. Then, in a clear, loud voice he said. "Hello, sir. My name is Scout. I am pleased to make your acquaintance." Scout thrust his hand out at the judge.

"Pleased to make your acquaintance, Scout. May I introduce a couple of old friends? This is Roamer Tresh and his nephew, Judson Walker Maravel."

Scout barely flinched. He turned, and with courage that brought a hot, dry lump to Roamer's throat he said:

"Pleased to meet you—both."

Jack roared. The cry was like a wild animal caught in a snare. "You bastard, Tresh. I thought you cared about Susan's brat, but all this time—you—were—waiting—for the *money!*" The sound echoed off the walls and reverberated through the library. Albert and the other servants came running, but Judge Mills waved them away.

"Now, now, don't take on like that, Jack. You tried, but it isn't going to work. I know that Roamer left here with Susan's child as an infant. He has raised the boy, all alone, since no other family wanted to involve themselves. Surely he would know his own nephew," Judge Mills said reasonably. "You have made a mistake, Jackson. It is understandable. After all, neither you nor anybody else in St. Louis has seen the child since he was an infant."

"No. It is a trick. That is not his nephew. This, this boy is Susan's child." The veins on Jack's neck were bulging and his eyes were wide. "His name is Judson Walker Maravel. I know it. He was living in a little dirt-water town—I took him."

"Really, Jackson, you are being foolish to admit such things to me, after all, I am still a friend of the court. What possible reason would Roamer have to deny his own nephew?"

"For the money!"

"That is silly. There is no money."

"What do you mean, there is no money?" Jack was nearly purple in the face. Spittle collected at the corners of his mouth.

"Young Judson has signed all his money away."

"What?" Jack made a strangled sound of rage. "Signed it all away?"

"Why, yes. I witnessed the document myself."

"Who? Who did he give it to?"

"Why he gave it all to charity. A private charity, I believe, to be administered by a Mrs. Samuel Smith." Judge Mills said quietly, letting his gaze shift to Roamer. This was not something they had agreed upon. Roamer narrowed his eyes. The judge had gone too far this time. He had put Mattie in more danger.

"So if you know where that lady is, I suggest you

keep her very safe indeed, because *she* has the power of attorney now."

Before the judge could even finish Jack had shoved Scout aside and bolted from the room. He knocked Albert and the other servants aside and ran from the house. His carriage had gone, but he didn't even pause to hail another. He started running, his feet slapping the cobbles in double-quick time.

Scout ran to Roamer. He wrapped his arms around Roamer's knees. "I knew you would come. Mattie said you would come."

"Scout, are you all right? Let me look at you." Roamer rubbed his hands over Scout's shoulders, his face, as if to reassure himself he was real—substantial and *here*.

"We did it, boys. We got Jackson to leave Scout of his own will. He won't be making demands on the boy or you anymore, Roamer."

"No, not me, but you have put Mattie squarely in Jack's crosshairs." Roamer stood up and glared at the older man. "Judge, if any harm comes to her because of this stunt, I will—"

"Instead of wasting time threatening me, I suggest you get out of here. I have taken steps to ensure her safety, but who knows whether my efforts will be enough? It is time to rescue your lady friend, Roamer. And I suggest you take my carriage to this address before Jack beats you there."

Twenty

Roamer wanted to climb up onto the seat and take the reins from Judge Mills's driver, to urge the horses to greater speed. It wasn't enough that the carriage had taken several turns on two wheels. He wanted more speed; he had to reach Mattie before Jackson did.

Of course he knew he was being stupid. Roamer didn't even know where the address on the slip of paper Judge Mills had shoved into his fist was. If not for the driver, Roamer could have been wandering aimlessly instead of closing the distance to Mattie.

Mattie. Dear, sweet Mattie. He was going to get down on his knees and beg her to abandon her husband and her marriage. He was ready to beg, to promise her a life of love and happiness.

Anything to have her with him and Scout. Roamer had managed to keep his feelings for her at bay while he worried about her and Scout. But now he was assaulted by his emotions.

He loved her. He wanted her, and if he had to move heaven and earth, he was going to have her.

Now Roamer simply wanted to find her, take her and Scout with him, and build a life. If it meant leaving McTavish Plain, then he was prepared to do that.

If it meant living in sin because Mattie was unable or unwilling to divorce her husband, then he was prepared to do that, too.

"Damn her husband!" Roamer said aloud. He had long since given up trying to decide if she had a happy marriage or if she was living like Susan had. "And damn Jack Maravel. If he gets in my way, he is a dead man."

The carriage left the smoother, tended cobbles of the more fashionable part of town. The ride was bumpy as the horses thundered through a run-down area of waterfront. The scent of too many people living on top of each other, and the decay of poverty, filled Roamer's nostrils. This was rough St. Louis—*dangerous* St. Louis. The scent of rotting wood and the stench of raw sewage were strong here.

Roamer thought of Mattie's neat little house in McTavish Plain. He thought of the passion they had shared, and of how he longed to care for her.

The carriage lurched to a halt so abruptly that Roamer slid across the gap until his knees touched the facing seat. He yanked open the door and bounded outside to find himself in front of a gambling hall. "Frenchy's" was painted on the window in uneven black letters. A crowd had gathered at the door, or what was left of the door. It seemed to be splintered and hanging by one hinge.

Seeing that group of people, hearing their astonished voices, made Roamer's gut clench.

"What's happened here?"

"A woman—somebody was wanting a woman, though why they thought they needed to take one by force is a mystery. Horrible sight it was, too, her kicking and screaming," one toothless woman said, crossing herself.

Roamer shoved his way through the throng to find most of them gaping at a little man with a heavily waxed mustache. A trickle of blood was coming from his nose. His head was resting in the lap of a woman with painted lips and cheeks.

"Mattie Smith—where is she?"

"Poor Pierre. Can't you see he's bad hurt? Leave him alone," the woman said.

The man blinked and looked toward the stairs while she dabbed at the blood and made cooing noises of comfort. "Oui, I am wounded. I tried to stop them, but—"

Roamer took the stairs two at time. He felt the air compressed from his lungs when he reached the landing and saw another door wrenched off its hinges.

"She put up a fight," one soiled dove said.

Roamer walked much slower now, needing to see but not wishing to see what might be there.

The room was empty. In one corner a pile of tattered and ruined calico caught his eye.

"Mattie's dress."

Roamer was stunned—too shocked to move for three full beats of his heart. And then a rage such as he had never known overtook him. He turned, wanting nothing more than to get Jack Maravel and tear him apart.

"Ha, we are both too late. The little strumpet has left us high and dry it would appear."

For a moment Roamer didn't know if the voice was real or a product of his imagination. It was Jack's voice—but what did he mean, *too late?*

Roamer turned. Jack was there, that same odd expression of horrified disbelief on his face as he lounged against the ruined door.

"What have you done with her?" Roamer growled, his hands itching to wrap themselves around Jack's throat.

"Not a damned thing. I guess someone else must've learned that she is the new heiress to the Maravel fortune. Good news travels fast. And being a woman, it didn't take her long to find somebody to share it with." Jack had a wild look in his eye. "What do you say we team up, Roamer, you and I. We could find her, get the money. You could live like a king."

Roamer hit him. It was a simple thing, his body moving of its own accord. He didn't have to think or plan. He simply let his hand ball into a fist and his shoulder drive that fist forward into Jackson's face.

It felt good—that initial gush of warm blood flowing over his hand. It felt right—just.

"You should've shot straighter, Jack. You should have put a bullet in my brain—made sure I was dead before you ran off like the yellow-bellied coward you are."

Once again he hit him, not too hard, just a little jackrabbit punch, quick and light on his jaw.

Jack staggered backward, nearly tipping over the railing at the landing; but Roamer didn't want him going over and getting hurt by the fall, so he caught him by the front of his shirt. . . .

And hit him again.

Blood spurted from Jack's nose. It wouldn't be so pretty now. In fact, to Roamer, Jack's slender nose now looked rather flat and wide, smashed into his cheeks as it was.

"Where is she?" Roamer asked again.

"I dunno! I mean it," Jack gurgled, blood filling his mouth as he spoke. "If I had her I wouldn't have waited around for you to come."

Roamer gathered him up by the front of his shirt. He half dragged him down the stairs. The crowd, now alert to more excitement of the bloody dangerous variety, had deserted Pierre and was watching Roamer with an expression of terrified glee. They parted as neatly as the Red Sea before Moses when Roamer hauled Jack through to the street outside.

In the street outside the dingy gambling parlor another crowd had gathered. Some of them were whispering, others were making bets—perhaps on whether Jack would live to see another day.

Roamer no longer cared. Mattie was gone. The pile of her torn clothing proved she wasn't coming back.

His heart tore in half. Pain, rage, and despair filled him. He loathed Jack for what he had done, but he also hated himself for being too much a coward to have thrown convention to the wind. He should have stood up to Ian and the town. He should have proclaimed his love for Mattie when he had the chance.

He shoved Jack down into the dirty street and kicked him in the ribs. The pain filled grunt was music to his ears. He watched Jack crawling in the gutter and wanted to make him suffer.

"Once I killed a man. I didn't want to. Not like I want to kill you, Jack."

"Please, Roamer, don't," Jack pleaded.

"He didn't have time to beg, you know. I hit him,

and though I didn't want it, he was dead as a mackerel."

"Roamer, I didn't mean it," Jack whimpered, and he crawled a few feet. Roamer took one stride and closed the distance.

"I hate you, Jack, but I will give you a chance. Tell me what you did to her and where you left Mattie, and I might not kill you."

"I don't know," Jack coughed, blood flecking his lips. "I swear it, Roamer. Two men were taking her away when I got here."

"Now why would two total strangers take her, Jack?" Roamer's voice was low, deadly. "Why would they take her, and where?"

"I don't know!" Jack looked around wildly. "Somebody help me. He's a madman!"

"Yes, I am mad, Jack. Mad with grief and disgust. I never meant to kill that other man, but I do mean to kill you."

Roamer bent and dragged Jack to his feet by the fabric of his coat. He no longer looked like a fashionable gentleman of St. Louis. He looked like the bullying coward that he was, groveling, whimpering. At last he was revealing his withered soul to the world.

"Please. For the love of heaven—"

"Heaven? You dare utter *heaven?* When my sister asked for mercy did you give it?"

"Susan?" Jack blinked, as if trying to remember his long-dead wife. "Well, I—"

"No. You gave her no mercy. Nor to Scout nor Mattie. All you wanted was what *you* wanted." Roamer slapped him, using his open hand. Blood and saliva sprayed from Jack's mouth.

"No," Jack whimpered.

"Did you hit her like this?" He slapped him open-handed again. And again, finally using the back of his hand. "Is that how you cuffed Scout?"

"I—"

"Don't bother to lie, Jack. I know you for the cur you are. And now, in front of God and these witnesses, I am going to put you out of your misery."

"Mr. Tresh!"

Roamer heard his named called, but he was intent upon Jack. There was a clamoring behind him. Hushed whispers and gasps of surprise filled the rotten air.

"Roamer, no, don't do it. He isn't worth it." Fingers grabbed at his clothes, his wrist. "Roamer, listen to me."

A voice like the trickle of a waterfall reached his ears. He was imagining things now—too far gone in his grief and sorrow to grasp harsh reality. He was hearing Mattie.

"No, Mattie is dead . . . Mattie is gone."

"No, I am here, Roamer." The voice penetrated his rage. "Roamer, look at me. I am here."

A hand touched his shoulder. He spun around. Two men stood there, one on either side of Mattie.

Mattie—sweet Mattie. With her hair loose around her shoulders, and in a dress that shimmered in the sun like the shiny scales of a fish. She looked prettier than he ever remembered—except for the livid bruise on her cheek.

"Roamer, it's me," she said softly, reaching out and placing her palm on the curve of his jaw. "He told me you were dead, but I knew you couldn't be dead. I would have felt it in my heart if you had been dead."

Roamer blinked. She didn't disappear. "Oh, Mattie!"

He yanked her to him, crushing her against him so hard that he could feel the stays of her corset. She was warm and alive.

He kissed her neck, buried his face in her hair. Tears, hot, salty, and painful, came from deep inside him.

"I nearly lost you, Mattie. I won't ever let you go again."

"Oh, Roamer . . ."

"No, let me say what I should've said long ago. I love you, Mattie Smith. I care not that some other man is your husband. If he was any kind of man he would've kept you with him. You are mine now—he gave you up when he let you come to McTavish Plain alone. I will not ever let you go."

"But Roamer—"

He cut her words off with a kiss. Then he lifted his head, violence and protectiveness shining in his green eyes. "Who did this to you?"

Mattie's eyes slid to Jackson in the gutter. Roamer's rage returned.

"You bastard. You dared touch her?" He made a move toward Jack but Mattie held his arm.

"No, Roamer. Enough. You have paid him in kind. That is enough." Her words were soft and soothing. And suddenly Roamer agreed. Jackson wasn't worth killing. He did not want to start their lives with the stain of death.

"Who are these two men?"

"Friends, Roamer. Sent by your Judge Mills."

"We wanted to tell you, sir, but you went by us like a bull on the charge," the man Mattie knew as Mick said with a grin. "We was to get the lady out of the gambling parlor as soon as the bloke left with the lad. That Frenchy wasn't no problem."

"You beat up the Frenchman?" Roamer asked.

"Just a little tap, like on the nose," Mick laughed, throwing a punch at the air. "The judge, 'e's a bit of a slippery fellow, like, ain't he? And he is a right sentimental bloke too. He sent this for you." Mick held out a small box.

Roamer took it and looked inside. There was a note from the judge. A key lay at the bottom of the box.

"The boy will be fine with me for a while. Take your lady friend and go to the Ambassador Hotel. The key is to room 107. Enjoy yourself, and if you have need of anything ask the hotel staff."

"The old coot. He does have a bit of romance in his blood, it would seem." Roamer drank in the sight of Mattie. "Come along, honey, there are things that need to be said . . . in private." Roamer stared down at Jack lying in the gutter. "We've finished with this."

"Yes, Roamer. I want us to start over fresh, and before we can do that, there is something I must tell you."

Mattie bit the inside of her lip as the carriage rolled smoothly toward the hotel.

It was time to tell Roamer the truth.

"Mattie, when we leave St. Louis, I want us to leave together—you, me, and Scout."

"Roamer, there is something that you need to know—"

"I know all I need to know. I should've told Ian and the whole blasted town how I felt about you, instead of being bullied into making that damned trip to Belle Fourche. If I had been with you as I should, Jack wouldn't have got his filthy hands on you or Scout."

"Roamer, you cannot blame yourself."

"That's where you're wrong, my love, there is no other person *to* blame. But I promise you, I will make it up to you and to Scout. We will leave McTavish Plain, find a new town, where we can be together."

"But, Roamer—"

"No, I don't care about your husband. You don't love him. You are not the kind of woman who would lie with one man and love another; I have known that from the start. There will be no more shrinking from what we feel, Mattie."

He pulled her onto his lap, and though the coach was swaying he gently cupped her cheeks in his hands. "I want you, Mattie, now and forever."

His lips were firm and demanding, and they conveyed every romantic thought, dream, and verse Mattie had ever wished for. Roamer loved her. She loved him. But how would he feel when she told him she was a liar?

Mattie's arms slid around Roamer's neck. She savored the feel of the heavy, corded muscles of his shoulders. Explored the nape of his neck beneath her fingers. He was a big man with a big heart.

And he loved her.

It was the culmination of all her dreams, her hopes, and all her guilty fears. She returned his kiss, wanting this moment to go on and on. When she felt his tongue gently nudge at her lower lip, she opened her mouth. Roamer moaned softly and pulled her tighter against his broad, hard chest. And beneath her buttocks she felt the firmness of his desire.

He wanted her.

The carriage stopped so abruptly that they nearly slid from the seat to the floor. Roamer grinned like a mischievous boy.

"I am glad the hotel was no farther away or I might have had you stripped and bedded here in this carriage." He gently placed her on the opposite seat. She could not help but see the bulge in his well-tailored trousers.

Mattie felt hot and prickly all over. She wanted him—wanted him with a carnal hunger deeper than she imagined, but she could not—*would not*—lie with him again under the cloak of her lie.

"Roamer, there is something I must tell you." Mattie said forcefully, straightening her obscenely low bodice as he opened the door and taking Roamer's hand as he assisted her from the carriage.

"Fine, tell me whatever you wish—in private."

Twenty-one

The hotel was quietly elegant. The carpet beneath Mattie's slippered feet was thick, and the drapery at the tall, paladin-topped windows was lush. The liveried doorman and bell captain were crisply efficient.

This was a hotel were the wealthy stayed.

A few couples stopped and stared. Mattie knew her dress was less than fashionable—in fact, it was barely respectable. What must they think?

That a fine gentleman had brought his mistress here for an afternoon of lovemaking? That she was a courtesan who had struck a bargain with a randy gentleman?

Mattie felt her cheeks flaming. It was a wonder she was still able to blush after all that had happened—all she had done, and the lies she had told.

Roamer went to the registration desk, a beautiful wooden cage carved by a master craftsman. Within moments he was back.

"Come, Mattie, our room is waiting. I have arranged for some food and drink to be brought up. And later a hot bath."

She nodded. Her mind was not on her stomach, or even on the lust she felt for Roamer.

It was time. It was time to tell him of her lies. She

only prayed that Roamer would not hate her when she had confessed.

The room was cool and dimly lit; the drapery at the window had been drawn to give it an intimate, private feel.

It was a huge room decorated in pale green silk, with furniture polished to a high sheen. The Aubusson carpet beneath Mattie's feet was thick as shearling fleece.

"Oh, Mattie." Roamer pulled her into his arms the moment the door was shut behind them. He held her as if she were a precious treasure. "Did Jack . . . hurt you?"

"He made more threats than anything else." Mattie said softly. "He said he shot you, Roamer. He told us you were dead."

"He tried," Roamer said in a flinty voice. "Whether he is just a lousy shot, or whether I was too ornery to give up the ghost, I don't know. I do know I was not prepared to meet my maker and leave you and Scout at Laughing Jack's mercy."

"Roamer, I thought about us—about what we did." Mattie pulled away from him and walked toward the bed. She gripped the ornately carved footboard for support.

"Mattie, I don't care anymore. Married or not, you are mine. . . . You have been mine since that night."

"That's what I am trying to tell you, Roamer, I have never been anybody else's."

"You mean you never loved your husband? I understand that—reckoned as much."

"I mean I've never *had* a husband."

Roamer stilled. It was more than just not moving; his whole body seemed to freeze, from his glittering green eyes to the hands he fisted at his muscular thighs.

"I can't begin to tell you how sorry I am," Mattie said softly. "It seemed so simple—so innocent. My sisters and I wanted to be part of McTavish Plain."

He continued to stare at her with his jaw clenched tight as a bear trap. Had he even blinked?

"We made up husbands for ourselves," she rattled on, swiping at the hot tears that filled her eyes. "Oh, Roamer, you don't know what it is like to be female. There are so many opportunities available to men that are denied women."

Mattie found herself gripping the footboard of the bed. It seemed as though time had halted all around her. Nothing—not even time, or Roamer—was moving. Her heart beat heavy inside her chest as she stared at him.

"Oh, say something! Say anything. Tell me that you hate me, but please don't simply look at me as if you no longer know who I am."

Roamer swallowed hard. His fingers flexed; he blinked.

"You *do* hate me." A rusty catch made the words rip from her lips in a painful sob.

"Hate you?" Roamer repeated softly. "*Hate* you? For lying?"

"Yes! Yes! I wanted to tell you that first time, but I was afraid of what Ian would do to my sisters. And I was even more afraid you would hate me. Now I see I should've gone ahead because you hate me anyway."

"Matilda Smith—no, that is not your name. What is your *real* name?"

"Green. I am unmarried Matilda Green." She held

up her left hand, the wedding ring twinkling on her finger. "My sisters and I bought rings from a passing tinker."

"Well, *Miss* Matilda Green, do you mean that when we lay together that first time you were a virgin?" He took three steps and closed the gap between them. His hands felt warm and heavy as he grasped her shoulders.

"Yes."

"And I thought you were—*we* were—cheating on your husband, a man that didn't even exist?"

"Yes."

"And you did this because . . . ?"

"Because my sisters and I wanted the same freedoms that men have. And because we all swore we would keep each other's secrets. I wanted to tell, but I couldn't. Especially when we heard Addie is carrying Ian's child."

"You thought Ian would cast her out?"

"Yes—no. Maybe. I think he is stubborn, and if he should ever find that Addie lied, and Lottie and me . . . it was a risk I couldn't take. Not with my sisters' happiness."

"So you were prepared to let me think you were a fallen woman in order to protect the secret you and your sisters share?"

"Yes."

He stood there, looking down into her eyes. Mattie wished he would say something—do something.

"You are a silly woman." There was the barest twitch of his lips. "You know the kinds of things I have done in my life. Do you really think I am the sort of man that would judge you so harshly for lying?"

"But I *lied*—to you."

"Yes, you lied, but you didn't intend to hurt anyone. Mattie, you don't give me any credit, and that breaks my heart. I wish you had felt you could trust me, could tell me the truth."

"I did, Roamer—when I told you now."

"Didn't you know you could trust me before? When I took your virtue and held you in my arms you should've known you could trust me." His hands were still resting firmly on her shoulders. She was no closer, but neither was he pushing her away.

"In a way I did trust you, Roamer. After all, I gave you my virginity, and I took the risk that Ian or someone might find out. I was also risking my sister's happiness by letting you think I was the kind of woman who would cheat on her husband."

"What do you want from me, Mattie?" Roamer asked.

"I—I want you to forgive me and I want you to love me as much as I love you."

His stern expression softened a little. "Forgiving you is no problem, for there is really nothing to forgive. And as far as loving you . . . don't you know? For a woman who reads poetry and thinks so much about romance, you seem a little thick. Can't you sense my feelings for you?"

"Oh, Roamer," she sobbed.

"Mattie, you silly woman," He pulled her to him until her head was resting on his chest. He smelled of finely milled soap and of *himself.* "Look at me, Mattie."

"I can't; I am too ashamed of myself."

"Look at me."

She looked up and found herself drowning in his emerald eyes.

"I love you, Mattie. Finding out you don't have a husband is the best thing I ever heard. I hated him, was jealous of him, thought he abused you. To find that I am the only man who has ever touched you, ever held you and shared your bed, is a gift from God. I love you, Matilda Green."

He scooped her up and kissed her while he brought her to the bed. With infinite care he laid her there and began to unfasten her tapes and hooks. The dress was soon off, and Roamer was staring at Mattie.

"Mercy," he gasped.

She glanced down and saw what had captured his attention. She was wearing the undergarments that Pierre had brought her—the small clothes of a courtesan.

"I never . . . that is . . . Lordy, Mattie, but you make a man's blood burn with desire."

She smiled, feeling flattered and aroused and beset with a million other emotions she couldn't put a name to.

Roamer reached out and flicked one of the sexy bits of ribbon with his forefinger. "I don't know a man alive that hasn't had a wild thought or two about the woman he loves in one of these riggings."

He grinned and raised a brow. "Or getting them *out* of one of these riggings."

Mattie smiled, feeling more womanly than she had ever felt in her life. "There are an awful lot of ribbons and bows. If you expect to have me out of this before dawn, you'd best get started."

Roamer made a thick sound of lust in the back of

his throat and shed his own fine clothing in the blink of an eye. His body was harder and straighter than the steel of his forge. His erection pulsed and seemed to strain toward Mattie as he slid onto the bed and lay beside her, propped on one elbow.

"If I pull this ribbon, what happens?" He said in a husky, low purr.

"Why don't you pull on it and find out."

He slowly pulled the ribbon until the bow came undone. And with that action one side of Mattie's silk chemise fell away, revealing the swell of her bosom above the black lace corset.

"Lordy. There is even more underneath."

"Uh-huh. Now you better make the other side match," she teased, feeling the hot curl of desire in her belly.

He did. With a wicked grin he very slowly pulled the other ribbon. The chemise slid down, held together in the center of Mattie's chest by one small blood red bow of satin.

Roamer plucked it with his teeth, coming away with the flimsy chemise held in his mouth like an eager hound. He flung it aside and dipped his head, feathering kisses across the mound of her breasts, made fuller and more prominent by the cut of the suggestive corset.

"Black lace suits you, Mattie."

"In what way?" she breathed, grasping his hair and pulling him closer. The feel of his hot breath and hotter tongue dipping into her cleavage was delicious. Mattie felt different—strangely powerful in these garments. She loved what Roamer was doing and wanted him to do more of it.

"A fallen woman should always wear black lace, I

think." His answer was no more than a whisper in her hear as he nuzzled her ear lobe, nipping, pulling it into his lips to suck it for a moment.

"Ohhh, Roamer." Mattie found her body arching to meet his, but he was playful, keeping himself just beyond her touch. It was exquisite torture for her, knowing that his hot, hard erection was just there, just a fraction of an inch away from the part of her that throbbed with equal desire.

"Mattie. The first time I thought I was having another man's wife, I hated myself for pulling you down into sin with me." His hands were busy exploring the bud of her nipple just under the stiff upper edge of the lacy corset. Now and then, between words his tongue would flick over her breast, causing her to stop breathing for half a heartbeat.

"This time we come together as free people. Free of the past, free of lies." He raised his head and stared into her face. His green eyes were dark with passion. "There will be no other man for you, Mattie, not ever—not after this. If you ever think or even consider taking to another man's bed, just remember I am a jealous brute."

"As if there could be any other man for me, Roamer." She kissed him, tangling her hands in his long hair, pulling him closer, wanting to be so close that they were one.

"And if we have to leave McTavish Plain and your sisters?"

"Then we will leave. Our love is too strong to be denied. If Ian insists you marry another—"

"No. Don't even finish. When I heard that you and Scout had been taken, it all seemed so silly, so stupid."

He kissed her hard, his tongue plunging inside her mouth. Then he began to bring it gently in and out of her lips, slowly, sensuously as his hips began to mimic the motion.

Each time his pelvis dipped toward her she found her body arching toward him, taut with desire, aching for him to be inside her.

She moaned.

His growl answered.

But he did not enter her. Roamer was intent on keeping up the dance of their bodies—close—so close and yet just beyond touching. He wanted this moment to last, for the perfect singing of their bodies to continue for a long, long time.

Mattie could practically feel the heat from him. She imagined how that warm, velvet tip would feel against her sensitive skin. . . .

In one mighty thrust, he entered her and slid deep, deeper, until again her body arched and she gasped in pure pleasure.

He was a big man, his erection matching the rest of him; and she took him all, wanting him all within her. They mated then in a hot frenzy of emotion and physical bliss that was beyond describing.

It was not like the first time. It was nothing like the first time.

This time the desire that coiled inside her burst in a delicious hot shower of sensation that made every nerve in her body tingle. Her body reached a pinnacle of sensation so intense, so perfect, that she thought she might be dying.

La petite mort. The little death. She had read those words in an old book of French poetry. Now she knew what the author meant.

She whimpered and ground herself against him, wanting the sensation to go on and on. Mattie found herself caught up in a whirlwind of excitement and need as the feeling built and grew. Her body knew what to do and did it. She bit Roamer's neck, she kneaded his muscular buttocks, pulling him into her with each stroke.

She was a wanton; she was in love.

And then, in a shattering overload of physical sensation, she climaxed. She thought she might have screamed, and she knew that Roamer roared. In the back of her mind she remembered that odd, dissatisfied feeling she had the first time they were together.

Now she knew what her body had wanted. Now she knew what lay beyond, no longer out of her reach. Now she knew what the future offered her and Roamer. They were one—connected, bonded, committed.

In the opulent pale green room, in the middle of the summer afternoon in St. Louis, they were alone in the world, alone with their lust and their love. And as their pulses calmed and as their heartbeats slowed, Roamer turned her in his arms.

Twenty-two

"You are a wild man," she said with a satisfied sigh.

"You once told me I was a beast." He ran his hand over her corset top. "I can't believe we did all that and I still didn't manage to get you out of that thing." He chuckled.

"I believe you had the most important parts of me uncovered and at your fingertips." She smiled and ran her hand over his chest. He was a study in human perfection—more manly than any statue and more heartrending than any poem.

"Mattie, there is something I need to ask you." Roamer raised up on one elbow and looked into her face, but a knock at the door brought both of them into a sitting position.

"Who could that be?" She gasped, fearing that Laughing Jack had found the courage and a way to retaliate.

"Only the judge and his men know where we are." Roamer hopped off the bed, pulling the top coverlet with him. He held it around himself as he padded from the bed up the step and opened the door.

The fresh-faced youth took one look at Mattie and turned as bright a crimson as his coat. "A m-message, s-s-sir." Hc thrust an envelope into Roamer's hand and vanished.

"I think we should've been a bit more discreet," Mattie said, adjusting the top of her corset. "You know what he thought."

"Yea, I know." Roamer winked at her.

He closed the door, let the coverlet drop, and ripped open the envelope. Mattie couldn't help but marvel at his beauty. His body was symmetrical, muscular, and sensual.

"Who is it from?"

"The judge. He wants us to meet him for dinner as soon as we can, uh, manage."

"Then I guess we'd better hurry." Mattie started to rise from the bed, but Roamer let the paper flutter from his hand as he strode to the bed.

"Not so fast. I want you again, and this time I am going to get rid of that wicked corset." He pinned her down and, with mock ferocity, plucked at the hooks until the black corset fell away.

"Now I will have a taste of you before we meet the judge for dinner."

Roamer dipped his head and suckled one breast. Mattie felt her body respond instantly. Her nipples peaked, her breath caught, and that strange, compelling heat between her legs ignited.

"Roamer," she gasped as he suckled the other breast, and then sipped at her belly, making her quiver as his tongue darted in her naval.

"You smell of me and our love, Mattie." Roamer said as he nuzzled the mound of hair, nipping and biting at the tender flesh of her. "And soon, very soon, I will taste you and see if you are as sweet as I imagine."

Mattie blinked, a little shocked at what he said—and even more aroused. Then he raised himself on his palms and entered her again. She was ready, meeting him thrust for thrust. This time it was fast, hot, and furious lovemaking that brought them both to shattering fulfillment too soon.

In a hired carriage they arrived at the judge's mansion as the sun was brushing the tops of the trees on the elegant street. Mattie felt garish in her gown of silk, but she took a little pleasure knowing that it looked much better since she and Scout had removed all the cabbage roses from it. She also enjoyed the slightly lascivious sensation she experienced each time Roamer's gaze flicked over her. It was easy to read the lust in his eyes—to know he was picturing her in the sinfully sexy undergarments of a soiled dove.

"I hope the judge doesn't think I am a loose woman," she said as Roamer handed her down.

"If he does then I will disabuse him of that notion. I am the only man who has ever touched you, and I will tell the world so."

"No. Oh, Roamer, no you can't." Mattie felt the cold sweep of panic. "I told you the truth because I love you and trust you, but we cannot, *must not,* reveal this to anyone else. It would ruin my sisters' lives. This secret—my *lie*—must remain with us. Addie and Lottie are still in jeopardy."

"But Mattie, surely Ian—"

"No, Roamer. I must have your promise. If Ian did forgive Addie—and I am sure he would, if for no other reason than for the child that is coming—that wouldn't help Lottie. She would either be forced to marry or to leave. Even if Ian did find it in his heart to allow it, how could she continue to live in town with everyone knowing she was a liar? Or worse, what if Ian felt he had to make an example of her to continue upholding his rule?"

"Ian is a sensible man—"

"Yes, and his rule has its merits. I understand what he is trying to prevent now that I have seen how prostitutes live and how degradation starts out as a small thing. A card game becomes a gambling parlor. A dance hall becomes a bordello. I do understand what Ian is trying to prevent. He is a man of principle, and he never intended his rules to hurt anyone. He doesn't want gambling halls full of whores and cheats like Jack and Pierre in town. If his rule fails, then it would only be a matter of time before McTavish Plain was like every other frontier town. There would be watered whiskey, women of the evening, and pimps, and soon McTavish Plain would see its first murder."

Roamer thought of the towns he had traveled through. Even the smallest one had tents for prostitutes and tents for gamblers. Mattie was right, but where did that leave them?

She was a single woman, free to marry at will. But to do that she would have to tell the truth. And telling the truth could ruin Addie's, Ian's and Lottie's lives.

Was their own happiness worth so much misery? Was their love enough to damn an entire town?

"Damn it, Mattie. I am not going back to McTavish Plain and pretend. I will not act like I don't love you. I won't deny it again."

"But Roamer, we cannot destroy others' lives."

Mattie suddenly felt a frisson of fear. Maybe she and Roamer weren't going to be together. She and

Scout had been through so much and grown so close, but she had never confessed her lie to him.

Now what was she going to say? That his teacher was a liar? That to get her own way she was as selfish and unscrupulous as Jack?

What would he say? What if he could not stomach the sight of her after that? Many obstacles still stood between her and Roamer being together.

A cloud of deep despair was hanging over Mattie and Roamer when Albert opened the door. She plastered a false smile on her face and followed the butler into Judge Mills's study. Scout was there, deep in conversation with the judge when they arrived. The moment he saw Mattie and Roamer, he exploded from his chair and ran to them, his bottom lip quivering as he tried to stay his tears.

"Uncle Roamer, Miss Mattie, I thought you would never get here."

"Well, we are here now. And together we are going to stay." Roamer tousled the boy's hair and met Mattie's sad gaze.

"Laughing Jack Maravel will never want to bother me again," Scout said, his expression turning solemn.

"No, but he may be after Mattie," Roamer said, giving Judge Mills a glare.

"Hello, my dear. I am Judge Mills, and since Roamer is too busy chastising me to introduce us, I suspect I will have to make my own introductions."

The silver-haired gentleman warmly grasped Mattie's hand, dispelling her fears that he would take her for a less than virtuous woman.

"Sir, it is a pleasure."

"And don't be too worried about Jackson. Mick

tells me you beat him right proper. There is no document, of course; that was all folderol. The money is sitting, waiting for Scout to claim when he has a mind to." The judge smiled at Mattie. "My dear, would you do me the honor? It has been a donkey's age since I had a beautiful young woman on my arm."

"Why, thank you, sir for the compliment and the offer. I accept." Mattie took the judge's arm and walked with him through the library and into the dining room. If she had thought the pale silk hotel room was beautiful, then this room was beyond her ability to describe.

Done in a pale shade of robin's-egg blue with gilt at every elaborately carved detail, the room spoke of money and taste.

A huge silver candelabra sat in the center of an enormous polished wood table, casting the warm glow of candlelight on the silver, crystal, and fine bone china.

"My gracious," Mattie gasped. "This is the most beautiful dining room I have ever seen."

"It pales in comparison to you, my dear," the judge said as he seated her. With every compliment the knot in her belly shrank a little.

Scout was seated opposite Mattie on the judge's left, and at a discouraging distance was Roamer, at the far end of the table.

"I will have to shout to talk with you," Roamer grumbled as the servants began to open a bottle of wine and serve the soup.

"Judge, I don't understand. Why would Laughing—I mean Jackson Maravel want to come after me?"

Roamer frowned darkly. "Part of the Judge's plan

was to tell Jack that Judson Walker Maravel, in the guise of a boy he switched for Scout, had signed his entire fortune over to you."

"What? And what on earth do you mean about a substitute Scout? I assumed you big, strong, powerful men simply *persuaded* Jack about the error of his ways." Mattie smiled when she saw a ruddy flush come into the cheeks of the three males.

"Well, it was a bit more complicated than that," Roamer interrupted.

"Complicated? It was foxy, sly, and the most ingenious plan ever conceived, if I do say so myself. My plan was foolproof and designed to have Jackson walk away from Scout of his own free will, and if at some later date he should want to go to court . . . well, I gave him something to think about." Judge Mills laughed heartily. "And I see Albert hovering by the door, so that means cook has prepared something wonderful for us." He picked up Mattie's hand again.

Mattie smiled, but her mind and heart were focused on the problem of her make-believe husband. She had found love—the kind of love that was real and honest, but her foolish lie still trapped her.

What could they do?

Through the soup and the fish Mattie was silent. Several times she glanced up to see Scout watching her with a half smile curling his lips.

"What is it, Scout?" she finally asked as the roast beef was being served.

"Oh, nothin'," he said, but she did not miss the wink the judge gave him.

"So, tell me, Mrs. Smith," the judge said suddenly. "What are your plans now?"

Mattie saw Roamer stiffen at the far end of the table. She knew he was thinking about her lie, her sisters, and all that kept them apart.

"My plans?"

"Yes, I was wondering if you are going to continue teaching school in McTavish Plain? Young Scout says you are a wonderful teacher."

Mattie smiled at Scout. Even though she had fought against it, he had become her particular favorite in all ways. In fact, she loved the boy. It was amusing in an ironic sort of way. The woman who only wanted romantic love was conducting a passionate physical affair with a man. Now, the foolish girl who swore never to have children had given her heart to a child.

Irony at its most sublime.

One of the pocket doors slid back to reveal Albert. "Sir, a letter has just been delivered."

"It can wait until after I have dined, Albert."

"Begging your pardon, sir. It is for the lady."

Both Mattie's and Roamer's heads snapped up. Their attention was riveted on the gleaming salver the black man held in one hand. Mattie knew she was imagining it, but his steps seemed abnormally slow as he traversed the oak server, came around the head of the table, and finally stood at her elbow.

She dabbed at her mouth, and then, as though time had become as slow as cold honey, she laid the fine linen in her lap and, with trembling fingers, picked up the paper.

The stationery was fine with a heavy watermark. It had been addressed to Mrs. Samuel Smith in care of Judge Mills, St. Louis, Missouri in a fine, bold copperplate that was not familiar to her. Mattie glanced up at Roamer. He seemed as confused as she was.

With a small sigh of resignation, she broke the seal and unfolded the thick paper.

Mattie's heart beat heavy in her chest as she read. Hot tears welled in her eyes.

"Mattie? What is it?" Roamer left his seat at the far end of the table and came around. He did not touch her but stood close enough for her to feel the heat of his body, the strength of being near.

"It—it is a letter."

"Yes, honey, I can see that. Who is it from?"

"There is no name." She looked up at Scout. A silent communication passed between them. "Though it says it is from a shipmate of my—my husband's."

"What?" Roamer leaned nearer.

"Yes, it informs me that my husband, Captain Samuel Smith, has perished in a watery grave at sea."

"Oh, my dear." The judge grasped her hand. "Albert, bring Mrs. Smith a brandy."

"Mattie?" She tilted her head and looked up at him. A thousand unspoken questions were in his eyes. "Does this mean—?"

"It means Mattie can marry someone—if they were to ask her," Scout said wisely.

"Marry?" The judge looked from Scout to Mattie to Roamer. His eyes twinkled and his grin widened. "And may I offer my services as judge if there is to be a wedding?"

"Before we have a wedding a lady must first have a proposal," Mattie said softly, looking up at Roamer.

He tilted his head back and laughed. Then he picked up her entire chair and turned her around to face him. Then, with a wicked gleam in his eyes, he went down on one knee and picked up her hand.

"Knowing how much you like for things to be romantic, Mattie, I think I better do this right and in front of witnesses." He winked at Scout. "Mattie *Smith,* would you do me the very great honor of being my wife? I want to protect you, shelter you, to spend the rest of my life with you. I will do my best to nurture every part of you, body, soul, and heart. I will even learn to spout poetry if that is what it takes."

Mattie swallowed hard. Happiness was a fount in her chest. Her tongue was tied and she could not speak.

"Yes, Mattie, will you marry us?" Scout asked from across the table. His eyes were wide with hope and expectation.

"Yes. I will marry you—both of you. But not here. This is a wedding that absolutely must take place in McTavish Plain."

Twenty-three

Addie's stone house looked more like a castle than ever before. The wedding of Roamer and Mattie promised to be the event of the year.

"Mattie, girl, it is high time you had some happiness," Gert said as she adjusted Mattie's veil. "The tragic death of your husband stunned us all. We know how you doted on that man."

"Yes, it was sudden," Mattie said, glancing at both Addie, who was round with child, and Lottie, who was doing the last-minute sewing on Mattie's trousseau.

There was a knock on the bedroom door. All the women turned and in one voice said; "The bride is getting dressed. You can't come in."

"You canna deny a man entry in his own home," Ian announced from the other side of the door.

Addie and Lottie rolled their eyes. "You may as well let him in or we won't have any peace," Mattie laughed.

"Cover yourself. He has no business seeing your dress before Roamer," Lottie said, tossing a quilt to Mattie.

"I suppose you are right." Mattie held the quilt in front of her, snugged up tight against her chin.

"Come in," Addie called.

Ian stepped inside, looking quite dashing in his beaded buckskin shirt with a tartan sash held in place by a huge brooch gleaming with the patina of centuries. Though his jaw was still scraped clean, he would always have the look of a wild highlander.

"Ian, you look dashing," Addie said with no small measure of pride in her voice.

"Ian always was a fine figure of a man. And speaking of men, I best go see if mine is ready," Gert said, excusing herself.

"You are a kind wife, Gert." He gave her a peck on the cheek and sidled up to Addie and squeezed her bottom.

"Ian!"

"If all you want to do is spoon with your wife, please take her outside. I have things to do," Lottie snapped.

"Ah, Charlotte, I am here on an errand of importance." Ian raised a brow. "As the head of this family, I have come to tell Mattie that I will be walking her down the aisle today."

"Telling her?" Addie repeated.

"Verra well, then, lass. I am *asking* your sister if I may have the honor of walking her down the aisle and giving her hand in marriage."

"I would be pleased, Ian," Mattie said, keeping the quilt up to her chin. Lottie was somewhere behind her doing last minute fluffing and stitching. She hoped she didn't get impaled on a needle.

" 'Tis the verra least I can do, since I wasn'a with you when you got word of your poor husband's death, or when Roamer proposed."

Mattie swallowed hard. "Ah, well—"

"Now how did that happen again, exactly?" Ian asked, screwing up his face. Addie gave him a soft kick in the shin but he ignored her completely. "I really want to know how you learned of the poor man's death all the way in St. Louis."

"A shipmate of my husband's saw me in St. Louis. He sent word. And then Roamer thought since you had insisted he take a wife . . . well, I was a widow, and he had been given an ultimatum by the town so—"

"Ah, yes." Ian gave Mattie a look that made her shiver. "We verra nearly forced him to find a wife—any wife, dinna we?"

Lottie was right. There was something in Ian's eyes that made Mattie think her brother-in-law knew far more than he was saying.

"Well, I will leave you ladies to it. Mattie, I will be waiting to give you to Roamer," Ian said.

"Where are you headed now?" Addie asked.

"I have a weddin' present to give to Scout," Ian said with a chuckle. "A verra special present for a special lad."

Scout was sitting on the steps of the church, tossing pebbles at an ant den. He was happy. He had almost everything that he wanted.

"Your uncle Roamer is one lucky son of a buck," Ian said as he walked up and sat down beside the boy. "He has a fine nephew, and soon he will have a pretty young wife. Even if her head is too full of romantic nonsense, Mattie has a good heart."

"I like Miss Mattie a lot," Scout said with a shy smile.

"Aye, I know you do. You like puppies too, do you not, lad?"

Scout's head snapped up. "Puppies?"

"Aye. You know I have some pups from Tay and Dee's litter. They are a ragged bunch of hounds, I admit, and far more trouble than they are worth. But there is one, a wee bit on the skinny side. I doubt anybody will want the sorry-looking critter. I was hoping he would find a good home—"

"I want him!" Scout was on his feet, nearly vibrating with emotion. "Please, Mr. McTavish, let me take him. I will train him and be the best master; I swear I will."

"On one condition only, lad." Ian looked stern.

"Anything."

"You start calling me Uncle Ian. Since I am married to your Aunt Addie I am now your uncle, lad. We are family—you are part of my American clan."

Scout stilled for a minute, thinking. "Is that true?"

"I wouldn'a lie to you, lad." Ian grinned.

"So now Uncle Roamer and I have a *family*? A—a *clan*?"

"Aye, such as this family is, lad. Though you know you are getting a sorry bunch. I am barely housebroke, and your aunts—well, they have been known to bend the truth a wee bit," Ian sighed in an exaggerated manner. "Those three sisters can be a trial, lad. I think me and you and your uncle Roamer will do well to stick together in this family."

Scout beamed. "A family, a mama, and a pup," he mused. "It is all I ever wanted—everything I prayed for."

* * *

Mattie stood facing Roamer in front of the Reverend Horace Miller while all of McTavish Plain looked on. Those who didn't fit into the tidy little church stood crowded at the open doors, and Mattie's schoolchildren pressed their noses against the windows.

"And do you, Mattie Smith, take this man—"

In the frontmost pew, Ian leaned very near to Addie and whispered in her ear. "Do you think it will be legal since she isn't using her real last name?"

Addie elbowed him in the ribs. "Behave." His pained grunt invited Scout's inquisitive gaze. The boy stood as still as he could manage, a silk pillow in his hands, and on it two gold bands.

"In front of God and in this company, I now pronounce you man and wife—you may kiss the bride, Roamer."

Once more Ian leaned close to Addie. "Well, one down and one to go. What poor defenseless man do you suppose we will have to blackmail into marrying your sister Lottie?"

Ian's next groan of pain was not heard over the happy cheers and laughter as the people celebrated another wedding in McTavish Plain.

Roamer pulled his bride into his arms and kissed her soundly. "I love you, Mattie."

"I love you, too, Roamer."

Epilogue

"Mattie is prettier every day," Gert said with a smile. "That silk and all that lace makes her look like an angel."

"Yes, she is an angel," Roamer agreed idly, watching his new wife, dressed in a fine silk dress of palest green, and he felt his loins grow warm. The color was almost identical to the color of the hotel room in St. Louis, and only he knew what kind of undergarments Mattie wore underneath.

He had taken such a shine to seeing his lovely wife in naughty French corsets that they had bought a quantity of lacy and completely scandalous small clothes before leaving St. Louis.

"I think it was tasteful of her to pick that pale green color for her second wedding. I'll tell you right now, Roamer, that lady of yours adds a bit of sophistocation to McTavish Plain. The young girls in her class have got a fine model to pattern themselves after," Gert said emphatically.

If only she knew about Mattie's corset! Her eyes would bug out and she would go crimson if she saw what the naughty waist-pinchers did to his innocent wife's figure.

He smiled just thinking about it. "Yes, she is a

beauty all right—for a schoolmarm. You know how straitlaced and proper those women are, but I'll tell you something for nothin', Gert: I intend to try and loosen her up a bit."

Scout punched Roamer on the arm. "Uncle Roamer, don't you go callin' Mattie straitlaced. She is perfect and she is a lady, and she is my mama." The boy grinned, but Roamer knew his words were serious.

Mattie had a champion in the child. And though they had never discussed who had written that letter, Roamer was certain Scout was somehow behind it all. He put his hand on the boy's head and tousled his fine, pale hair.

"Whatever you say. I wouldn't want to get on your bad side." They laughed together until the volume of the clapping and tempo of the music made Roamer seek out his bride.

He found her speaking with Lottie by a long table laden with summer food.

" 'Scuse me, Gus," Roamer said as he wove his way through the dancing couples. He heard Lottie's words as he approached.

"Well, Matilda, I think it's funny. Addie is big as a barn with her baby, and you're married off with a caution of a boy to look after and a big husband to cook for. Who would've thought it?"

"Love makes fools of us all," Mattie said with a bemused smile, looking over her sister's head at Roamer.

"You are the only one of the Green sisters left, Charlotte. I wouldn't boast too long or too loud, for fate and life have a way of making us eat our own words."

"Ha. I am smarter than you and Addie. I don't

intend to get caught up in some web of romantic foolishness. No, thank you very much, ma'am. I intend to enjoy my life, and I intend to do it without some man tracking up my carpets. I don't need a man for anything."

"Hello, sweetheart." Roamer slid his arm around Mattie's waist and pulled her into a hot, long, hard kiss. When he pulled away Lottie was watching them with big eyes.

"Don't be too sure, Lottie," Mattie said, leaning her head against Roamer's chest. "There are some things that men are quite necessary for—and very good at."

Then she turned and tilted her head, inviting her husband to kiss her again while Lottie laughed and gave her a sly wink.

If you liked MATTIE AND THE BLACKSMITH, be sure to look for Linda Lea Castle's next release in the Bogus Brides series, LOTTIE AND THE RUSTLER, available in May 2001 wherever books are sold.

Lottie is quite satisfied to live without a man. Taking the name Shayne Rosswarne from a wanted poster, she has invented a long-lost—and conveniently absent—husband and is running her successful dress shop in peace. Until the real Shayne Rosswarne shows up—and wants some answers. . . .

COMING IN MAY 2001 FROM ZEBRA BALLAD ROMANCES

__MY LADY IMPOSTER: The Sword and the Ring #1
by Suzanne McMinn 0-8217-6875-1 $5.50US/$7.50CAN
Upon his return from the king's campaigns in France, Damon of Sperling found his father dead and his demesne ravaged by plague. Now he must restore order to his estate, and to the lives of his four orphaned sisters—a task that seems best accomplished by wedding Lady Lorabelle of Orrick, to whom he has long been promised.

__BEAUTY AND THE BRAIN: The Dream Maker #2
by Alice Duncan 0-8217-6879-4 $5.50US/$7.50CAN
Actress Brenda Fitzpatrick is accustomed to hiding her intelligence behind the facade of a featherheaded blonde. But not when it comes to Colin Peters, a research assistant on the new romantic movie she's starring in. Now Martin Tafft has asked Brenda to loosen Colin up. It isn't long before attraction blossoms into a love more real than any fantasy.

__ANNE'S WISH: The Wishing Well #3
by Joy Reed 0-8217-6810-7 $5.50US/$7.50CAN
Anne Barrington's hopes for escaping life in the court of Queen Charlotte are shattered when the courtier she loves jilts her for an heiress. Her devastation is witnessed by James, Lord Westland, who offers marriage as a solution to both of their dilemmas: Anne desperate to leave the Queen's service; James needs a wife to provide him with an heir.

__REILLY'S PRIDE: Irish Blessing #3
by Elizabeth Keys 0-8217-6811-5 $5.50US/$7.50CAN
Quintin Reilly had come home to run his family's shipyard. The last thing he expected was to find himself with a wife! Shannon Murray was little more than a child when he'd gone off to sea. Now she was a widow boldly proposing marriage! Quin hesitated, until "Reilly's Blessing" convinced him that this beauty was meant to be his bride.

Call toll free **1-888-345-BOOK** to order by phone or use this coupon to order by mail. ALL BOOKS AVAILABLE MAY 1, 2001.

Name____
Adress____
City_____________________State_______________Zip_______

Please send me the books that I have checked above.

I am enclosing $______
Plus postage and handhing* $______
Sales tax (in NY and TN) $______
Total amount enclosed $______

*Add $2.50 for the first book and $.50 for each additional book. Send check or money order (no cash or CODS) to: **Kensington Publishing Corp., Dept. C.O., 850 Third Avenue, New York, NY 10022.**
Prices and numbers subject to change without notice. Valid only in the U.S.
All orders subject to availability. **NO ADVANCE ORDERS.**
Visit our website at **www.kensingtonbooks.com**

Put a Little Romance in Your Life With
Janelle Taylor

__Anything for Love	0-8217-4992-7	$5.99US/$6.99CAN
__Lakota Dawn	0-8217-6421-7	$6.99US/$8.99CAN
__Forever Ecstasy	0-8217-5241-3	$5.99US/$6.99CAN
__Fortune's Flames	0-8217-5450-5	$5.99US/$6.99CAN
__Destiny's Temptress	0-8217-5448-3	$5.99US/$6.99CAN
__Love Me With Fury	0-8217-5452-1	$5.99US/$6.99CAN
__First Love, Wild Love	0-8217-5277-4	$5.99US/$6.99CAN
__Kiss of the Night Wind	0-8217-5279-0	$5.99US/$6.99CAN
__Love With a Stranger	0-8217-5416-5	$6.99US/$8.50CAN
__Forbidden Ecstasy	0-8217-5278-2	$5.99US/$6.99CAN
__Defiant Ecstasy	0-8217-5447-5	$5.99US/$6.99CAN
__Follow the Wind	0-8217-5449-1	$5.99US/$6.99CAN
__Wild Winds	0-8217-6026-2	$6.99US/$8.50CAN
__Defiant Hearts	0-8217-5563-3	$6.50US/$8.00CAN
__Golden Torment	0-8217-5451-3	$5.99US/$6.99CAN
__Bittersweet Ecstasy	0-8217-5445-9	$5.99US/$6.99CAN
__Taking Chances	0-8217-4259-0	$4.50US/$5.50CAN
__By Candlelight	0-8217-5703-2	$6.99US/$8.50CAN
__Chase the Wind	0-8217-4740-1	$5.99US/$6.99CAN
__Destiny Mine	0-8217-5185-9	$5.99US/$6.99CAN
__Midnight Secrets	0-8217-5280-4	$5.99US/$6.99CAN
__Sweet Savage Heart	0-8217-5276-6	$5.99US/$6.99CAN
__Moonbeams and Magic	0-7860-0184-4	$5.99US/$6.99CAN
__Brazen Ecstasy	0-8217-5446-7	$5.99US/$6.99CAN

Call toll free **1-888-345-BOOK** to order by phone, use this coupon to order by mail, or order online at **www.kensingtonbooks.com.**
Name ______________________________
Address ______________________________
City ______________ State __________ Zip ______________
Please send me the books I have checked above.
I am enclosing $______________
Plus postage and handling $______________
Sales tax (in New York and Tennessee only) $______________
Total amount enclosed $______________
*Add $2.50 for the first book and $.50 for each additional book.
Send check or money order (no cash or CODs) to:
Kensington Publishing Corp., Dept. C.O., 850 Third Avenue, New York, NY 10022
Prices and numbers subject to change without notice.
All orders subject to availability.
Visit our website at **www.kensingtonbooks.com**

Put a Little Romance in Your Life With

Rosanne Bittner

__Caress	0-8217-3791-0	$5.99US/$6.99CAN
__Full Circle	0-8217-4711-8	$5.99US/$6.99CAN
__Shameless	0-8217-4056-3	$5.99US/$6.99CAN
__Unforgettable	0-8217-5830-6	$5.99US/$7.50CAN
__Texas Embrace	0-8217-5625-7	$5.99US/$7.50CAN
__Texas Passions	0-8217-6166-8	$5.99US/$7.50CAN
__Until Tomorrow	0-8217-5064-X	$5.99US/$6.99CAN
__Love Me Tomorrow	0-8217-5818-7	$5.99US/$7.50CAN

Call toll free **1-888-345-BOOK** to order by phone or use this coupon to order by mail.

Name ____

Address ____

City ____________________ State ________ Zip ______________

Please send me the books I have checked above.

I am enclosing $______________

Plus postage and handling* $______________

Sales tax (in New York and Tennessee) $______________

Total amount enclosed $______________

*Add $2.50 for the first book and $.50 for each additional book.

Send check or money order (no cash or CODs) to:

Kensington Publishing Corp., 850 Third Avenue, New York, NY 10022

Prices and Numbers subject to change without notice.

All orders subject to availability.

Check out our website at **www.kensingtonbooks.com**